CRISIS OF IDENTITY

William A. Simms

Waverly House Publishing

Published by:
Waverly House Publishers
P.O. Box 1053
Glenside, Pa. 19038

Copyright 1997 by William A. Simms

All rights reserved.
No part of this book may be reproduced or transmitted in any form or by any means, electronic or mechanical, including photocopying, recording or by an information storage and retrieval system without written permission from the publisher or author, except for the inclusion of brief quotations in a review.

Library of Congress Catalog Card Number: 97-60710

ISBN: 0-9650970-1-3

Copy Editor: Nora Wright

Cover design and illustration:
Kirk Gaines
Gaines Production and Associates

Printed in the United States of America

Also by the author:

Zuro! A Tale of Alien Avengers

Chapter 1

If you were to apply the European standard of beauty, Gina Marlene Epps would easily measure up. She was a stunning, African-American woman in her mid-twenties. Originally, her hair had been a deep, dark brown in appearance, although a closer look at a single strand of it under light would have revealed it as being very dark red. She had not been satisfied with her hair in its natural state and had dyed it a brilliant flame red, but at the roots, you could always see the real color, struggling to be noticed. In an effort to achieve symmetry in her appearance, she wore reddish-orange contact lenses to match her hair. She was a light-skinned woman with a small pointed nose, small lips and high, pronounced cheek bones. She couldn't quite pass for white (although she would have if she could), but from the back you could easily mistake her for a white woman. She knew she was considered very attractive and didn't hesitate to flaunt her looks, dressing in tight, alluring clothing to draw attention to her voluptuous body.

Gina worked at a prestigious law firm in downtown Philadelphia, Pennsylvania as a legal secretary. Every morning, after dropping her car off at the parking lot, she had to walk a block before reaching her job, and she would put on a show for all who would watch. This morning was no exception. She walked very seductively with hips swinging from side to side, looking straight ahead with her nose up in the air, bag over her shoulder, and arms moving in perfect synchronization with the rest of her body. She left no doubt in anyone's mind as to the effect she was trying to achieve on her onwatchers. There were all kinds of remarks shouted out: "Damn, baby, how'd you get in them clothes? Looks like somebody melted you down and poured you in-um!" . . .

"You lookin' for me, Baby? I'm right over here." . . . "Come to Papa, come to Papa! I got just what you want and more than you need!"

Gina appeared to be ignoring her admirers, but the slight smile on her face was an indication of some secret feeling of triumph.

When Gina entered the building where she worked, she received the same attention as outside, but much more subtle in expression. Nobody said anything to her; men and women alike waited until she passed them on her way through the lobby before turning their heads to stare and make murmured remarks.

The firm she worked for, Dillenbeck, Talley and Grundage, occupied the entire top floor of the building and had its own elevator for employees. A few of Gina's co-workers were waiting for it to arrive, and she greeted them all with good mornings and then asked, "Are we too late for the ride up?"

Someone answered, "No, you just made it - it's on its way down now."

Gina had asked the question because her employer held very rigid views about getting to work on time and had arranged with the building management to set the elevator to run only at certain hours of the day - from seven in the morning until nine, twelve noon until one, and three until five in the afternoon. In this way, close tabs could be kept on where the employees were and what they were doing.

When the elevator came, everybody waiting got on. Because Gina was the last one in, she was right at the elevator door, facing it. All the men behind her were looking her up and down, from the back. All the women were staring at the men in disgust . . . except for one woman who seemed to enjoy the view as much as the men.

Chapter 1

At the top floor, the elevator stopped, and everyone got off and rushed to their work stations, hoping to appear as if they had been at work for quite some time. Gina headed straight for her office, and just as she entered, she heard a voice behind her. "Chil', have I got some juicy stuff to tell you."

Gina quickly turned her head, saw who it was and responded, "Girl, don't scare me that way, and what you got to tell me that's so juicy?"

"Well, before I tell you . . . how many guys did you turn on this morning with that sexy walk of yours, huh?"

"Ah, shut up, Beth, you ain't got no room to talk."

Marybeth Turner (known to her friends as Beth) was a white woman, but if you were in another room and heard her talk for the first time, you would swear she was black; she was so fascinated by black people that she had made a point of copying their accent almost to perfection. Perhaps she didn't realize that this appeared condescending - as if she believed that blacks would not understand what she was saying if she spoke standard English. Gina didn't like this about Marybeth when she first met her because she never spoke anything but standard English herself; however, as she grew to value Marybeth's friendship, she started talking like her when they were together in order to please her.

Like Gina, Marybeth was a very attractive woman by European standards. She didn't dress quite as provocatively as Gina did, but she could turn as many heads as Gina whenever she felt like it. She was a bleached blonde with blue eyes, a typical Anglo-Saxon nose, and rather large lips for a white woman. Actually, they weren't that way naturally; she had undergone cosmetic surgery to enlarge them because she was attracted to African-American men, and on occasion some had said that they didn't enjoy kissing her because her lips were too small.

Marybeth and Gina were as good friends as two women could be. Unlike most friends, whose relationship is usually a symbiotic one, these two women seemed to have a genuine like for each other, despite the fact that one was white and the other black.

In response to Marybeth, Gina asked, "So, what's this juicy stuff you have to tell me?"

"Well, Honey, you're not gonna believe this. Guess what? . . . the firm just added a new senior partner!"

"So, what's so juicy about that?"

"Wait a minute, Chil', listen! You haven't heard it all yet . . . he's black!

Gina sniffed, "So, what do I care . . . you know I'm not interested in black men."

"Girl, what's wrong with you? I wish I had a tape recorder so you can hear how you sound sometimes."

"Please, Beth, don't start with me this morning."

"Look . . . look, Gina," Marybeth whispered, "Speak of an angel, and he will appear." She gave a low, growling sound, "g-r-r-r-r," and said in a sultry voice, "Damn . . . look at him! He is s-o-o-o fine!"

The object of her admiration was Steven Richards, recently recruited as a senior partner because of his very successful record in criminal defense, a new area of law for the firm. He was a dark and handsome African-American man of medium height with a receding hair line which complemented the shape of his face. His eyes were deepset, dark almond in color. He dressed expensively and with a flair and originality rarely seen at the rather stodgy firm of Dillenbeck, Talley and Grundage. There was that distinctive air of casual confidence about him which came from being recognized as being very good at what you do. Although he was the finished product of an Ivy League school, he had not quite forgotten that he had been born and raised in one of the roughest areas in North Philadelphia, and on more than one occasion had supplied free legal representation to people from the old neighborhood.

Gina, not at all impressed by Steven, responded, "M-m-m-m, I guess he dresses nice, but that doesn't make any difference to me. I'm not at all interested, and I wish you would stop trying to hook me up with . . ."

Marybeth cut in on Gina. "What makes you think I'm trying to hook you up? If I can reel him in, this catch is mine, so hands off, Sweetheart."

"You don't have to worry about me. Like I said, black men don't turn me on." Gina added, "It looks like you're gonna get a chance to show your stuff sooner than you thought, 'cause he's coming this way."

Marybeth gasped and said, "Ooooh, he shore is! I wonder what he wants? What are we gonna do, Gina?"

"I don't know what you're gonna do, Beth, but I wish you would stop acting like he's coming to ask one of us to go to bed with him."

Just as Gina said, Steven was headed right for her office. He knocked on the door at the same time as he was pushing it open. "Hello, Ladies. My name is Steven Richards. I was told that I would be able to find a Ms. Epps in this office. Is that so?"

Marybeth immediately loved the sound of his voice. It had a slightly hoarse quality, and years of education had not stripped him of sounding like a black man when he talked. In her excitement, she spoke up first and out of turn. "You have the right place, Sir . . . may we be of help to you?"

Steven, not knowing any better, extended his hand to Marybeth and said, "I'm glad to meet you, Ms. Epps."

"The pleasure's all mine, and you can just call me Beth."

Gina spoke up. "Mr. Richards, I'm Gina Epps, and this is

my office, and this woman does not belong here. Goodbye, Beth, I'll see you for lunch."

As Beth was leaving the office, she turned and said in a soft, teasing tone, "Be careful of her, Mr. Richards. She's a real man-eater."

Steven paid no attention. You could tell right away that he was really flabbergasted by Gina's beauty. He took her hand and said, "I'm sorry about the mix-up. I hope you'll forgive me."

"Oh, it wasn't your fault. How were you to know? You'll get to know Beth after a while - she's really a fun person."

He smiled. "Oh, I'll bet she is."

Steven was unaware that he still had Gina's hand in his, but, quite the contrary, Gina was completely aware of it. She tried several times to break the grip but to no avail. She finally had to tell him, "You can let my hand go now."

Steven once again apologized and then laughed. "I've only known you for a couple of minutes, and I've apologized to you twice already."

Gina wanted to get to the reason he was in her office and said, "I understand they made you a senior partner in the firm."

Steven answered, "Yes," but before he could say another word, Gina asked snappishly, "And why did they send you to me?"

"They said that you would be the best one to acquaint me with how things get done around here, and, until further notice, you've been assigned to me."

Gina was furious; she lost her temper and shouted out, "What! They can't do that. I work for Mark Souderton . . . and he needs me, so you can forget that."

Steven asserted himself. "Well, Ms. Epps, for the third time, I'm sorry, but that's the way it is."

Chapter 1

"Well, we'll see about that. Would you please wait outside my office for a moment?"

He left the room, and she snatched up the phone and asked the receptionist to connect her to Dan Dillenbeck, a senior partner and founder of the firm. As soon as he came on the line, Gina blurted out, "Mr. Dillenbeck, what's the idea of taking me away from Mark Souderton to work with this new guy?"

"Gina, first of all, he is not just a 'new guy' - he's a full partner in this firm and deserves some respect. I know this move came as a surprise to you, but the decision was not mine alone, and I'm afraid you're stuck with it. And, Gina, I don't want to hear any more about it. Do you understand?"

Gina slammed the phone down. With her finger, she summoned Steven to her. He re-entered her office just as the phone rang. When Gina picked it up, it was Mr. Dillenbeck. He said to her in a stern, gritted-teeth manner, "Gina, if you ever slam the phone down in my ear like that again, your days of working for this firm will come to a rapid conclusion. Is that understood?"

Gina had her back to Steven, facing a large window which looked out over Philadelphia. He could tell by the whispering tone of her voice that she was embarrassed by what was being said to her, so he pretended that he wasn't listening by holding his head down, studying the floor, with his hands behind his back.

The last thing he heard her say was, "Yes, Sir, I understand." This time, she gently hung up the phone and then sarcastically said to Steven, "I'm at your command, Sir ... within reason. By that, I mean I don't fetch coffee, and I don't run errands. I don't do anything that takes me outside the realm of my job." Gina tried to keep the tears from flowing, but was unsuccessful.

Steven looked at her with pity and said, "Ms. Epps, I wish I could undo what's been done, but I'm afraid it's too late. We'll just have to live with it until . . . maybe after I . . ."

"After you what?"

"Well, what I was going to say . . . after I've been here for a while, maybe I can recommend that you be assigned back to Souderton."

"Please do. For now, I guess we're stuck with each other. I just hope you don't come in here with any nigger shit."

"Nigger shit! What does that mean? That word's not even in my vocabulary. Okay, Ms. Epps, that's it. I've tried to be as nice to you as anyone could, but it seems that you're hellbent on getting this relationship off to a bad start. From here on out, I don't want to hear that word coming from you again - at least not as long as you work for me."

Gina stood there seething, her hands on her hips, her eyes blazing, while he continued. "Ms. Epps, things between you and me can be as bad or good as you want them to be. When I first saw you, I thought you were the prettiest thing that God put on this earth, but the more I hear you talk, the uglier you become to me. And make no mistake, I will fire you if I have to!"

He turned to leave her office, and Gina impulsively said, "Well, excuse me, Mr. Thang."

He came back at once. "My office is off the south corridor, Suite 21. Get your things moved up there before the day is over. Oh, just one more thing - you address me as Mr. Richards, and don't you forget it." He left, slamming the door behind him.

From the hallway, Marybeth had heard everything that had gone on, and now she started to follow Steven. Almost immediately, she heard a familiar voice say, "Beth, whatever

is going on, I want you to stay out of it." She stopped in her tracks. "But, Sir, I was just going to see if there was anything he needed."
It was Marybeth's boss, Martin Pollock. He was a stout man with rather coarse features and dark hair, cut in a closely-cropped style. "I think he can manage without you," he said sternly. "Now be in my office in five minutes . . . I have some dictation."
"Yes, Sir," Beth replied and reluctantly returned to her desk.

On the way to his office suite, Steven thought about his encounter with Gina. He felt there had to be more to her behavior toward him than just her anger at being assigned to him. A couple of reasons why she would act that way crossed his mind, such as the fact that he was black and in a superior position to her, but he dismissed them. He didn't want to believe that she could be thinking that way, even though she had told him not to come in there with any nigger shit. That had really left a sour taste in his mouth.

Meanwhile, Gina was seated at her desk, still in a tizzy over her reassignment when Mark Souderton, her now former boss, came in. "Gina, I heard what took place this morning, and I'm very sorry about it."
Gina looked up at him, enraged and sobbing. "Mark, why did you let this happen? You know how well we work together!"
"Now, hold on a minute here, Gina. Don't blame me. I wasn't even here this morning when they called this shot, and it came right from the top. Remember, I'm not a partner in this firm, and they don't have to ask me anything. I know sometimes you think I'm larger then life around here, but when I look at my paycheck every week, that tells me

something else." Mark put his arm around her shoulders and tried to comfort her by saying, "Look at it this way. You'll now be working for one of the senior partners, and that may mean a hike in pay for you. Who knows?" Then he smiled and said sympathetically, "When I get my own firm someday, you'll be the first one I call. I've never worked with a secretary as efficient as you."

Gina looked at him for a brief moment, her eyes glazed with tears, and then spoke. "Mark, it was foolish of me to think you would go behind my back that way. I'm sorry . . . I'm so sorry . . . would you forgive me?"

"Oh, sure, no problem . . . don't worry about it."

"Let me ask you a question, Mark."

"Sure, go right ahead."

"Are there any strings you can possibly pull to get me out of this mess?"

"What mess, Gina?"

"Oh, you know, this mess with Steven Richards."

Mark didn't understand Gina's problem with Steven and said, "He seems to be a pretty nice guy to me. What's wrong? Is there more to this than meets the eye? Your attitude toward him is rather extreme, not to mention strange."

Just then, Marybeth entered the room, saying, "I'll tell you what's wrong with her, Mr. Souderton. She doesn't want that black man to be her boss. Isn't that right, Gina? Tell him. Come on, be truthful with yourself, if no one else."

Mark cut in, "Is that true, Gina?"

"No, she doesn't know what she's talking about; she's always running off at the mouth."

"Well, never mind - I don't want to go there . . . you guys are going to have to work that out yourselves. How 'bout a farewell lunch today, Gina?"

"No, thanks. I've got to move my stuff out of here."

Chapter 1

"Okay, maybe tomorrow," Mark responded. He then left the two women together.

Before he could close the door behind him, Gina was all over Marybeth. "Why'd you have to come in here and say that?"

"Say what?"

"You know perfectly well what I'm talking about. You didn't have to say that I didn't want that black man to be my boss. Even if it's true, you should have kept your mouth shut."

Marybeth answered, "Gina, I love you like a sister, but there's one thing about you that really bothers me - you can't accept your blackness. It's who you are, and there's nothing in the world you can do about it."

"You got it wrong, Sister. I do love what I am and how I look."

"But you obviously have a problem with what *he* is!"

"Well, you're right about that," Gina acknowledged.

"But why is that, Gina?"

She answered in a whining tone, "I don't know, Beth, that's just the way it is . . . I can't help it. Anyway, we've gone over this a thousand times before, and I don't want to talk about it any more."

"That's right, Gina, close me out, like you always do."

Gina laughed and said, "Oh, Girl, I'm not closing you out . . . do me a favor, Beth. Go and get the handtruck for me. I think it's in the storeroom. I want to load this stuff on it and get the hell out of here."

Marybeth looked at Gina with an affectionate smile and said, "No problem - at least I have you laughing again."

The argument they had just had was pretty commonplace between them, but, as usual, did not have any effect on their relationship.

When Marybeth returned with the handtruck, the two women loaded it with Gina's belongings. Then they passed through the large common area of the firm with Gina moving her body in a seductive manner, at the same time pulling the cart, waving, and saying goodbye, while Marybeth was bent over pushing the other end of the cart, with her cheeks jiggling up and down . . . up and down. You would have thought both of them were leaving for good. Between the two of them, they had the whole staff laughing. As a matter of fact, Gina and Marybeth were always just about the only entertainment available in the stuffy atmosphere of Dillenbeck, Talley and Grundage.

When they got to Steven's offices, Marybeth was obviously excited and said, "Ooh, Gina, let me come in for a minute. Please?"

"Well, Beth, you really shouldn't . . ."

"Oh, please, please? I want to see what your new home looks like."

"You mean you want to be newsy . . . Beth, you've been all through this place. You know what every square inch of it looks like. You just want to get a peep at him again, and right now I want to be alone . . . I want to work this out myself. Some other time, okay?"

"Sure, Honey, I understand."

One of the practices of the law firm was the placement of a one-way mirror in all executive offices in order to keep an eye on secretaries and staff. When the two women came in, a buzzer had gone off, alerting Steven. He rose from his desk, went over to the mirror, and watched them talking. After Marybeth left, he continued to watch Gina. She was still breathtaking to him, but he knew he had to maintain control over the relationship. When he saw her coming toward his office door, he ran back to his desk, picked up the phone and pretended to be talking to someone. She knocked, and he called, "Come in, the door's open."

He began speaking on the phone to no one. "Okay, that's fine with me . . . I'll have to call you back; someone just came in. I'll tell you what, why don't you call me tonight, and we can talk more about it . . . alright, bye now." He then turned his attention to Gina. "Ms. Epps, I see you managed to get yourself and your belongings here."

Gina didn't say anything; she just gave him a quick smirk of a smile and asked, "Where's my desk?"

"The one just outside this room is yours . . . and why is it that I believe you already knew that?"

Gina simply said, "Thank you, Mr. Richards. While I'm here, is there anything else I can do?"

"Well, for now, get yourself situated, but the first thing tomorrow morning, I have applicants coming in, and I'll need your help with them."

"Very well, Mr. Richards."

Although Steven had told her to address him as Mr. Richards, now he found himself softening toward her, and he said, "Gina, not so formal - you can call me Steven if you want to."

"Well, Mr. Richards, it's not up to me - it's what you want. If you want me to call you Steven, I'll call you Steven; if you want me to call you Mr. Richards, I'll do that. It's up to you."

"Well . . . call me Steven."

"Okay. You're the boss."

Steven laughed to himself and thought, "I hope so." Given Gina's singular effect on him, asserting his authority might not always be easy!

Chapter 2

At a country club in Abington, one of Philadelphia's suburban towns, Martin Pollock, Jr., a part-time law clerk at Dillenbeck, Talley and Grundage and the son of a junior partner there, was finishing a game of racquetball with one of his best friends, Jeffrey Burroughs. Jeffrey's father was a well-known African-American surgeon, and Jeffrey himself was a medical student.

Martin grabbed a towel to wipe the sweat from his face and said, "That was a good workout, Jeff."

Jeffrey laughed. "The only time you say that is when you beat me, and here lately that seems to be all the time. You know what they say - never say die - one of these days, I'm going to get my swing back and beat the crap out of you."

"Yeah, yeah, I know. For now, let's hit the showers - maybe it'll make you feel better after getting whipped."

As they were showering, Martin called over to him, "Yo, Jeff, why don't we drive into Philly tonight?"

"And do what?"

"Well, there's going to be a little get-together over at Lenny's. How's that sound?"

"No, I don't think I should go. I promised my dad I'd help him find his way around the internet tonight. Myself, personally, I don't think he'll ever understand it - he's already forgotten what I've shown him before."

"Well, I just wish I had any kind of relationship with my old man," Martin responded sadly.

While Martin and Jeffrey were talking, a third person had slipped into the shower room. Both young men were facing the wall and had no idea that someone other than themselves was in the room. The intruder moved quickly and quietly into

Martin's stall, put his left hand over Martin's mouth to keep him from crying out, and stuck a six-inch stiletto deep into his back. He immediately pulled it out and put it to his throat and slashed it twice from ear to ear. Martin had enough life left in him to turn around. He slid down against the tiles of the shower stall, and the look on his face was one of shocked recognition of his assailant. He murmured a single word, "Why?"

His attacker carefully put the knife down on the shower floor and slipped out of the room as quickly as he had come in.

During the attack, Jeffrey was still talking to Martin, completely unaware of what was taking place. "You know what, Martin, I was just thinking - maybe we should get together tonight after all. It'd be a lot more fun than putting up with Dad."

There was no response from Martin. Jeffrey called out, "Yo! Are you still with me?" Still no answer. "Martin, are you there?" Jeffrey assumed that Martin had left and thought no more of it. By now he had finished his shower so he stepped out, reached for a towel and started to dry himself. He could hear that the water in Martin's stall was still running, and he glanced quickly into the stall. From where he was standing, he could only see a small portion of it, but what he saw made his hair stand on end. He saw that the water on the floor was a pinkish-red. Suddenly afraid of what more he might see, he moved cautiously, peering into the stall slowly until he could see it all - Martin's bloodied body slumped against the wall, his head sagging to one side and his legs twisted beneath him.

Jeffrey cried out in horror, "Oh, my God, what the hell happened?" He stepped into the shower. He immediately tried to find a pulse, but there was none. He saw the murder weapon lying beside Martin, picked it up and then hastily dropped it. In a panic, he rushed out of the shower room, wrapped in his towel, into the corridor of the club. He ran to the front desk, yelling, "Call the police. Somebody call the police! Martin Pollock's been murdered! He's in the shower room."

Fifteen minutes later, Jeffrey was seated in the club lounge, being questioned by Detective Sean Dickens. Jeffrey's account of what had happened didn't add up to Dickens, and he said to him, "Son, you're in a pretty precarious situation here. Mr. Pollock was slashed to death with a knife with you right there. The only thing separating you two was the wall of a shower stall, and you mean to tell me you didn't hear anything? You need to help me here. If I don't find any prints on the knife, I won't have anything to go on. I've got to be honest with you . . . since you're the last one to see him alive, you're my only suspect."

Jeffrey responded, "I was afraid you were going to tell me something like that. And what's worse is that my fingerprints probably will be on the knife. When I went in the stall, right after I looked for a pulse, I saw the knife lying beside his body and, not thinking, picked it up."

"Well, in that case, I think you have a problem," Dickens said.

Jeffrey protested, "That's my best friend lying in that shower room, and you're going to tell me that you believe I did it?"

"No, I didn't say I believe you did it. I said you were my only suspect . . . at this time."

"Then I don't think I should say anything else to you - maybe I should get a lawyer."

"That would be wise."

Chapter 2

After the conversation with Dickens, Jeffrey went straight home. When he entered the house, his mother, Helen, immediately saw the distraught look on his face and said, "Son, what's the matter? You look like you just lost your best friend!"

"Mom, you don't know how true that is. You know Martin Pollock . . . the guy I had over to dinner last week? Well, he was murdered today. We were taking a shower at the club, and somebody murdered him right while I was in the stall next to him! And that's not all, Mom . . . the police think I did it!"

"Oh, my God, Son! Are you alright?"

"Yeah, I'm okay, but I've got big problems - I just lost a friend today, and now I'm being accused of killing him."

Helen said, "Maybe we should call Ted Carpenter."

"But, Mom, all he handles is wills and stuff - I think I'm going to need a criminal lawyer for this."

"Well, we can call him and at least get some advice." She rushed to the phone and dialed. "Is Mr. Carpenter there? This is Helen Burroughs . . . No, I have to talk to him right now . . . this is an emergency!" While Helen was waiting, she said, "Jeffrey, your father is going to be very upset by this."

"Mom, I can't concern myself with Dad being upset! That's the least of my worries."

"Well, you know how he is."

Mr. Carpenter came on the line.

"Ted, this is Helen Burroughs. I'm sorry to have interrupted you, but my son believes that he's being accused of murder."

Mr. Carpenter expressed shock. "What! There must be some sort of mistake. I know Jeffrey's not capable of something like that."

"Yes, I know, but the police don't share that same view. Right now, he needs help."

"Helen, you know I'm not a criminal lawyer."

"I know you're not, Ted, but maybe you can steer me to someone competent who handles these kind of things."

"Let me see . . . oh, yeah, there was a real smart young man at the firm where I used to be - the last I heard he had gone to Dan Dillenbeck's firm."

"Do you have his number?"

"No, but I'll try to get hold of him and see if he can call you right away."

Five minutes after Helen hung up the phone, the doorbell rang. She looked out the side window to see who it was. "Jeffrey, it's the police! What should I do?"

"Let 'em in, Mom. I didn't do anything, so I don't have any reason to hide."

Helen opened the door. It was Lieutenant Dickens, accompanied by two uniformed officers. Dickens asked, "Is this the residence of Jeffrey Burroughs?"

Jeffrey joined his mother at the door and asked, "What's the matter? Did you want to ask some more questions?"

Dickens replied, "I'm afraid it's not that simple, Jeffrey. I have a warrant for your arrest."

"A warrant for my arrest?" Jeffrey's heart was pounding at the thought of it.

At that moment, Jeffrey's father, Dr. Ozzie Burroughs, came in the front door and demanded, "What's going on here?"

Dickens asked, "Who are you?"

"No, the question is, who are you and what are you doing in my house?"

Helen cut in. "This is Jeffrey's father."

"Well, Mr. Burroughs, your son is under arrest for the murder of Martin Pollock."

Chapter 2

"Murder! You have to be kidding. My boy would never do anything like that."

"Well, if he didn't do it, you don't have anything to worry about."

"No, you're wrong. Given the boy's color, I think I do have something to worry about."

Dickens ordered one of the policemen to handcuff Jeffrey and read him his rights. He then steered him out the door.

Ozzie hollered out, "Don't worry, Son, we'll be down to get you out as fast as we can." He turned back to his wife, "We've got to get a lawyer - let's call . . ."

Helen interrupted. "Honey, I've already taken care of that. I'm waiting for a call from an attorney that Mr. Carpenter recommended."

Ozzie was beside himself. "What the hell's going on? I come home and find cops in my house, my son's been dragged away - what the hell's going on, Helen?"

She explained what she knew, and he cried out, "Goddamn it, there's no way you're going to get me to believe my son could commit a murder!"

At that moment, the phone rang, and Ozzie picked it up. It was Steven Richards who asked, "Is this the Burroughs residence?"

"Yes, it is. To whom am I speaking?"

"This is Steven Richards, and I'm with the firm of Dillenbeck, Talley and Grundage. Ted Carpenter said you might want to talk to me."

"Yes, we do . . . would you speak to my wife? She knows more about this than I do." He handed the phone to Helen.

Steven introduced himself to her and said, "I don't think this is anything we can talk about over the phone; you'll have to come in and see me."

"Oh, Mr. Richards, you don't understand. My only child has just been arrested - I don't want him to spend a minute longer in jail than necessary!"

"Okay, Ms. Burroughs, where did they take him?"

"The Abington Police Station."

"I'm in Philadelphia - it'll take me about thirty-five to forty minutes to get out there. Could you meet me there?"

Helen gratefully agreed.

Steven hung up the phone and went into the outer office and asked, "Gina, are you pretty well set up here?"

"Yes, I guess I'm as settled as I'm going to be."

"Well, this may not be customary procedure in the type of law you're used to, but I'm going out to see a client now, and I'm going to need you to come along and take some notes for me."

"I'm sorry, Sir, but are you telling me to go or asking me to go?"

"I'm telling you that you have to go because I'm asking you to. And that's the way it is. I'm leaving now, Gina."

Gina said, "Could you hold on a minute? I'm just going to powder my nose," and started toward the ladies' room.

Steven stopped her. "Gina, we don't have time for that. I told you I was leaving right now. You can do it in the car."

"I can take my car and follow you."

"No, Gina, we're going to take one car, and that's mine."

In the car on the way out to Abington, both of them were very uptight, and the air was thick with tension. During the whole trip, Gina spent the time looking in the mirror, fussing with her make-up, and not a word passed between them. When Steven pulled up to the police station, he got out quickly so that he could open Gina's door for her, but before he could get around to her side of the car, she jumped out. At

that point, he slowed his walk so as not to appear to be rushing to assist her and said, "You're pretty fast, Gina. I won't try that again."
Gina gave him a victorious smile.
When they entered the police station, they went directly to the front desk, and Steven asked if Jeffrey Burroughs was being held there.
Jeffrey's parents were sitting on a bench near the front desk, and when they heard their son's name, they knew who Steven was. Both of them jumped up anxiously and hurried over and introduced themselves.
Helen said, "We asked them to let us see him, but they wouldn't."
Steven responded, "Don't worry about it, Ms. Burroughs. I'll take care of it from here."
The officer on the front desk had made a phone call and now told Steven, "Yes, he's here, but he's being interrogated. Who are you?"
"I'm his attorney, and this is my assistant."
"I don't know whether you can see him now."
"No, I can see him now and I want to see him now," Steven responded forcefully.
The officer called the interrogation room, and Dickens answered the phone. "Lieutenant Dickens, a Steven Richards is out here - he says he's Burroughs' lawyer , and he wants to see his client."
"Okay, you can send him back."
Steven asked Helen and Ozzie to stay put and said he hoped that when he came out, he would have Jeffrey with him. He was relieved to hear that Lieutenant Dickens was handling the case. He had encountered him before and thought that he was pretty rational . . . for a cop.

As Steven and Gina entered the room where Jeffrey was being held, Dickens was asking Jeffrey, "Are you sure you don't have anything else you want to tell me?"

Steven broke in. "He doesn't have to tell you anything more at all, and if you don't have proof enough to hold him, I think you should release him."

"Hello, Richards. On the contrary, we do have enough for an arrest. His fingerprints are on the murder weapon."

Steven asked, "Would that be true, Jeffrey?"

Jeffrey explained to Steven how his fingerprints happened to be on the knife, and Steven said to Dickens, "Well, really, since he told you about this even before you examined the weapon, I don't think you have any reason to hold him. I think you should release him into my custody."

Dickens surprised Steven by saying, "Well, Richards, I've known you for a spell and trust your judgment, so for now, I'm gonna let him go." He turned to Jeffrey and said, "You're free to go, Son."

As Jeffrey, Gina and Steven were leaving, Dickens said, "Richards, can I see you a minute?"

"Sure, why not?"

Dickens said quietly to Steven, "You know, between you and me, you're wrong - I do have enough to hold him. I'm letting him go because I don't believe the kid did it. But judging from the evidence so far, I may have to haul him back in here at any time."

Upon entering the outer room, Jeffrey's mother and father rushed up to him. Helen cried, "Are you okay? Did they hurt you?"

Ozzie said, "Helen, stop that. Can't you see the boy's alright?" but he hugged his son very tightly.

Steven said, "Well, Gina, that's all we can do here for now; let's get back to the office," and then told Jeffrey, "If anything else comes up, make sure you call me. I have to tell you - right now, it doesn't look all that good for you."

"I know that, Sir, but believe me, I had nothing to do with killing my best friend."

"Well, Jeffrey, if it means anything, I believe you, so don't worry about it." Then Steven smiled and said, "Besides, you're in good hands now! I don't like to lose!"

On their way back, Steven asked, "Well, what do you think, Gina?"

"What do I think about what?"

"Oh, you know, the case . . . weren't you there?"

"Yes, I was there . . . and I think he's guilty."

"Gina, what is there about it that would bring you to such a speedy conclusion of guilt?"

"Well, isn't the fact that his fingerprints were all over the place proof enough for you?"

"No, Gina, that's not enough proof, and I'm really surprised that a woman as intelligent as you appear to be could rush to judgment so quickly."

"Oh, don't give me that condescending, liberal stuff about innocent until proven guilty. You don't care if some creep kills an innocent person in a carjacking or for a vial of crack. As a defense lawyer, you just want to worry about their rights to continue to do as they please and get away with it."

"Gina, let me ask you something. And please try to be as honest as you possibly can. I need to know this. Do you believe Jeffrey Burroughs is guilty because he's a black man?"

Gina glanced toward him, and, for a moment, their eyes met in silence. She turned away, but not before Steven had seen the look on her face - the look of someone about to reveal their true feelings. She spoke out. "Well, who's committing all the crimes? I don't see any white people coming into our neighborhoods doing these terrible things. Who's . . . who's doing all this stuff? I'll tell you who it is - it's us - it's our own people - and, to be honest . . . I'm afraid of them!"

"First of all, Gina, this case has nothing to do with anything you just said. This is a black man going to medical school whose friend was murdered in a suburban country club to which they both belong. Now you tell me how that relates to what you were talking about? Which raises my next question - is that your problem with me - that I'm a black man? Or am I completely off base?"

Gina replied, "I don't feel I should have to answer that - what I feel is my own business."

"Gina, your answer won't reflect on what I think of you as an employee. We really need to be completely honest with each other, and I think we'll work much better together."

"Steven, I don't want to talk about this now. Will you drop it . . . please?"

"Just one more question. Have you ever dated a black man?"

"I can't recall."

Steven sighed. "Well, I can see I'm getting nowhere. We've both had a long day - let's go and close up the office and then get a bite to eat."

"Are you inviting me to dinner?"

"I guess I am. Will you accept?"

"Well, if there's any way that I could consider an invitation to dinner as sexual harassment, I would. In other words, I'm suggesting that you be careful in what you say to me."

"Gina, I think I understand exactly where you're coming from, and I'm sorry that you see things the way you do. You

Chapter 2

have my promise. From this day on, our relationship will be on a strictly professional basis."

When they neared the office, she asked, "Is it necessary for me to come up with you?"

"No, you're finished for the day. I'll see you tomorrow. Oh, those notes you took back at the police station - have them typed up and on my desk first thing in the morning."

Steven pulled over to the curb, and as he watched Gina getting out of the car, he couldn't help noticing her short skirt rising to the very top of her thighs. His eyes followed her until she got to the parking lot. Before she walked through the entrance, she turned to see if he was watching.

Chapter 3

Every morning that they had the time, Gina and Marybeth had coffee and doughnuts in the building coffeeshop before they went upstairs. This morning, Gina was already sitting at a table when her friend came in. "Hi, Gina! How ya doin'?"

"I'm fine."

"How did it go yesterday with your new boss?" Marybeth asked in a coy voice. "Did he come on to you?"

"Oh, Beth, don't try to turn everything into something sexual. He was the perfect gentleman."

"Well, what do you think of him?"

"Oh, he's okay."

"He must be more than okay. You wouldn't leave anything out on me, would you?"

"Beth, you know how I feel, so don't even go there."

"Well, you could do worse than landing a full partner in Dillenbeck, Talley and Grundage!"

"I'll tell you what I did do. I threatened to sue him for sexual harassment if he did or said anything that I considered grounds for it."

"You didn't! Why did you do that? Did he or didn't he make a pass at you? I thought you said he was a perfect gentleman."

"Well, I just wanted to keep him on his toes."

Gina and Marybeth talked a while longer. Suddenly Gina jumped up and cried, "Oh, my God, it's almost time for the last elevator - let's get out of here." They made a dash for it. As they stepped out on the 37th floor, Martin Pollock was passing and asked irritably, "Marybeth, do you ever catch anything but the last elevator up?"

"Mr. Pollock, it is my own time. Will you give me that?"

Chapter 3

"Well, sometimes when you purposely do things at the last minute, you miss out. Keep that in mind." He went on down the hall.

Marybeth whispered to Gina, "Damn, you'd think he'd take a couple of days off - after all, his son just got murdered."

Gina replied, "Well, for some people, work is therapy."

"Not me, Honey. I'd take all the days off I could get. I'll see you later."

Gina went to her office and typed up her notes from the day before. She took them in and handed them to Steven, asking him, "Do you have a minute?"

"Yeah, go right ahead, Gina."

"I thought about what you said yesterday as far as you and I needing a good working relationship. I'm sorry I came across so cold, but I can't help feeling the way I do. So I'm asking you to try and accept me as I am."

Steven was curious. "Just for the record, Gina, how *do* you feel? What are you really saying to me?"

"I guess the truth is I've never had any interest in dating black men, and furthermore, I don't like having a black man in authority over me. But that's a fact that I can't change unless I decide to quit, and I'm not about to do that so I'll just have to get used to it. Starting now, I'll do the best job that I can possibly do for you."

"Gina, I hear you, and if that's the way it is, so be it. If you ever have any problems, I'll be here for you."

The buzzer at the entrance to the suite rang. Steven said, "You'd better see who that is. And, Gina . . . about screening the job applicants . . . I want the best qualified; you have to leave your personal opinions out of this."

"You don't trust me to do that, Steven?"

"To be honest with you, Gina, from what I've just heard, no - I don't trust you to be objective. As a matter of fact, I want to see all the resumes."

Gina went to the outer office and opened the door for a man who was applying for the position of investigator on Steven's staff. As she read over his resume, another applicant came into the office, and Gina asked, "Are you applying for one of the positions?"

"Yes. My name is Andrea Hall."

"Just put your resume in the basket there, and I'll be with you shortly."

When Gina finished with the first applicant, she called, "Ms. Hall?"

Andrea Hall was about five foot three with a petite well-shaped body. Her facial features were a mixture of African and European, and she had a beautiful brown complexion and wore very little make-up. She was rather plain in appearance, but looking closely at her, you could see that if her make-up and clothing were more flamboyant, she could easily give Gina a run for her money.

Gina asked, "Ms. Hall, I see here you're applying for the researcher position. Why did you leave your last job?"

"The company was down-sizing, and I was one of the last to be hired."

Just at that moment, Steven came out of the office and said, "Gina, after you finish there, could you get Jeffrey Burroughs on the phone for me?"

When Andrea saw Steven, she appeared awe-struck by him and found it difficult to stop looking in his direction. He went back into his office, and Gina laughingly said, "Ms. Hall, your interest in Mr. Richards is pretty evident - try to compose yourself!"

Chapter 3

Andrea was embarrassed and said, "Oh, I'm sorry! Was my staring that obvious? I've heard so much about him. He's pretty well-known in the legal world."

Gina asked Andrea a few more questions about her resume and then told her, "That'll be all, Ms. Hall. We'll let you know in a couple of days if an interview with Mr. Richards will be scheduled."

Just as Andrea was about to leave, Steven popped his head out of his office door. "Excuse me, Ma'am, but are you applying for one of the positions we have open here?"

Not sure if Steven was talking to her, Andrea looked around the room to be certain there was no one else he could possibly be addressing. When she saw that there wasn't, she asked, "Are you talking to me, Sir?"

Steven shook his head up and down affirmatively. "Uh-huh, I'm talking to you!"

Andrea nervously answered, "Yes, Sir, I am."

"Which position?" Steven asked.

"Researcher, but Sir, I. . ."

Steven cut her off. "Good, you're just the one I need to see . . . will you come into my office, please?"

"Right away, Sir."

Gina put her thumb and forefinger together in a circle, held it up to Andrea and winked an eye, as if to say, "Good luck!"

In his office, Steven extended his hand to her. "My name is Steven Richards . . . and you are?"

"Oh, I'm Andrea Hall."

"Well, Ms. Hall, I'm glad to meet you."

Andrea felt a warmth go all through her body as she held Steven's hand. She didn't want to let it go, but she remembered how obvious her attraction to him had been to Gina and quickly pulled her hand away.

"Have a seat, Ms. Hall . . . and I might as well tell you, if you can do what I need you to do right now, the job is yours."

"Oh, Mr. Richards, thank you very much for the opportunity. Just tell me what it is you want, and I'll do the very best I can."

"I'm telling you, Ms. Hall, if you can't do this, you don't have the job."

"I understand, Sir."

Steven had no way of knowing it, but Andrea had a lot of experience in the field of criminal law research and was completely confident in her ability to do whatever he might ask of her.

"I want you to go to the law library and look for case law.'" Steven handed her a list of issues he wanted researched.

"No problem, Mr. Richards."

"Good luck! I hope you can find what I need."

Andrea stood there sort of mesmerised for a moment, and Steven said, "That's all, Ms. Hall."

"Oh, I'm sorry, Sir. I'm on my way."

As she left the office, Gina asked her, "How'd you do?"

"He said if I can do the assignment he gave me, I'll have the job. I'm pretty sure I'll be able to."

"Well, if you come back in time, maybe you'd like to have lunch with me and a friend of mine."

"Oh, that'll be great!"

Andrea left and, so overwhelmed by the fact that she had been given a chance at the job without having to be concerned about other applicants, on her way down the hall she lost control of her emotions, put a little skip to her stride and yelled out, "Whoopee!" With that, she drew the attention of the few people in the corridor; they looked at her as if she were crazy. When she noticed their stares, she brought her hand up to her mouth as if to try and control herself, acting as if she were ashamed of her outburst, but continuing to make a spectacle of herself by saying out loud, "I think I'm going to like this job - I like the people here."

One of the passers-by murmured to himself, "Yeah, I'd like to see how she feels a couple of months from now!"

The phone rang in Steven's office. It was Gina. "Steven, I have Jeffrey Burroughs on the line."

"Hi, Jeffrey, how're you doin'?"

"I'm fine, Sir. You wanted to talk to me about something?"

"Yes. Jeffrey, how long had you and Martin been together on the day of the murder?"

"I picked him up in the morning, the same as I do just about every day. We had breakfast and then went straight to the club."

"How many people in the club saw you together?"

"Oh, just about everyone. We go there on a regular basis."

"Did you guys have any disagreements or arguments that someone within earshot might misconstrue as being threatening or violent in nature?"

"Not that I can think of, Sir."

"Now, this is important, Jeffrey, so try and remember. Any little thing you can think of may be of some help to us."

Jeffrey thought a bit and then said, "Oh, yeah, I don't know whether this is important or not, but I used to beat him in racquetball all the time, but here lately he'd been beating me, and we were discussing that, but it wasn't what I would call an argument. He was more like joshing or teasing me, the same as I did him when I was winning."

"Was it loud and boistrous?" Steven asked.

"Well, I suppose someone listening might hear it that way. I think I said I was going to beat the crap out of him someday."

"Oh, great," Steven groaned. "Well, Jeffrey, I guess that'll be all. You haven't heard anything more from Lieutenant Dickens, have you?"

"No, thank goodness!"

"I don't think it's going to go away, Jeffrey. We're going to have to be prepared so I'll probably be calling you from time to time."

After Steven hung up, he buzzed for Gina on the intercom. "Gina, Talley has a brief he wants me to review. Could you please pick it up? I'd like to have that as soon as possible."

There was no response from Gina. A minute or two passed, and he buzzed her again, but still no response. He got up from his desk and looked out through the one-way mirror but didn't see her anywhere. He went into the outer room, looked around, but still no Gina. The entrance to Steven's suite had a door, the top half of which was framed smoked glass, and through it, he could see two silhouetted figures standing very close together. The one figure he knew was Gina's, and the other figure was obviously that of a male. His heart started beating rapidly, and he found himself feeling afraid of discovering that Gina was already spoken for. Fearful of what he might find, he slowly approached the door and just when he opened it, he saw Gina on her toes, stretching, trying to equal the height of a tall, dark-haired, white man in order to kiss him on the lips. Opening the door startled them, stopping them from engaging in what might have become a steamy, passionate moment.

Chapter 3

Steven was both nervous and angry - nervous because he didn't want to show any sign of jealousy and angry because Gina had not been at her work station where she belonged when he needed her.

Gina obviously was shook up by Steven's presence, and before he could say anything, she immediately jumped from the man's arms and said, "Oh! I'm sorry, Mr. Richards. I'd like you to meet Bob Rosenberg. Bob, this is my boss."

Bob extended his hand to Steven. "Glad to meet you, Mr. Richards."

Steven just nodded his head in a not-so-friendly manner and then turned his attention back to Gina. "I want you in my office right away," he said. Trying to exercise restraint and not show his anger, Steven carefully turned away, although not without a slight jerking movement, and quickly went back to his office.

Gina and Bob stood there momentarily. She shrugged her shoulders as if to say, "Well, I have to go now," and Bob tilted his head and turned one corner of his mouth up, indicating to her, "What can I say?" They both walked away.

When Gina got in Steven's office, before he could get a word in, she started apologizing in a rapid monotone, "Steven, I'm very sorry about that, and I promise you that it'll never happen again."

Even though what he had just seen upset him a lot, he didn't want to risk any remote chance he might have with Gina and told her in the mildest way possible, "All I ask is that you leave your love life outside of this office. What I was really more disturbed about is you not letting me know you were going out. Alright, Gina, let's get beyond that. Now, what I called you for - Talley's secretary has some papers I want you to pick up right away. She's expecting you."

It was almost lunchtime, and as Gina was leaving the office, Marybeth was coming in, "Oh, Gina, I know I'm a little early, but I came to find out where we're going to have lunch today."

"Not now, Beth. I'm in a rush. I have to go down to Talley's office and pick up something. Why don't you come with me?"

"Oh, I'll just wait here for you."

"I'd prefer you went with me."

"Gina, I'd rather stay here."

"I know what you're up to . . . Girl, don't bother that man in there!"

"Oh, get outta here, Gina. You're always thinking the worst of me!"

As soon as Gina left, Marybeth knocked on Steven's door. Steven had seen who it was through the one-way mirror and called out, "Come in, it's open."

She entered the room and walked over to his desk, moving in a provocative way. "How do ya like being a partner in DTG so far?"

Although Steven felt Marybeth was being a little disrespectful, the fact that she was Gina's friend tempted him to play along, and he answered, "So far, so good," and then, in order to remind her of his position in the firm, said, "By the way, that's DTGR - R for Richards."

"Oh, right. How's it coming with Gina?"

Steven thought to himself that if he had been white, Marybeth would not have been so presumptuous as to believe that such a question would be tolerated, and he said, "I don't know what you mean by that question, Beth."

"Oh, you know. I noticed the way you were looking at her when you first saw her."

Steven asked, "How do you think Gina would feel if she knew you were in here questioning me this way?"

"You don't understand Gina's and my relationship. Even if Gina was here, I wouldn't have any problem asking you the same questions."

"You ladies are really close, aren't you?"

"You got it. As close as mice tits."

At that moment, Gina entered the office and demanded, "As close as what?"

Steven said, "Well, Beth here was just telling me - in her own unique way - how close the two of you are as friends."

Gina said, "Oh . . . here's the brief you wanted. Beth, are you ready to go to lunch?"

Marybeth answered yes, but before they left, she said, "Oh, and, Steven, when you get tired of chasing Gina around the desk, you can come chase me around mine for a while!"

As they were leaving, Gina wailed, "Beth, why do you always have to be so crude?"

"I thought you didn't care what he thought."

"I don't," Gina snapped.

"Girl, that man is a hunk, and you are a real fool!"

As they were getting on the elevator to leave the building, Andrea was getting off. Gina greeted her. "Oh, Andrea, I forgot all about you! How'd you make out?"

"It was a breeze. I think he'll be satisfied."

Gina introduced Andrea to Marybeth and then said, "I'll tell you what, we'll wait down in the lobby for you."

"No, you guys go ahead - I'll just grab something quick at the snack bar. I'm sure we can do this another time."

Gina and Marybeth got on the elevator, and Gina said, "I know she just wants to be with Steven alone - that's why she turned the lunch down."

Marybeth laughed. "Gina, you crazy. She gonna take that man right from underneath you. All those white guys you like to date - ain't none of 'em goin' take you home to Mama - including that one you got now."

"Oh, Beth, speaking of Bob, let me tell you the awful thing that happened today!"

Andrea returned to Steven's office and gave him the information he had requested and said, "I hope you'll be satisfied."

After Steven had quietly looked over the papers, he said, "You did a very good job, Andrea, and I'm satisfied . . . but I'm afraid it's not in my client's favor."

"I'm very sorry to hear that, Sir."

"Well, it comes with the territory. By the way, I hope you won't be sorry to hear that you have the job!"

A smile lit Andrea's face, and she exclaimed, "Oh, thank you, Mr. Richards. Thank you very much. I hope I'll be able to live up to your expectations."

"I'm sure you will."

Andrea started to leave the room and then turned back and asked, "Which desk will be mine?"

"You have your choice since you're the first to be hired - just don't take Gina's."

Andrea said, "Oh, of course not," and left the room.

Steven's phone rang, and he picked it up.
"Hello, Mr. Richards; this is Dickens."
"Hi, Lieutenant. How may I be of help to you?"
"I'm afraid it's not very good news as far as your client goes. I have to bring him in on a charge of first degree murder."
"But you don't even have a motive."

Chapter 3

"I don't need a motive. The murder weapon says it all, Richards. In addition, someone heard him threaten Martin."

"Well, I can assure you that so-called threat has already been explained to my satisfaction. I just don't understand the rush to arrest him. He's not going anywhere. I'm willing to guarantee that."

"I'm being pressured to bring him in, but I would like to spare his family the embarrassment of arresting him at the house and taking him away in handcuffs - so I was thinking maybe you might want to deliver him. Can I depend on you to do that?"

"You sure there's not another way we can handle this? I mean, this kid is innocent, and I think it's a darn shame that he would have to go through this just because you guys don't want to look for anyone else."

Dickens bristled angrily. "Right now, Richards, all I'm interested in is whether I can depend on you to bring Burroughs in."

Steven reluctantly agreed. "Yeah, you can depend on me."

Gina had come back from lunch, and she was telling Andrea all about the firm when Steven came out of his office and said, "Andrea, I need you to go with me to a client's house." To Gina, he explained, "They want to arrest Jeffrey Burroughs, and I'm going out to bring him in."

Gina's previous job did not include her leaving the office on business. She secretly enjoyed the idea of it and so was somewhat disturbed by Steven asking Andrea to go instead of her. While Andrea had gone to get her coat, Gina called Steven to her desk and said, "I thought I would be the one to go with you when you go out to see a client."

"Gina, now that I know the way you feel about me - and black men in general - I would rather not have you accompany me. I hope you understand. And besides, this is why I hired Andrea - she has more experience in this area than you do. I think our interests will be best served by your staying in the office and holding down the fort." Steven added, with a smile, "And I wouldn't want to give you any opportunity to sue me for sexual harassment!"

Just then, Andrea came back with her coat and said, "I'm ready, Mr. Richards."

"Please, Andrea . . . just Steven."

At that, Andrea blushed with delight.

As they walked out together, Gina watched them go, looking more than a little annoyed.

Chapter 4

In Dan Dillenbeck's office, a meeting had begun among Dillenbeck, Andrew Talley and Simon Grundage, along with Martin Pollock, Sr. After they had expressed to Pollock how sorry they were about his son's death, Grundage said to Pollock, "I don't know if you know it or not, but Richards, our new partner, is defending your son's murderer."

Pollock looked shocked. "How could that be?"

Grundage responded, "It had to be an outside referral - we would never have agreed to represent the son of a bitch."

Dillenbeck broke in. "Now wait a minute! Before you go off half-cocked, we added a criminal law department to the firm to broaden our capabilities. We got Richards because he's one of the best; he's heading up that department, and if he thinks the case can be won, he has the right to take it."

Pollock responded, "Yeah, yeah, I know you think Richards is hot stuff, but there's plenty of good white lawyers around - why did you have to choose a black one to bring into the firm?"

"Well, Pollock, we felt it was useful to demonstrate some commitment to affirmative action - after all, he is the only black attorney we have - and besides, most of the criminal caseload is going to be coming from blacks, and Steven will be able to attract them to us and make them feel comfortable once they're here."

Pollock didn't seem at all satisfied, saying, "I still don't understand how we're going to sit by and watch our firm defend the man who murdered my son."

Talley spoke. "Just a minute, Gentlemen, can I say something? First of all, when Richards took the case, he didn't even know that Martin was a member of the firm. And,

Martin, I hope you know that I'm as sorry as anyone here about the death of your son, but as lawyers, of all people, we should remember that a defendant is innocent until proven guilty. So far we know nothing about the case and therefore should reserve judgment." Talley had recommended Richards to the firm and was somewhat on the defensive about him.

Dillenbeck chimed in, "You're right, Andrew, and what's done is done now. To tell you the truth, I don't care how good Richards is - I don't think he's going to get him off. It looks like an open-and-shut case to me. Well, Gentlemen, that's all for now. Martin, do you have a couple of minutes? I want to talk to you about something."

"Sure, Dan," Martin replied. As the others were leaving, they again expressed sympathy for Martin's loss.

Back in her office, Gina was on the telephone with her mother who had called to tell her that Gina's father had been hospitalized because of a slight stroke. Gina immediately went to Marybeth and told her about it, asking her to let Steven know why she had to leave.

"Do you want me to drive you, Gina?"

"No, I can handle it. I'd rather you didn't."

At the hospital information desk, Gina inquired, "What room is Mr. Gilbert Epps in?"

"How long has he been here?" the receptionist asked.

"Oh, he was just admitted today for a stroke."

"He would probably be in the intensive care unit." She consulted her monitor. "Ah, here he is right here. What relationship are you to him?"

"A good friend."

She instructed Gina to sign in, and Gina signed "Gina Mills," and was given a visitor pass with that name on it.

Chapter 4

Gina's father was a very dark-skinned African-American, and whenever Gina found herself in public circumstances such as this, she was always reluctant to acknowledge that she was his daughter.

When she entered her father's room, she found her mother by his bedside. Florence Logan Epps was of the same stature as Gina, but had a lighter complexion. You could tell that Florence, when she was younger, must have looked just like Gina now.

The first thing Florence noticed when Gina entered the room was that her name tag had "Mills" printed on it. She didn't indicate her reaction except for a slight shake of her head. "Gilbert, Gina's here."

"Oh! . . . oh, my baby's here. . . my Gina's here," Gilbert said in a feeble voice. "Come here, Baby." Gina went over and placed her hand in his. He pulled her down close to his face and asked her in a whisper, "Did you tell them you were my beautiful baby? Did you, Honey . . . did you, huh?"

"Of course I did, Daddy."

Florence glanced again at Gina's name tag, and Gina's eyes met hers, and in shame, she turned away. Florence sadly shook her head again, but this time murmured, "Gina . . . my child . . . when are you gonna learn?"

Gina bent over her father and kissed him gently on the forehead and then asked her mother to join her outside the room. In the hall, she said, "Mom, Dad is pretty bad off - I thought you said this was just a slight stroke."

"Well, Gina, I didn't want to upset you because I know you must love your father . . . even though your attitude toward him is terrible. You've been denying that he's your father since you were in grade school. It's time you put an end to that nonsense. He may not be with us for much longer, and nothing would make him happier than if you acknowledged him publicly as your father. Don't you realize how awful it is - not to use your own name when you've come to visit him in the hospital?"

Gina burst into tears and sobbed, "Yes, Mom, I realize how awful it is, but I can't help it - it's the way I am. I've tried. Lord knows, I've tried."

"Well, maybe you should get some sort of counseling."

"Counseling's not going to help me, Mom. All they're going to do is tell me what I already know about myself. Listen, I can't stand to see him like this, Mom. I have to go."

Florence was really very angry with Gina and said stiffly, "Maybe you should," and went back into the room.

Before Gina could reach the elevator, she heard her mother cry out, "Gilbert! Gilbert!" and saw the nursing staff rushing to her father's room. She went back and found that her father was dead. Mother and daughter held each other, and Gina cried, "Mom, I'm sorry, I'm sorry. I'm really sorry. I feel responsible."

"Don't start blaming yourself, Baby! You have enough problems. You didn't have anything to do with his death. Here recently he's not been well and wouldn't listen to me or his doctor. Anything that was bad for him, it seemed he couldn't get it down in his body fast enough. You know, he was always talking about dying; maybe this is the way he wanted it."

After staying with her father's body for a while, Gina called her office to see if Steven and Andrea had gotten back. When there was no answer, she called Marybeth. "I have real bad news."

"What is it, Gina . . . what is it?"

Gina told her about her father's death and asked her to let Steven know that she would not be in for a few days.

When Steven and Andrea returned to the office from turning Jeffrey over to Lieutenant Dickens, the phone was ringing. It was Dillenbeck. "Oh, hello, Richards. I've been trying to reach you for the last hour and a half or so."

"Sorry I missed your call - I was out seeing a client."

"You wouldn't be talking about Jeffrey Burroughs, would you?"

"Yes, how did you know that?"

"Steven, after you've been here for a while you'll learn that there's very little that goes on in this firm that old DB doesn't know about. Let me ask you something. Did you know that there is a Martin Pollock Senior - the father of the murdered young man - and that he's a junior partner in this firm?"

"No, I didn't, Dan."

"Well, there is, and I think we may have a problem."

"I don't understand. Of course I'll make full disclosure of the facts to my client, but I feel sure it won't make any difference to him."

"But, don't you see, Steven? This will pit you against one of your own . . . one of our partners. Can't you see how that may create difficulties?"

"Not really, Dan. With all due respect, you brought me in to attract criminal cases, and that's just what I'm doing. Dan, I need to know right now . . . is every case I take on gonna be scrutinized this way?"

"Oh, of course not, Richards. Don't be so sensitive. I just like to keep peace in the family, and you defending this guy may create some bad feelings between you and Pollock."

"Well, I hope that's not the case, and it's sure not my intention."

"Enough said, Steven. Let me ask you this before I let you go. Based on what you know so far about the case, what do you think of his guilt or innocence?"

"Personally, I think he's innocent. It looks to me like he's been set up."

"Set up . . . what do you mean, set up?"

"Well, Dan, what I said . . . I believe he was framed. Someone knew that Jeffrey would be there as the fall guy."

"Do you have some particular reason why you would believe that?"

"Oh, no . . . nothing more than a hunch. It just doesn't seem to me that Burroughs is capable of such a heinous crime. Besides, the two men were very good friends . . . you know what I'm saying . . . one of those rare relationships between a white man and a black man . . . you know."

"Sure, sure, I've heard of things like that," Dillenbeck said, not sounding very sure at all. "Well, anyway, good luck with the case, Steven. I think you're gonna need it."

When Steven hung up, he sat there for a moment thinking about the conversation he and Dillenbeck had just had when the phone rang again. It was Andrea announcing a call from Marybeth.

"Thanks, Andrea. Put her through . . . hello, Beth, I was just getting ready to call you. You wouldn't happen to know where Gina is, would you?"

"Yes, I do. That's why I called. I'm afraid there's been a death in her family."

"Oh, no! Who was it?"

"Her father. She told me to tell you she would be taking a few days off."

"Oh, sure, sure . . . no problem. Tell her I said to take her time. And please, give her my condolences. Oh, and Beth, thanks for letting me know."

"Well, I'll tell you what, Steven, you can show your appreciation by letting me take you to lunch." There was a

Chapter 4

moment of silence before Marybeth said, "Well, Steven, what do you say?"

"I'll tell you what, Beth - only if you'll behave yourself." She answered in a soft, sultry voice, "Why, Steven . . . what on earth do you mean by that?"

"You know what I'm talking about, Beth. Just what you're doing right now . . . pouring it on with the sex and flirtation. We can go to lunch together if you don't do that."

"Oh, I promise, Steven, I really promise. I won't come on to you."

Because Marybeth knew that Steven was interested in Gina, she had never expected him to accept her invitation to lunch and now was very excited by the prospect. However, it was precisely because Steven was interested in Gina that he wanted to have lunch with Marybeth who might be able to tell him more about her.

When lunchtime rolled around, Marybeth came strutting into Steven's suite. "Hi, Andrea. Will you tell Steven I'm here?"

Steven came out of his office. "Are you ready, Beth?"

"Ready as Freddy," she answered flippantly.

Steven smiled and shook his head as if to say, "This woman is really crazy!" He turned to Andrea and said, "Could you do me a favor? I'm going out with Beth, so could you take your lunch at one? That way someone can be here in the office."

"You go right ahead, Steven. I'll take care of things here for you."

"Thanks, Andrea. I know I can depend on you. I'll see you when I get back."

Andrea watched them intently as they were leaving. At the door, Marybeth turned to see how she was reacting. Andrea quickly looked in another direction, but not before

Marybeth saw what she was looking for - an obvious expression of envy on Andrea's face.

Marybeth took Steven to a place where many business executives wined and dined their prospective clients. It was a swank, expensive place with a romantic ambiance that made you feel as if you were being unfaithful or doing something wrong even if you weren't.

Steven looked at the menu and then asked the waiter to make him up a cheeseburger and a Pepsi.

Marybeth peered over the top of her menu and said, "Steven, order anything you want; I'm paying for it."

Steven was annoyed by Marybeth's assumption that he was bothered by the prices and snapped at her, "Beth, I don't see anything here I want. I like cheeseburgers . . . now, what are you going to have?"

The waiter was a tall, thin, white male, somewhat effeminate with a supercilious attitude. He looked down at Steven and Marybeth in disgust and rolled his eyes to the back of his head and said, "Would you like more time to decide?"

Beth could hear the impatience in his voice and hurried up. "I'm ready. I'll have the shrimp scampi, please."

The waiter retrieved the menus and scurried off.

Marybeth asked Steven, "How do you like this place?"

"I like it fine, Beth . . . just fine." Although Steven had been to the restaurant on several occasions before, he went along with her. Racism comes in many forms, and he believed that Marybeth was engaging in one of the more subtle ones by assuming that, because he was a black man, he had never been to such a classy place and that the prices were too rich for his blood. The fact that he was a senior partner in

Chapter 4

the firm that employed her seemed to have gotten past her. Steven kept his thoughts to himself.

Marybeth asked, "So, how's the case going?"

"What case?"

"You know, the Pollock murder . . . that one."

"Word sure travels fast around the firm, doesn't it?"

"Well, what do you expect? I do work for the victim's father. You know they were gay, don't you?"

Steven was really taken by surprise. "Who are we talking about now, Beth?"

"Burroughs and Pollock . . . they were a gay couple."

"What? . . . What are you talking about, Beth? Are you sure of that?"

"Of course."

"Beth, how do you know? You can't just say things like that."

"Well, the rumor was all over the firm that Pollock's son was gay and he and Burroughs were lovers 'cause they were always together. Once I came on to Burroughs, and it was just something about the way he turned me down that made me realize he was gay."

"Beth, if what you're saying is true, I think you've just added a new twist to this case."

After lunch, Steven was sitting in his office, trying to figure out how he might be able to use what Beth had told him to Jeffrey's advantage. At this point, he realized that if this were true and the police became aware of it, they might just chalk the murder up to the result of a lover's quarrel. He decided that he just had to confirm what Beth had said.

Andrea was not back from lunch yet so he dialed Ozzie himself. After a bit of a third degree from Burroughs' receptionist, she put him on hold and then Ozzie came on the line. "Hello, Steven. Is everything okay?" he asked anxiously.

"Well, really, nothing's okay until we get your son out of jail. Doc, I'm sorry if I called at an inconvenient time, but I need to ask you a question which I hope won't offend you."

Ozzie laughed and said, "I hope it doesn't offend me either . . . go ahead."

"I heard a rumor that Jeffrey is homosexual. That you know of, is there any truth to that?"

"Yes, there is. We've known it since he was a very young boy, and his mother and I support him wholeheartedly."

"Dr. Burroughs, I have to make something clear here. You, Jeffrey and your wife have to be completely honest with me. I don't need any surprises. If we go into the courtroom, and something comes up that I don't know, that lessens my ability to defend him. If you support your son's sexual orientation, why didn't you tell me about it before now?"

"I didn't think it was relevant to anything."

"In a murder case, everything is relevant. Now, before we go any further, is there anything else that I should know about?"

"No, at the moment there's nothing I can think of. I'll tell you one thing, Steven.

"What's that, Doc?"

"I'm glad to see that you're right on the case."

"Well, that's what I get paid for."

"Steven, before you go . . . how's my son holding up? You hear so many stories about what can happen in jail - and he's no tough guy, that's for sure."

"Oh, he's doing pretty good," Steven assured him. "I just hope we can get bail set at the arraignment tomorrow and get him out of there."

Ozzie asked, "Do you think that could be a problem?"

"I don't know. It might be - we have to remember - they're gonna see him as someone black who killed a white person in the heart of suburbia, and the impact of that can't be underestimated. We'll just have to wait and see."

At Jeffrey's arraignment the next morning, the prosecution entered a charge of first degree murder and asked the judge that bail be denied. Steven argued strenuously against the prosecution's request - so emotionally that he interrupted the judge on several occasions and was cited for contempt and fined two hundred dollars. Bail was denied.

Ozzie and Helen were horrified; Jeffrey looked terrified. Steven tried to console them. "Try not to worry - Jeffrey's innocent, and I'll work as hard as I can to prove that."

Martin Pollock, Sr. and his wife, Jody, along with Dillenbeck and his assistant, had attended the arraignment. On the way out of the courtroom, Pollock glanced over at Steven and rolled his eyes. At the same time, Dillenbeck went to Steven and put his arm around his shoulders and said, "You didn't get your way, but you put on a great show. I think Talley chose just the right man to head our criminal law department."

Chapter 5

The death of Gina's father had made her take a closer look at herself, but that was all. It hadn't really changed how she felt about people of color, and, more especially, about being one herself. But every time she heard her father's last words to her, "Gina, did you tell them you were my beautiful baby?" she felt guilty about the denial of her own people.

Today would be Gina's first day back at work since her father died. On this morning, Gina was not dressed provocatively, and this was noticed by her usual admirers on her walk from the parking lot to the office. As she passed by them, one of them called out, "Hey, Baby, you're not your sexy self this morning. What's wrong?"

Gina just held her head down and moved right along.

When she got to the office, she went to Steven's door and knocked.

"Come in, it's open."

When Steven saw who it was, his heart skipped two beats. He jumped up from behind his desk. "Oh, Gina, it's you! I was so sorry to heard about your father. Are you sure you're ready to come back to work?"

"Yes, I am. I thought maybe my being here would help take my mind off things. But, if it's okay with you, I'd like to leave early today. I have something I need to take care of."

"Oh, sure, Gina . . . whenever you want."

As she was leaving his office, he stopped her and said, "Gina, tell Andrea I want to see her."

When Andrea came in, he told her, "I'm going to see Jeffrey Burroughs again, and I'd like you to come along."

"Sure, Steven. What time are you leaving?"

"In about a half an hour."

Chapter 5

Jeffrey was no longer in the Abington jail; he had been transferred to a more secure facility in the county. Andrea and Steven were in a room reserved for prisoners to consult with their attorneys. While they were waiting for Jeffrey to be brought in, Steven complimented Andrea. "I like the way you have your hair today."

Blushing deeply, she said, "Oh, do you really? I wear it this way every day. It's funny you hadn't noticed before."

Just then, the guard brought Jeffrey into the room. Steven immediately acknowledged his presence, but Andrea had been so overwhelmed by Steven's offhand compliment that she hadn't taken her eyes off him and didn't even realize that Jeffrey was now in the room with them until Steven said, "Jeffrey, you remember Andrea, don't you?"

At that point, Andrea stopped staring at Steven, and Jeffrey said, "Of course. How could I forget such an attractive woman?"

Steven explained to Jeffrey, "From now on, Andrea will probably be with me when I talk to you, but don't let her presence inhibit you from saying whatever needs to be said. She's on the team."

"Oh, her being here doesn't bother me."

"Good. How have they been treating you?"

"Ah . . . as well as can be expected, I guess," Jeffrey replied despondently. "After all, this is a prison."

"Well, Jeffrey, I'm here because we need to confirm something I recently heard. I've already talked to your father about it; I just need to hear it from you. Are you a homosexual?"

"Yes, I am," Jeffrey replied. "What does that have to do with anything?"

Steven said, "It may have plenty to do with it. In a situation as serious as this, that kind of information can't be ignored."

"Well, I wasn't trying to hide anything."

"I'm not saying that you were, Jeffrey; it's just that, like I told your father, I need to know everything there is to know in order to defend you properly. Was your relationship to Pollock that of a lover?"

"Well, we had an off-and-on relationship."

"But, what was it at the time of Martin's death?"

"It was more of a sexual nature than anything else."

"What exactly does that mean?"

"Well, let me put it this way. We've always been good friends, but we never wanted the commitment of living with each other."

"I see," Steven said and then asked, "In any relationship, one of the parties is usually more involved than the other. Who do you think that was in this case?"

While Jeffrey hesitated to answer, Andrea glanced at Steven. She found the question very intriguing since it certainly applied as well to her relationship with Steven.

Jeffrey answered. "Oh, I would probably say, it was Martin. Why all the questions? You sound like you don't believe I'm innocent."

"Well, since you're an admitted homosexual, the prosecution is going to find out, and with that kind of information as ammunition, they would eat you up and spit you out in the courtroom. There's going to be times when it will sound as if I doubt your innocence, but I'm just trying to prepare for any eventuality. Do you understand?"

"Yeah, I guess I do."

Steven then asked, "Now, Jeffrey, is there anything else you haven't mentioned that might be relevant?"

"No, there really isn't."

"Okay, Jeffrey, I guess that's all for now."

Chapter 5

Andrea and Steven said goodbye, and as they were leaving, Andrea looked back and saw Jeffrey still standing there, watching them go. Her heart went out to him - he looked so vulnerable and so completely out of place in the harsh prison setting.

In the days since Andrea had been hired, Steven had become quite aware that she was interested in him. Now, on the way back in the car, Steven was thinking to himself, "I'll have to be careful not to lead her on," but in the next breath, he said to her, "I know it's still a bit early yet, but would you like to have lunch now?"

Andrea couldn't quite believe what she was hearing and said in a high-pitched voice, "You mean with you?"

Steven turned his head and looked all around the car and said, "I don't see anyone else in here."

Andrea felt foolish, but smiled and said, "I would love it."

"Is there any place you would prefer to go?"

"Oh, a fast food place will suit me just fine."

"Any one in particular?"

"No, not really. Just stop at the first one you see. That was a fascinating interview with Jeffrey, wasn't it?"

"In what way, Andrea?"

"Oh, the way he so easily admits that he's a homosexual is really something."

"Well, his parents have known about it since he was young, and they don't seem to make a big deal out of it - being raised that way, I guess he hasn't made a big deal out of it either."

Andrea said, "He must really have great parents to just take him for what he is and not be judgmental." Then she slyly looked over at Steven and asked softly, "You're glad Gina's back, aren't you?"

Steven, surprised by the question, quickly turned and looked at her. "Why did you ask that?"

Andrea grew nervous, feeling she'd gone too far, and said, "Oh, you know, you probably have a lot of typing to get done."

Steven laughed, saying, "Well, in a pinch, I'm a pretty good typist myself." He had been made uncomfortable by Andrea's question and decided to turn the tables on her. "Now what about you? Are you married? Do you have someone you're seeing on a regular basis?"

"No. Right now, I'm living at home with my parents, but I want to get from underneath them. Talk about judgmental - they're really driving me crazy."

"Ah, you don't know how lucky you are - living at home where you know someone truly cares about you. There's been many a day I wished I were back home again. But, Andrea, getting back to you, I can't believe an attractive woman such as yourself hasn't found the right guy yet."

"Well, there's not very much to pick from these days, and the way white cops are planting evidence and framing black men all over this country, after a while, there won't be any at all to pick from."

"Do I hear a hint of social consciousness there? I like that in a woman."

Andrea turned to look at Steven and said sarcastically, "Oh, you do? I would never have known. "

Steven realized that she must be referring to his interest in Gina, who was hardly an advocate for social justice, and said, "Now wait a minute here, Andrea, hold on. Don't even go there . . ."

Before Steven could finish, Andrea realized how she must have sounded and said, "I'm sorry, Steven . . . I was way out of line. I'm . . . I'm really sorry."

Chapter 5

"Andrea, I accept your apology, but I want you to know that I don't think you know me well enough to make those kind of remarks."

"I understand . . . I won't do that again."

There was a dead silence for about a minute until Andrea broke it, asking, "Do you live alone?"

"Yeah, I have a suite at the Four Seasons."

"Oh, my goodness! I always wondered what it would be like to spend even one night there."

"Oh, it's just another hotel. Someday I might invite you up. Can you cook?"

"I'm one of the best in Philadelphia!"

"I mean some real down home cookin'. . . pig feet, potato salad, collard greens and some good ol' fried candied yams. You know what I'm sayin'?"

Andrea replied in a southern drawl, "Why, Steven, honey, where y'all think I'm from? Born and raised in the deepest part of the South."

Steven laughed and asked, "Where 'bouts yew from, Sugah?"

Andrea felt that his laughter meant that he was no longer annoyed with her. She decided to continue the joking a little longer and answered, "Souf Carolina."

Steven reacted. "Hush yo mouf, Chil', yew lyin' . . . ain't dat sumpin' - dat's just where ah's from." He stopped laughing at that point and said, "Well, it's a date, Andrea . . . I want you to hold me to that . . . y'all hear me?" That's when he turned to look at Andrea and found her looking at him strangely. He quickly returned his attention to the road and thought to himself, "Oh, my God, I've probably done just what I was afraid of doing. I really didn't want to lead her on."

And Andrea said wistfully, "That would be nice, Steven."

At that point, Steven spotted a restaurant and was glad for an opportunity to change the subject. "Look, Andrea, there's a Wendy's - is that good enough?"

"Sure."

After they ate, Steven told Andrea, "You know, I really enjoyed that - it's the first time I've been in one of these places since I was a kid."

Andrea laughed. "In that case, the next time, we'll get you a kid's meal!"

Steven smiled. "Very good, Andrea . . . very good! You know . . . you're alright, Girl!"

When they got back to work, Gina was not there, and Steven remarked anxiously, "She left earlier than I expected her to." As he walked into his office, he said, "She's probably just gone out to lunch." He put his head back out the door. "Andrea, if Gina comes back, tell her I want to see her." He turned to go back in, saying, "I wonder where she is."

Andrea just looked at him sadly, acutely aware of his preoccupation with Gina.

Steven went to his window to look out. As he was taking in the view of Philadelphia, he happened to look down. That's when he saw a woman that he thought might be Gina. He ran back to his desk, pulled out a pair of binoculars from one of the drawers, and quickly returned to the window. When he focused the lens, he could clearly see that it was she. Bob Rosenberg, the same man he had seen kissing her at the door of his office suite, got out of a small white convertible, went around to the passenger side, and embraced and kissed her before opening the door to let her in. Steven was angered by what he saw. He thought right away that Gina had lied to him about having some business to take care of. He also realized the relationship she had with this man must be pretty

Chapter 5

serious which would mean he didn't stand much of a chance with her himself.

That afternoon, Andrew Talley, one of the senior partners, got a phone call from the firm's accountant, Irv Rhyner. "Hi, Irv, what can I do for you?"
"Well, Andy, I have a slight problem here and thought maybe you would be able to straighten it out for me."
"Go ahead - shoot."
"Well, I didn't want to bother you about it at first, but I can't seem to balance things out here . . ."
Andy cut in, "Irv, will you stop the hemming and hawing and get to the point?"
"Alright, I can't find out where three hundred and sixty thousand dollars has gone. It's just disappeared. I've gone back eight months now and that's where it first starts to show up missing."
"Irv, you've got to be kidding with me!"
"No, I'm not kidding, Andy. It looks like someone's been skimming the cream off the top."
"How sure are you about this?"
"Pretty darn sure."
"Does anyone else besides you and me know?"
"No, just my assistant and I."
"Well, for now, let's keep it under wraps, okay? Irv, I'll tell you what - I'll have to run this past the other partners . . . in the meanwhile, you keep looking for something you might have missed that would explain it."

As soon as Andy hung up, he contacted Dan and Simon and told them to come to his office as soon as possible - that it was a matter of urgency. The other two men were in Talley's office within a few minutes.

Grundage opened the gathering with, "Well, Andy, what are we here for?"

"Gentlemen, I'm afraid somebody in the firm might be doing some embezzling. I just had a talk with Irving Rhyner and he's pretty sure that someone's been dipping in the till. I told him to doublecheck anyway."

Dillenbeck reacted angrily. "What? I don't believe this! That goddamn Irv, he's been wrong before, the dumb bastard! We've got to hire another accounting firm. I don't have time for this fuckin' shit."

Simon cut in, "Dan, Dan, what are you getting so excited about . . . Irv isn't absolutely sure, is he?"

Dan snorted, "Well, if he isn't, that's just one more indication of his incompetence . . . Andy, how much are we talking about here?"

"We're talking to the tune of three hundred and sixty-thousand over a period of eight months."

Simon muttered. "Wow, that's a lot of money for such a short period of time."

Then Talley said, "If this is true, I guess you know we're all gonna have to be investigated. This sort of thing could only be done by someone close to the top. I don't mean to be insulting to either of you, but I can tell you right now, it's not me. So if it's one of you guys, it would save us a lot of embarrassment if we tried to settle this in-house. What do you say, Gentlemen? Am I out of line?"

By this time, Dillenbeck had settled down a bit and said "No, Andy, you're not out of line. Somebody had to say it."

Simon horned in, "Well, if this is confession time, I can assure you, it wasn't me."

"What about you, Dan?" Andy asked.

"No, not me. But if none of us is the culprit, then who?"

Talley suggested, "Well, guys, now that we have it out in

Chapter 5

the open, I think we should just wait for Irv to call us back. And Dan, I hope you're right in saying that Irv is an incompetent, and this is all just one big mistake."

Chapter 6

After spending the afternoon taking care of some business for her mother in connection with her father's death, Gina went back with Bob to the apartment they shared. She hadn't yet gotten over the sudden death of her father and was preoccupied by it. While she was tossing a salad for their dinner, Bob came over and kissed her on the back of the neck, and she hunched her shoulders as if to repel him. He was very annoyed. "What's the matter with you? Why'd you do that? You haven't been very receptive to me all day. Is it that new boss of yours?"

"Oh, no, Bob. He has nothing to do with it. I just lost my father - give me a break!"

"Your father's been dead for almost a week now. And you hardly ever saw him when he was alive, so who do you think you're fooling? What the hell is it?"

"I don't know, Bob - his death has made me think a lot, and I don't like some of the things I see in myself."

Bob took her in his arms and said, "Oh, I'm sorry, Baby. Maybe I should be a little more understanding. Believe me, everything's going to be alright."

He gradually guided her over to the couch, where he took Gina in his arms again and kissed her once on each eye, then on each cheek, and then her lips. As he did so, he was steadily pushing her to a prone position on the couch. He began fondling her. As he progressed in this, Gina slowly became more and more uncooperative until she actually pushed him away, and Bob jumped up in a rage. "What the hell's wrong with you? I think something *is* going on between you and your boss."

Chapter 6

"I told you - it's nothing like that. I'm just not in the mood. Don't I have that right once in a while?"

"Goddamn it, Gina, I saw the way he looked at you when he saw us together. There's no way you can tell me that nothing's going on. And the way you dress in those little tiny skirts, he'd have to be crazy not to notice you."

"Bob, I'm getting tired of these jealous fits you go through. I don't need that in my life right now."

"What you mean is you don't need me in your life. Isn't that right?"

Gina didn't respond fast enough for him, and he shouted, "Goddamn it, isn't that right, you nigger bitch, you?"

Gina was paralyzed by the rage in him and just stood there, unable to respond.

Her lack of response made him even angrier, and he struck her across the face.

Gina cried out, "This is the last time, Bob. I'm not going to let you treat me this way again. This is it!" She grabbed her purse to walk out.

Bob snatched her by the arm and pulled her back, and with a jolting blow, knocked her to the floor. He pounced on her, grabbed her by the hair and beat her face with his fist.

All Gina could do was scream.

He finally stopped and stormed out of the apartment.

A little later that evening, Steven was relaxing after work in his suite at the Four Seasons. He had just pulled out a Pepsi from the refrigerator and was about to pour it over a glass of ice when his phone rang. To his great surprise, it was Gina. "Steven, I'm downstairs in the lobby. I need to see you."

"Stay right where you are, Gina. I'll be right down."

"No, I'd rather come up."

"Fine. I'm in 426."

In a few moments, Gina was knocking on his door. Steven opened it at once, and saw her standing there, her face beat to a pulp.

"What the hell? What happened, Gina?"

"Steven, I don't want to talk about it, and I don't want you to misunderstand my being here. I couldn't find Beth, and I can't go to my mother's like this. You were the only one I could think of. You said if I needed your help, you would be there for me, and I'm taking you up on that."

Steven said, "Of course! Come in."

Gina entered and then told him, "I need some place to hole up for a couple of days until I look presentable again."

"Who in the hell did this to you?"

"It's not important, Steven. I just want to take a shower and go to sleep."

"I think you need a doctor - let me call one."

"No, Steven, don't do that. It would have to be reported, and I'm not interested in creating problems for anyone. I'll be okay. Just leave me alone."

"Is this the first time this has happened to you?"

"I told you I didn't want to talk about it. If you're going to continue this badgering, I'm going to leave."

"Leave and go where? You came here because you didn't have any place else to go. Let's get something straight right now, Gina. You can stay here as long as you want, but I'm not going to let you treat me like I'm dirt under your feet. What you're going to do right now is go in the bedroom and lie down, and I'll put a cold compress on your face to try to take the swelling down."

"Steven, this is not the way I want you to help me. I want you to . . ."

"This is my place, Gina, and we're going to handle this my way . . . not yours."

Chapter 6

Gina reluctantly allowed him to lead her into the bedroom. After he took care of her, he said, "Leave this on your face for a while - the area around your eye looks pretty bad. Then you can take a shower - do anything you want - just make yourself at home."

Later, while Gina was in the shower, Steven took the opportunity to look in her purse for Marybeth's phone number and called her. "Beth, Gina's here. She's been beat up. Do you know anyone who would do anything like that to her?"

Beth was upset. "Oh, my God! Is she alright?"

"Well, her face looks terrible, and there's a lot of other bruises, but I think she'll be okay. All she probably needs is a little time to heal. But who could have done this?"

"Didn't Gina tell you?"

"No, I couldn't get anything out of her."

"Well, why are you trying to get me to go against her wishes?"

"Beth, this is serious! Someone has assaulted her. Is that how you guys live your lives? You're supposed to be her best friend - why won't you tell me?"

"Steven, I have an idea who did it, but I really don't think it's my place to tell you."

"But you know what often happens to someone who's being abused this way. They end up dead. Do you want to take a chance on that?"

"Okay. Steven, you have to promise not to tell her I told you."

"Promise, I promise. Just tell me."

"She has this man she's been living with for a while, and this isn't the first time this has happened. I told her not to take that shit off him, but she doesn't seem to understand that he might do some serious damage to her."

"This guy we're talking about - is his name Bob?"

"Yes, how did you know?"

"Well, he showed up at the office the other day."

Beth said, "Steven, I really don't know what to do about Gina. She seems rather self-destructive."

"I've got to hang up now, Beth. I just heard her come out of the bathroom."

"Well, Gina's very lucky to have someone concerned about her the way you are. I should be so lucky!"

He chose to ignore her remark and just said, "I'll keep you informed of how she's doing."

As soon as Beth hung up from speaking with Steven, she got a phone call from Bob who asked, "Is Gina there?"

She answered him coldly, "No, she isn't."

"Beth, you're lying to me. She is there."

"Did you beat her up tonight?"

"Goddamn it, Beth, now I know she's there! I'll be right over."

"Don't bring your ass over here!" Marybeth shrieked, but Bob didn't hear her; he had already hung up the phone.

Beth called back Steven who had been joined in the living room by Gina. "Oh, Steven, Bob just called here - he sounded raving mad. I told him she wasn't here, but he didn't believe me and said he was coming anyway. What do you think I should do?"

Steven glanced in Gina's direction. He didn't want her to know it was Beth. He just said, "Give me your address. I'll be right over."

"1129 Pine, second floor. Turner's my last name."

Steven hung up and told Gina, "I'll be right back. I have to make a run. He went out without bothering to change from his jeans and tee shirt.

Chapter 6

About ten minutes had gone by, and Bob was ringing Beth's doorbell. Over the intercom, she asked, "Who is it?"

Bob shouted, "You know fuckin' well who it is; I'm here for Gina. If you don't let me in, I'm going to break this goddamn door down."

"Gina's not here. I'm calling the cops on you - you're an uninvited guest!"

Bob leaned up against the wall, pondering his next move. At that moment, Steven came in and recognized him. "You're Bob Rosenberg, aren't you?"

"Yeah. Do you have a problem with that?"

Steven responded hotly. "Look, let me tell you something, Buddy. I saw what you did to Gina, and if I ever hear that you've laid a hand on her again, you're gonna have to answer to me personally."

Bob was frightened, but felt he had to answer boldly in order not to appear cowardly. "What business is it of yours?"

"Technically, none, but I'm making it my business. You got that?"

Just then, Bob heard a police siren and rushed out of the building. Before Steven knew it, the police were in the lobby and all over him. "Up against the wall, You - what the hell are you doin' here, anyway?"

Steven protested. "Hold on a minute, Officers. I think there's some mistake here. I'm just calling on someone in the building."

One officer said, "Shut the fuck up, Nigger, before I blow your goddamned brains out."

Beth suddenly appeared in the lobby and shouted, "Stop that! You have the wrong man. He's not the one I called you about. Let him go!"

The cops glared angrily at Steven and reluctantly released him.

Steven was upset by the roughness with which they had handled him and snarled, "If you guys weren't so anxious to beat up a black man, you'd probably solve more of the crimes being committed by whites in this country."

One of the cops retorted, "If you know what's good for you, you'll keep your goddamned opinions to yourself, or we'll run your fuckin' ass in and create some charges against you."

Marybeth broke in, "I wouldn't do that if I were you. This man is a lawyer and a partner in one of the most prestigious law firms in this city."

"Yeah, and I'm doin' some moonlighting for F. Lee Bailey. Now what do you say to that?"

The other officer had taken Steven's wallet during the time they were searching him. He nudged his partner and showed him Steven's credentials. Both men's faces turned red as a beet. They then began to apologize. "Oh, we're sorry to have inconvenienced you, Mr. Richards . . . why didn't you say something? You could have saved yourself a lot of trouble."

Steven responded, "No, the only thing you're really sorry about is that I wasn't just another powerless black man on whom you could impose your cowardly acts of brutality."

The two officers just turned and walked away while Steven was still talking.

After they were gone, Marybeth threw her arms around him and said, "Oh, Steven, are you alright . . . are you alright? I was so afraid they would hurt you!"

Steven didn't respond to her embrace; he just stood there with his arms dangling at his side and said, "Beth, please, I'm okay . . . really."

Marybeth let her lips slide from his neck across his face until they met his, and she began to kiss him passionately.

Chapter 6

Steven couldn't resist her tongue eagerly searching for his, and his mouth slowly opened. Marybeth had only a nightrobe and panties on, and Steven's hands moved to the inside of her robe. He began to caress her, and she started breathing in little grunts and moans, but Steven suddenly pulled away.

"What's the matter?" she asked. "Oh, I know, you're afraid someone might walk in on us. Is that it? Let's go upstairs to my place where we can have a little more privacy."

"No, Beth, that's not what's wrong. This isn't what I want. I admit, I was turned on by you, but when I have a relationship with someone, feelings have to play a major part, or I just walk away with a lot of guilt. So let's think about what just happened before we make a mistake both of us might regret. Okay?"

"But, Steven, I know you want me. Why fight the feeling?"

"Beth, do you want me to be really honest with you? If I thought you wanted me because you knew me and sincerely liked me as a person, I might respond to you a little differently. But I think I'll just be another notch on your belt, and I don't want that. And another thing, you're into a lot of competitive behavior."

"You haven't known me that long, Steven, so how can you say that?"

"For starters, why did you turn to look at Andrea so triumphantly when you and I went to lunch the other day? I'll tell you why. I think you know that Andrea is attracted to me, and although there's nothing going on between you and me, you wanted to give her the impression that there was. Isn't that so?"

By this time, Marybeth had cooled down a little and answered with a mischievous smile, "You don't miss very much, do you, Steven?"

He just grinned at her and said, "I try not to . . . but I do like you, Beth." He took her hand in his and said, "Let's be friends."

"I don't know, Steven. I'm not very good at being friends with a man, but in your case, I'll try - only because you're a very special guy." As he was leaving the building, Beth called out, "Steven, take good care of her, she needs you more then she realizes."

When he got back to his place, Gina was relaxing on the couch. He walked past her without a word, went straight to the kitchen and picked up where he left off before his quiet evening at home had been interrupted by nothing but pure chaos. He got another Pepsi from the fridge and poured it over a glass of ice cubes, drank it halfway down, and gave a sigh of satisfaction: "Ah-h-h-h!" Then he went back into the living room and told Gina, "I said you could sleep in my bed; I'll sleep out here."

Gina noticed that he was somewhat disturbed about something and inquired, "Who ruffled your feathers?"

The way he was feeling at the moment, if anybody other than Gina had asked him that question, he would probably have snapped their head off, but instead, he just quietly answered, "Oh, nobody. I'm tired and just want to get some rest."

Gina wasn't satisfied with his response and pressed on, "Was that all about me?"

"Was what all about you?"

"Well, you know . . . the reason you left out of here so fast after that phone call - and now you've come back angry and looking like you were in a fight for your life."

Chapter 6

"Gina, don't be such an egotist - the world doesn't revolve around you, you know! And besides, why would anybody call here for you if no one knows you're here?"

"I don't mean for it to sound that way, Steven, but I have a feeling that my being here has caused you problems."

"Well, don't worry about that."

Gina then summoned him to her, "Steven, come here for a minute. I want you to look at my eye to see if it's any better."

Steven felt strangely nervous but slowly walked over to the couch and stood over her, squinting his eyes. "Yes, it seems to look a little better now."

Gina patted her hand on the couch and said, "Sit down here, Steven, for a closer look - you can't possibly see my eye from up there."

He was hesitant, but nonetheless, he sat down on the couch beside her, and Gina gently took him by the neck and pulled his face closer to hers. She could feel how tight he was and told him, "Steven, please, would you try and relax? I'm not going to bite you." She then touched his lips with hers and began to nibble at them. The nibbling became more and more intense, and before long they were doing some serious kissing. All of a sudden, Steven pulled himself away from her, the same way he had earlier that evening reacted toward Beth, but for a different reason.

Gina was shocked at this. "What's wrong? Isn't this what you wanted?"

"Yes, Gina, this is what I wanted, but I've learned that you don't like black men, so with that, I would say there's only a couple of reasons you would be doing something like this. You either feel sorry for what you believe to be a lovesick puppy, or this is your way of thanking me for taking you in. What is it with you and Beth anyway? First she tried to seduce me tonight, and now here you are trying the same thing. Is sex the only way you girls know how to express yourselves?"

That enraged Gina. She jumped up and shouted, "To hell with you, Steven, I was just . . . just trying to be nice to you . . . trying to make up for . . ."

"Make up for what?" Steven asked.

"Oh, what the hell's the use, you wouldn't understand. Goodnight!"

As Gina stormed toward the bedroom, Steven yelled out to her, "I understand more about you than you realize, Gina Marlene Epps."

When she got to the bedroom door, she turned and glared at him, and he glared back at her. Then she went in the room and slammed the door.

In a minute, she popped back out. Steven had his trousers halfway down, getting ready to settle in on the couch, and when he saw her, he quickly grabbed them and pulled them up. She said, "Excuse me, but I just realized . . . that's where you went - over to Beth's place! Just how much did my little friend tell you about me?"

Steven clapped his hand to his forehead and mumbled, "Oh, shit, what did I do now?" and then said, "Look, Gina, Beth had nothing to do with it." After Steven explained the events of that evening, Gina stomped off to bed. She was angry - angry at Steven for involving Marybeth behind her back, angry at Marybeth for turning it into a sexual encounter, and angry with Bob for trying to track her down.

Chapter 7

The next day at the firm, Andrew Talley went to see Dillenbeck. While he was in the outer room, he heard loud, angry voices coming from Dillenbeck's office. He asked the secretary, "What's going on in there?"

"I have no idea, Mr. Talley. It's been like that for the last twenty minutes now."

"Who's in there with him?"

"Mr. Pollock and Mr. Grundage."

Just then, the door opened, and Martin Pollock came out. In the background, Dillenbeck was heard shouting after him, "Over my dead body, Pollock! Over my dead body!"

Pollock left the area, and Talley went in to Grundage and Dillenbeck. "What's going on? What's all the shouting about?"

Dillenbeck said, "For some reason or other, that goddamn Pollock thinks he should be made a senior partner in this firm."

Talley said sarcastically, "And of course our usual response to such a request is 'over my dead body,' right?"

"Well, the son of a bitch was too goddamn arrogant," Grundage replied. "He gave us an argument. Maybe we should get rid of him."

Andrew thought it was rather strange that Dillenbeck and Grundage had responded to Pollock's request in such a crude way, but decided not to pursue the subject further and went on to say, "Well, anyway, the reason I'm here is that Irv Rhyner said he wanted to set up a meeting to discuss our little problem. I need to give him a time that all four of us are available."

Dillenbeck said, "By that, I assume he's still insisting that there's a problem."

"Well, I guess he is."

Grundage said, "If it's okay with you guys, I think we should get together tonight around six after everyone's gone home. We don't want it to get out that there's anything wrong. Are you in agreement with that?"

They both agreed, and Talley said, "Then six it is."

Just then Dan remembered something Talley had said and asked, "What do you mean - the four of us?"

"Well, I mean us and Steven Richards - after all, he is a senior partner."

Dillenbeck said, "Oh, I don't want him to hear about this just yet - I don't want him to think he's joined up with the wrong firm."

"But I've already invited him," Talley protested. "Now what am I supposed to do?"

"You didn't tell him what the meeting was about, did you?"

"No, I just told him it was a meeting with the accountant."

"Well, then, just don't say anything - he doesn't know what time we're meeting."

Talley seemed a little anxious. "Uh, I don't know - this doesn't sound right to me."

Grundage said, "Andrew, we're doing the right thing - don't worry about it."

"Okay. Whatever you guys say."

In Steven's office, Andrea had just arrived and went in to see him. "Good morning, Steven. Is there anything you want me to do?"

Chapter 7

"Yeah. Gina's not going to be with us for a couple of days, and I want you to prepare the papers for Jeffrey's preliminary hearing. Are you familiar with how that's done?"

"Yes, I can do it."

"I guess there isn't much that you can't do, is there, Andrea?"

Andrea surprised him by answering, "Yes, there is something I can't do. I can't seem to find the right man!"

Steven was sympathetic. "Oh, Andrea, he'll come along - just when you least expect it. It's a matter of recognizing him when he finally does show up in your life."

In response, she laughed and said, "Actually, I think I've found him, but I'm just waiting for him to recognize me!"

Steven looked somewhat uncomfortable.

Then Andrea asked, "Is Gina alright?"

"Of course, why do you ask that?"

"Oh, I heard that there was a problem last night, and she's staying at your place."

"Who in the hell told you that? Never mind, you don't have to answer; I know who told you. I wish that Beth would keep her mouth shut."

"I don't know why she should keep her mouth shut - you don't have any reason to hide anything from me, do you?"

Steven responded, "Look, Andrea, there are some things we need to get out in the open. I guess you know how I feel about Gina, and I think it's fair for me to say I know how you feel about me."

Whether he was right or not, Andrea was disturbed at Steven's assumption that he knew how she felt about him and replied, "How do I feel about you?"

"Well, I thought we could talk about it, but by your question, I see that we can't."

She thought for a moment and then spoke, "No, Steven, you're right - we should talk about it. I do have very strong feelings for you, and I guess I'm not very good at hiding them. But I hope you don't mind me saying this; I don't think Gina will ever have the same feelings for you that I have - and I think you're wasting your time with her."

"Do you think you're wasting your time with me?"

"I may or may not be."

"Well, if you can't give me a definitive answer to that, how can you say for sure that I'm wasting my time with her?"

"Maybe it's because that's the way I would like it to be."

"But, Andrea, you don't know me at all - we only met a few days ago."

"So what's that matter? My parents got married a week from the day they met. But I'll tell you what, Steven, if you want, from now on, I'll try to keep how I feel to myself. I have a job to do, and right now, that's more important than anything else."

Steven was fascinated by the strength of Andrea's interest in him, and the thought of what it might be like to hold her in his arms crossed his mind. He got up from his desk, went over to her and, taking her hands in his, pulled her up from her chair. He spoke softly to her. "Andrea, I would like to kiss you - would that be okay?"

"Why would you want to do that?"

"Because your fondness for me makes me wonder what it would be like."

Andrea looked at him intently, wondering if this were the moment that she might be able to win him over. She consented. "Yes, Steven, you can kiss me."

He hesitated for the briefest of moments, and then lightly brushed her lips with the tip of one finger. At his touch, Andrea drew her breath in sharply, and her body swayed slightly. As if to steady her, he put his arms around her. He bent his face to hers and quietly kissed her on the mouth, and

Chapter 7

then allowed her to be the one to press forward and seek deeper contact. They stood absorbed in the kiss for about a minute until Steven slowly drew away, saying, "You almost made me forget where I was - we're lucky no one came in!"

Andrea laughed nervously and smoothed her hair with her hands.

Neither wanted to look at the other, feeling somewhat uncomfortable with their mutual arousal, and Andrea left the room, saying, "I'll get those papers ready for you," while Steven went and sat at his desk. He did reflect on the closeness that he and Andrea had just shared, smiled fondly at the memory and said to himself, "Not bad . . . not bad at all."

In the outer office, the event had a completely different effect on Andrea. She sat down at her desk and started daydreaming about all kinds of romantic situations she and Steven might be caught up in. While she was deep in thought, Marybeth came into the office and stood over her desk and said, "Andrea." There was no answer, and Marybeth repeated, but louder this time . . . "Andrea!"

Andrea looked up with a start. "Oh, oh, I'm so sorry, Marybeth. Can I help you?"

"My God, Chil', that must have been a hell of a man you were thinkin 'bout. I don't know where you were, but you weren't in this office! You wanna tell me who he is?"

Andrea smiled bashfully and said, "No, I don't, Beth."

"Well, let me guess."

She wanted Marybeth to stop probing and tried to think of a way to change the subject, but before she could say anything, Marybeth said "I'll bet you were thinkin 'bout Steven, right?"

"Oh, stop it, Beth. What are you here for?"

"Honey, I'm just teasin' you. I just wanna know if Steven's here."

"Just a minute, I'll see if he's free." She picked up the phone and said, "Steven, Beth is out here. Do you want me to send her in?"

Steven didn't want Marybeth to come in his office, so he told Andrea to tell her that he would be right out.

In a minute he appeared and said, "Good morning, Beth. Can I help you?"

"Don't be so formal with me, Steven."

"Oh, okay. What do you want, Beth? Is that informal enough?"

"Yeah. I was just passing by your office and thought I would stop in to see if you wanted to have lunch with me today."

Steven made up a quick excuse. "Oh, Beth, I'm sorry. Andrea and I are going to be out of the office on some business and won't be back until after lunch."

Marybeth exclaimed, "Oh, darn it, my luck!"

"Some other time, maybe . . ." Steven responded.

Marybeth said, "There better be!" and left.

Andrea was delighted to hear Steven turn Marybeth down and to hear that she and Steven were going out of the office together, but her hopes were quickly dashed when he admitted to her that he had just lied to Marybeth to get rid of her. He told her that he needed her to finish the papers for Jeffrey's hearing. Later in the afternoon after Andrea had completed the task, she took them in to Steven and he looked them over. Seen in black and white, the case for Jeffrey seemed very poor. He said to Andrea, "We don't have enough here to even convince me that Jeffrey didn't commit this murder. C'mon, get your coat - we're going to visit him again. I want another crack at seeing if he can give us anything more to go on."

Chapter 7

Andrea smiled - they were going out after all!

At the prison, Steven started off by telling Jeffrey, "I'm here because right now, judging from what we have, there's not enough to keep you from being convicted of first degree murder. So I need you to think hard about anything that might help us get you out of this mess you're in. You guys were pretty close - can you think of anyone who might have hated him enough to want to kill him or have him killed?"

Jeffrey thought for a moment and then said despondently, "No, I can't come up with anyone - I mean he's had petty arguments with a few guys around the club - mostly centered around his being gay. I never paid any attention to it myself, but he let it bother him."

Steven said, "Jeffrey, take your time. Think about it."

Jeffrey was quiet for a few minutes and then said, "This may not mean anything, but he and his father didn't get along. In fact they hated each other, but that was . . . you know . . ."

"Oh, is that so? Well, what was the problem between them?"

"The same thing - him being gay - his father just really hated Martin's lifestyle - he kicked him out of the house because of it."

"Is there anything else they might have quarreled about besides that?"

"Well, you know he worked at the same firm as his father. And for the last couple of weeks, he's been disturbed about something on the job. I tried to get it out of him, but he refused to talk about it - just said it was something about a lot of money."

Steven asked, "This thing at work that concerned him - do you know whether or not it involved his father?"

Jeffrey replied, "I'm pretty sure it did."

"Why do you say 'pretty sure'?"

"Well, I told him, I said, 'you know, you gotta talk to somebody about it,' and he just said, 'I don't know, Man, I don't know - it's my Dad - I think there's gonna be some trouble', but he wouldn't go any further than that." Jeffrey paused and then asked, "You don't think his own father would have anything to do with his death, do you?"

"Jeffrey, anybody who knows the victim is a possible suspect in a murder case." Steven went on to ask, "Is there anything else?"

"Not that I know of."

"Well, okay, Jeffrey, we have to get back now." Steven rose and extended his hand and said, "Don't worry - we're doing everything we can. I'll keep you informed if anything new develops."

"I know I haven't been much help," Jeffrey replied.

"Oh, I wouldn't say that - you may have been more help than you realize."

On the way back to Philadelphia, Andrea asked, "Do you think he's innocent?"

Steven responded, "I feel sure of it."

"I do, too. So what's next?"

Steven gave a long sigh. "Well, Andrea, I'll tell you. I really think I'm gonna have to talk to Martin Pollock, Senior. I don't think that's going to be an easy job - he's already angry that I'm defending Jeffrey, but he may be able to shed some light on the case."

When they got back to the firm, Steven didn't waste any time. He got right on the phone and called Martin Pollock's office. "Beth, this is Steven. Is Pollock in?"

"Oh, Steven, will you hold for a minute, please? I'll see if he can talk to you."

Chapter 7

Steven held on until Marybeth came back and said, "I'm sorry, Steven. He said he's not in."

"Oh, is that so? Okay, well, tell him I called and would like to have a talk with him . . . bye, bye."

Steven jumped up from his desk, put his suit jacket on, and went out and told Andrea, "Hold down the fort. I'll be right back." He proceeded down the hall looking at the names on the doors until he saw Pollock's. He went in, and there was Pollock talking to Marybeth with some papers in his hand. They both turned to look at Steven. As soon as Pollock saw who it was, he said, "Hey, what gives you the right to come barging in my office?"

Steven ignored Pollock's question and angrily remarked, "If you were gonna lie to me, you could have at least told me you were in a meeting instead of saying you weren't in at all."

Pollock cut in on Steven, "You have a hell of a lot of nerve wanting to talk to me. What do you think I'm supposed to do - forget that you're defending the man that murdered my son?"

"The man that you say murdered your son is innocent. I'm just as sure of that as I am standing here. Now do you wanna help find the real murderer, or do you just want to hang the man that's been accused? You're supposed to be a lawyer, Pollock . . . you know better than that."

Pollock's only response to Steven was "Get the hell out of my office, Richards . . . get out! Get out now!"

While they were arguing, Marybeth became concerned that they would eventually come to blows, and she called Dillenbeck's office. "Mr. Dillenbeck, this is Marybeth in Mr. Pollock's office . . . I think you should come over right away. Martin and Steven Richards are getting ready to fight! Please, come right now!"

The yelling could be heard all over the firm. As Dillenbeck came running out of his office, he met Grundage who asked, "What the hell's going on?"

"Oh, I don't know, it's Richards and Pollock . . . I gotta get there before somebody gets hurt."

The onlookers in the hall moved aside as Dan and Simon ran past them. There were heads sticking out of doorways, people asking, "What's wrong . . . what's going on?" No one seemed to know.

When they got to Pollock's office, Andrew was already there, telling Martin, "Calm down, Man. Whatever it is, this screaming and hollering isn't gonna help."

"I'll calm down alright . . . when he gets the hell out of my office!"

Just then Dillenbeck called out, in a tone of authority, "I want this nonsense to stop, right now. The both of you, cut it out . . . now! Steven, I want to talk with you." Dan put his arm around Steven's shoulder, led him to the door and whispered, "I want you to understand one thing, Steven; I'm not taking sides, but I think the best way to handle this is for you to go and wait for me in my office. I'll be there with Martin in five minutes, and we'll settle this on neutral grounds, so to speak."

After Steven left, Dan asked, "What the hell is this all about, Martin?"

"He wanted to talk to me about my son's death. I told him he was out of line and to get out."

Andrew Talley broke in. "What's it gonna hurt to answer a few questions, Martin? The man's only doing his job."

"I'll tell you what it's gonna hurt - that bastard Burroughs murdered my son! I think it's insensitive of him to expect me to help get his client off. After all, I am the victim's father."

Chapter 7

Dan cut in. "Martin, Steven is waiting for me in my office. I know it'll be a bit uncomfortable for you, but I want you to join us there so that we can clear the air."

Martin responded negatively, "But, Dan that's . . .!"

"No but's about it, Martin. That's an order."

After Martin and Dan left, Talley turned to Grundage and said, "Don't forget - we have a meeting with Irv tonight at six. Be sure to remind Dan."

Pollock and Dan arrived at Dan's office. Upon entering, Pollock glared at Steven who was sitting on the couch, looking quite relaxed. Dan said, "Look, I'm going to cut to the chase. I understand how you feel, Martin, but Steven here is doing the job we got him for and, as partners, we should be giving him the utmost cooperation. I know the circumstances are quite unusual in this case, but I think it would be best if we tried to treat this as we would any other case. I suggest that you find a mutually agreeable time to meet and go into whatever detail Steven feels is necessary. Now, let's shake hands and cut this shit out."

Steven rose and reached out for Pollock's hand. Pollock was very slow to respond, but eventually took Steven's hand in his and gave a very limp shake, barely touching him. Steven noticed that, after the handshake, Pollock quickly wiped his hand on the side of his pants. They arranged to meet the next day.

As Steven was leaving, Dan said, "Martin, you stay. I want to talk to you."

Steven wondered what more Dan had to say to Pollock.

When Steven returned to his office, Andrea looked at him with concern and asked, "Are you alright? I heard you almost came to blows with Martin Pollock."

"Oh, I'm fine. I just don't feel like talking about it right now. I'll be in my office, and I don't want to be disturbed. I'm leaving early today."

As soon as Steven was at his desk, he called his apartment, and Gina answered, "Richards' residence."

"Gina, this is Steven - is everything okay there? Did I get any phone calls?"

"Everything's okay. Your mother called and said for you to call her when you got in. She wanted to know who I was."

"What did you tell her?"

"Oh, I told her I was your latest fling."

"Did you really?"

"Yes - she seemed a little upset by it."

Steven laughed. "You have to watch what you say to Mom. She's rather protective of me."

"Oh, you're a mama's boy, huh?"

"No, not really. That's what she would like, but it's not the case. How're you coming along - do you feel any better?"

"I still look terrible."

"Well, you'll be alright. I'm going to come home a little early tonight."

"Not for me, I hope."

"There's your ego, working overtime again. I'll see you when I get there." Steven hung up the phone, thinking that it seemed as if Gina's attitude toward him had changed somewhat for the better, and he couldn't wait to get home and see her.

Andrea came in and asked, "Would it be okay if I left when you do?"

"Oh, sure, why not?"

"Steven, may I ask you a question? Are you leaving early for personal reasons?"

"Why do you ask that, Andrea?"

Chapter 7

"Well, I was wondering . . . you know . . . I don't have anything to do, and I was wondering if I could treat you to dinner tonight."

Steven was made very uncomfortable by her invitation and replied, "No, I'm going home - I just want to get some rest."

"Oh, I really wanted to fix dinner for you at my place, and I wanted you to meet my parents. Do you think I'm being too forward?"

Steven looked exasperated and said, "Andrea, I hope you're not going to make me sorry about what I did this morning. I enjoyed it, but I don't want it to haunt me . . ."

Andrea was insulted by Steven's choice of words and cut him off by saying, "Didn't what we shared have any effect on you at all?"

"Yes, Andrea, but you promised you would try to keep your feelings to yourself . . . I know what you're doing - you know that Gina's at my apartment, and you're trying to keep me from going home."

"Steven, I can't turn my feelings on and off like a faucet. And you're right, I don't want you to go home to her."

"I'm not going home to her - I'm going home to my apartment - it's where I live. She happens to be staying there. Now will you stop it, Andrea?"

Andrea angrily turned around and went back out to her desk.

Steven was very annoyed with her and even thought for a moment about asking her to resign because the situation was getting too complicated; however, the thought was immediately erased from his mind - aside from his fascination for the way she felt about him, he also knew her experience and abilities would eventually make her a real asset to his office. After a couple of minutes, Steven left, saying to Andrea, "Goodnight; I'll see you in the morning."

Just as he got to the outer door, he turned and said, "Andrea, I'm sorry."

She replied stiffly, "You don't have anything to be sorry about. Have a good evening."

Chapter 8

At six that evening, Irv Rhyner arrived promptly at Dillenbeck's office. When everyone was settled, Dan asked, "So, Irv, what do you have to tell us? Do you still think we're headed for the poorhouse?"

"I'm sorry to say, nothing has changed. I've reviewed the accounts over and over again and still come up with the same figures. It looks like someone has hit the accounts for three hundred and sixty thousand dollars. I need to know what direction you want me to take in this."

There was a moment of silence in the room, and then Talley asked, "Do your findings point to anyone in particular?"

Irv said, "No, they don't. Whoever did this was very smart - they knew what they were doing. There's been quite a bit of commingling and transfer among accounts - I guess you'd say laundering. The amount of money is not going to break you guys, but there is the serious issue of embezzlement. As you all know, I'll be obligated to report this in the financial statement."

Talley responded, "We have to get to the bottom of this. You're directed to do whatever it takes."

Grundage broke in. "Now hold on a minute. If we call in anyone from the outside to investigate, the story's going to be all over the legal community by the next day. The reputation of the firm would be ruined. Is that what we want?"

Dillenbeck immediately answered, "Hell, no. I say close down the goddamn accounts in question so they can't be fiddled with anymore, increase your internal controls, and let's forget about it. And as for your financial statement, make sure this is buried somewhere deep in the backup - you understand?"

Talley protested, "But if you handle it that way, Dan, we'll be living with someone among us who would rob us blind if the opportunity ever presented itself again."

Irv added, "And further, Dan, it's a matter of concern to me - I wouldn't want to be implicated in any sort of coverup. The only thing I can do is give you some time to look into this on your own."

Dan exploded. "Damn you, Irv. When you opened up your doors, we were the first to give you some business. And since then, you haven't looked back."

Irv calmly replied, "I appreciate the fact that you got my business off the ground, but what you want could run my business into the ground. I can't do it."

Dan shot back, "If that's the way you feel, maybe when this is over, we should be looking for another accounting firm!"

"I'd be sorry to lose you as a client," Irv said quietly, "but I have to do what I have to do."

Talley spoke. "Dan, Irv's only the messenger of bad tidings. I don't know why you're giving him such a hard time."

Grundage said, "Oh, I'm sure Dan's just letting off some steam. Irv's suggestion is a good one, and I'm sure we can bring this to resolution on our own."

Dan reluctantly agreed and forced himself to apologize. "Forgive me, Irv; I didn't mean what I said. I'm just a little upset over the whole goddamn thing. I can't believe this is happening to us."

Irv nodded his head in acceptance of Dan's apology and said, "Well, Gentlemen, I've done everything I can do here. I hope this turns out for the best, and I'll be waiting to hear from you."

Chapter 8

While his partners were meeting, Steven was on his way home to the Four Seasons. When he got off the elevator at his apartment floor, he smelled an aroma and thought to himself, "Damn, that sure smells good; someone on this floor must really know how to put it together."

By the time he reached his place, the smell had gotten much stronger. He said to himself, "No, it couldn't be - I know that isn't coming from my place." When he opened his door, he called out, "Gina, it's me . . . where are you?"

"In here, Steven . . . I'm in the kitchen."

He headed for the kitchen, talking all the while. "Holy smokes, Gina, you have the whole floor lit up. When I was coming down the hall, there's no way you could've told me that that it was coming from here . . . whatcha got cookin?" He lifted the lid to a skillet. "Oh, man, my favorite, liver smothered in onions." He looked further and discovered a pot of wild rice and a small pot of broccoli with cheese sauce on it.

Gina smiled at him. "Go and wash up, Steven . . . by the time you're finished, dinner will be ready."

In the shower, Steven sang like a hundred birds. He thought once more to himself, "Gina must really be changing . . . she likes me, I know she does."

At the same time, Gina was sitting in an armchair in the living room, reflecting on her father's last words to her, and the pain she had caused both her mother and father.

When Steven came out, they sat down and started to eat. Steven said, "M-m-m, this is really great - how did you know that liver and onions was my favorite meal?"

"Oh, I don't know - just a coincidence, I guess!"

Steven then remembered that his mother had called earlier that day and realized that Gina must have asked her for suggestions for the meal. He decided to see how far Gina would go in her little deception and said, "Oh, I don't think it could have been just a coincidence. Maybe it's a sign that fate has brought us together."

"Oh, no, that's not it at all," Gina quickly replied. "Don't get the wrong idea. I think I'd better tell you how I knew."

"No, let me tell you! My mother told you, didn't she?"

Gina laughed. "I confess - that's it!"

"Ah, at least that tells me you cared enough about me to ask her what I liked!"

When they had finished eating, Gina got up to do the dishes. Steven asked her if she wanted help, but she said, "No, find something else to do - I'd rather do this by myself."

Steven went into the living room and worried a bit that Gina seemed to be cooling off and wasn't as warm as she had been on the phone or when he first came home.

When Gina finished the dishes, she joined Steven in the living room, sitting on the sofa opposite him. They were both quiet, not knowing what to say to each other.

Steven rose and said, "I'm going to get something to drink. Do you want something?"

"No, thanks."

Steven returned with a glass of ice in one hand and a can of Pepsi in the other and said, "You sure you don't want anything?"

Gina again responded, "No, thanks."

Steven set the soda and ice on an endtable and went over and sat beside Gina. He took her hand in both of his and gently stroked it. When she didn't resist, Steven was encouraged to go further. He put his hand behind her neck and began to massage it. Gina still didn't pull away. Steven drew closer, kissed her on one side of her face and then the other, and then began to kiss her on the lips. Gina began to breathe quickly and opened her mouth slightly, letting him touch her tongue with his. The gentle kiss was slowly

Chapter 8

progressing to greater intensity until Gina suddenly pushed him away. Surprised, Steven asked, "What's the matter? Did I do something wrong?"

"No, Steven, you didn't do anything wrong. It was me who was wrong. I didn't want my gratitude to go this far."

Steven was stunned by the coldness of her words and said, "Gratitude! Is that what this is? I don't know how anyone can be as passionate as you just were and say something like that. And I told you last night, I don't want you to feel sorry for me or obligated - I want you to want me for me."

"You don't understand. I can't want you for you. You're too dark."

"Is it just that I'm too dark or you refuse to have anything to do with any black man? Which is it?"

"I just don't date black men. I will not go out with a black man."

"Why - tell me why? Are white men better at beating you up?"

"Don't be ridiculous."

"Well, then, do they make love better?"

"I wouldn't know."

"You mean to say you've never had a black man?"

"Right, and I don't intend to."

"Give me a reason - tell me the difference between black and white men."

"It's their hair, their lips, their darkness . . . oh, I don't know . . . I just think everything about them is ugly. When I have children, I want them to have straight hair and be light-complected."

"Gina, let me ask you this. Was your father a black man?"

The question enraged Gina, and she smacked Steven sharply across the face, shrieking, "Don't talk about my father! Don't you dare talk about my father. He has nothing to do with this!"

Steven stood up and held his hand to his face. "I must have really hit a nerve there, Gina. I must have really hit a nerve. You just told me more about yourself than you know. But I'll tell you one thing, I would never strike you, and I don't want you to feel that you have the right to strike me. Don't ever do that again."

Steven grabbed his coat and headed for the door.

"Where are you going?"

"You're a very ugly person tonight, Gina, and I don't want to be with you. Tonight, I'll sleep somewhere else."

After Steven left Gina, he went down to the lobby of the Four Seasons, found Andrea's home number in his address book and called her. "Andrea, is that you?"

"Yes. Who's this?"

"It's Steven."

Andrea's voice immediately perked up. "Oh, Steven, it's you! How are you and to what do I owe this call?"

"Remember - you asked me to have dinner with you. I already ate, but would you like to go out for a drink?"

"What time is it?"

"It's nine-thirty. That's not too late, is it?"

"Oh, no, by no means. Where should I meet you or do you want to come here and pick me up?"

"I'll be there in about a half an hour."

"Do you know where I live?"

"Yes, it's in my book."

"Okay, I'll see you soon."

Andrea was thrown into a tizzy by the call. She bounded up the stairs two at a time to the bathroom, rushed in and took

Chapter 8

a quick shower and then spent the time remaining trying on four different outfits, struggling through the buttoning and unbuttoning, zipping and unzipping, much to the amusement of her younger sister, Adele. "What's up, Girl? Is Denzel Washington coming to 2000 East Upsal Street?"

Andrea laughed. "No, something better. You know my boss, the one I was telling you about? He just called and he's coming over tonight. I hope you'll get a chance to see him."

When Steven rang the bell at Andrea's house, she opened the door and asked him to come in to meet her family.

"No, Andrea, I don't feel up to meeting anyone right now. I just need the company of someone who understands."

Andrea got her coat from the hall closet and left with him. In the car, she asked, "What's wrong, Steven?"

He didn't say anything to her and just shrugged his shoulders.

Andrea said, "Should the someone who understands be quiet or try to find out what's wrong?"

"Oh, Andrea, I'm sorry to be such a bore; just being with you is good enough right now."

Steven was quiet until they were seated at Quincy's, a night spot in the Adams Mark Hotel, and he told her about the events of his evening with Gina.

Andrea listened intently and then asked, "If you're not going back there tonight, where will you sleep?"

"Oh, I don't know. I'll probably stay right here, I guess."

"You can spend the night at my house - we have a finished basement."

"No, I wouldn't want to put your family to that trouble."

Andrea thought for a moment. She was afraid to ask her next question, but started it anyway. "Can I . . ." Steven cut her off, saying, "It's getting pretty late; I guess I'd better take you home." Andrea was relieved that Steven had stopped her from finishing her question; nevertheless, she knew she had to ask it. Just when she started to ask again, Steven cut her off again. To her, it was as if he already knew the question and was trying to prevent her from asking it. He rattled along in conversation, but Andrea kept hearing the question over and over again in her head until she finally blurted it out. "Can I stay with you tonight?"

Steven went on talking for a moment and then looked up sharply and said, "What did you say?"

Andrea repeated it, but this time more slowly and softly. "Can I stay here with you tonight?"

"I thought that's what you said. Andrea, there's nothing I'd like better right now, but I think it's only fair to tell you - just as you said earlier, I can't turn my feelings on and off, and after a night with you, I'm still going to feel the same way about Gina."

"Well, I'll take my chances. I promise I won't try to hold you to anything."

"I understand," Steven responded. "I'll go see about a room."

"Okay. While you're gone, I'll just run to the powder room. I'll meet you in the lobby."

Andrea had used going to the ladies' room as an excuse so that she would have a chance to think about what was about to take place between Steven and herself. When she got there, she went to the mirror over the sink and looked in it for a minute and then slowly brought her hands up to clasp her face and said wearily to the image in the mirror, "Don't be a fool, Girl. You're acting pretty darn desperate at this point." She quickly grabbed her purse off the sink and hurried out of the bathroom.

When she got to the lobby, Steven was there waiting for her. He gave her a big smile and said, "I got the room - are you ready?"

"I have to talk to you, Steven." She led him over to a couch by the window of the lobby. "Sit down a moment. I've thought about this, and I don't think it's right under the conditions you've given me. The work relationship is too close - I'll be seeing you every day, and when Gina comes back, I think it will be an uncomfortable situation, especially with me being on the losing end. I think I'll pass on this."

Steven stared at her for a short time, and then smiled and said, "Andrea, that was a very sensible decision you just came to, and I respect you for it. My heart wasn't in this either, but I guess my male ego wouldn't allow me to say no. And with that, I'll take you home."

"Steven, I'm so glad you understand."

Outside of her home, before Andrea got out of the car, Steven leaned over to kiss her, and Andrea said, "I don't think you should do that, Steven."

"You're right again, Andrea. I'll see you in the morning."

Chapter 9

The next morning, Steven went back to the Four Seasons to change his clothes before going to work. When he arrived at his suite, he found that Gina was gone. He looked on the dresser and saw a note which read:

Dear Steven:
I'm very grateful that you were kind enough to let me stay in your home, but I'm afraid it's not working out very well. We're only going to end up enemies if I stay any longer. Don't worry. I'm going to my mother's. I'll be alright.
Sincerely, Gina
P.S. Even though I've never wanted to sleep with a black man, you really did turn me on last night.

Steven was both sad and relieved that Gina was gone. The things she had said to him had hurt him deeply. Feeling somewhat despondent, he sat down on the side of the bed and thought about what had occurred in the last couple of days, not only with Gina, but with Andrea as well. He called his office and told Andrea that he would be in about noon, and then lay back on the bed and sighed, "Why me, why me? A couple of weeks ago there wasn't a woman in my life, and now there's two after me, and I'm chasing a third." After a while, he laughed at his melancholy behavior, got up from the bed, and fixed some breakfast before going into work.

At the office building, as he was getting on the elevator, Marybeth was getting off on her way to lunch. She spotted him and pulled him back off the elevator. "Oh, Steven, wait

Chapter 9

a minute. Catch the next one up. I wanna talk to you. Where's Gina? I called your place last night and didn't get any answer."

"She's okay. She went home to her mother."

"What's the matter - you guys couldn't make it?"

"Yeah, that's right, Beth. We couldn't make it, and I don't have to tell you why, do I?"

"Yeah, I know. That creep Bob called me last night looking for her again. I didn't say anything about where she was, but I think he knew she was at your place 'cause he asked me, 'Is she still with him?'"

"Well, Beth, if you want to find out how she's doing, you can reach her at her mother's."

"Steven, can I see you tonight?"

"About what, Beth?"

"About nine o'clock."

Steven laughed and thought to himself that recently his encounters with the opposite sex had produced virtually no end result, but a lot of frustration, and perhaps it was time for a little gratification. He said, "Sure, why not, Beth? Where do you want me to meet you?"

Marybeth was surprised. "Are you serious?"

"Serious as a heart attack."

"Okay. You haven't forgotten the way to my apartment, have you?"

"Of course not. Nine it is."

Steven's appointment with Pollock was at one o'clock. When he arrived at Pollock's office, Dillenbeck and Grundage were there as well as Pollock. Steven said, "Oh, I wasn't expecting to see you and Simon here. Is there a reason for this?"

Dillenbeck said, "Uh . . . yes and no, Steven. Uh, the way you guys carried on yesterday, we thought we would be here to keep the peace. Just pretend we're not here and fire away. Sit down and make yourself comfortable."

"No, I'd rather stand." Steven began his questioning by asking Pollock, "Martin, were you aware of your son's homosexuality?"

Martin responded, "Yes, I was quite aware of it."

"And how did you feel about it?"

"Goddamn it, what does that have to do with anything?"

Dillenbeck cut in. "Martin, I think you should just answer the questions - even if you don't think they're relevant."

Martin was quiet, and Steven asked again, "Well?"

Martin knew what Steven wanted, but forced him to ask the question again by saying, "Well, what?"

"How did you feel about your son's homosexuality?"

"I really don't know what you mean. He was my son, and I loved him - it didn't make any difference what he was."

"Isn't it true that you and Martin, Jr. argued about it all the time?"

"No, that's not true, and I don't know who's filling your head with this stuff."

"Wasn't it the reason you put him out of the house? As a matter of fact, from what I understand, you hated your son because of it. Isn't that true?"

Martin jumped up from his chair. "Goddamn it, I don't have to take this fuckin' shit from you or anybody else - especially you!"

Steven asked, "What does 'especially you' mean?"

"That's for you to figure out. And whatever you think it means, that's what it means."

"Why are you getting so uptight? I don't understand. You're beginning to make me believe there's something you don't want me to find out. Is there?"

Martin gritted his teeth and said, "This meeting is over."

Chapter 9

"Fine with me - I got what I came for." Steven walked out of the office.

Andrea was on her way to the xerox room when she saw Marybeth approaching her in the hallway. She said to herself, "Oh, God, here comes Beth. Why would I have to run into her? She's such a blabbermouth."

When Marybeth came near, she said, "Oh, Andrea, how're you doin', Girl? Didja' hear?"

"Hi, Beth. Did I hear what?"

"Oh, I guess Steven didn't tell you. Well, don't tell him you got this from me, but Gina's not staying at his place any more."

"Oh, no kidding!"

Marybeth said coyly, "I had a feeling you'd be glad to hear that."

"Beth, it's no secret that I'm attracted to Steven, but I wish you wouldn't throw it in my face every time you see me, okay?"

"Oh, I'm sorry, Honey. I don't mean no harm. Still friends?"

"Beth, I can't be angry with you, but if I don't tell you how I feel, you'll never know. I gotta go now and get this copying done. I'll see you later."

"Oh, wait a minute, Chil', I forgot to tell ya - I finally got a date with him - tonight's the night!"

"Got a date with whom?" Then Andrea felt a sharp pang of realization. "Never mind, I don't want to hear it, Beth. I have to go." She rushed away.

While Andrea was out of the office, Steven had returned. After a few minutes, Dillenbeck came in and said, "Hi, Steven. I need to talk to you for a minute."

"Sure, Dan, what is it?"

"What were you driving at with those questions you asked Martin?"

"Well, I'm wasn't really driving at anything, Dan. I'm just trying to get some background information on Martin, Junior. But he's made me suspicious now - of what I don't know."

Dillenbeck asked, "Are you suspicious that he's just not telling the truth or do you believe he actually had something to do with his son's murder?"

"Well, at this point, I don't believe he's telling me the truth. I have a client that I know is innocent - I don't think it, I know he's innocent. And he's told me that Martin, Junior and Martin Senior didn't get along at all - that the father hated the son's lifestyle. Why would Pollock feel the need to lie about it? I just feel that something more is going to come out before this is all over. As a matter of fact, I'm glad you're here, because I need to find out something. If this leads back to this firm - or anyone in this firm - I need to know where I stand. Is the firm ready to back me regardless of what the outcome may be?"

Dillenbeck was taken back by Steven's straightforward approach to him, and he momentarily grappled for the appropriate response to his question. He finally said, "Sure, sure, Steven - we're behind you a hundred and fifty percent - you are us." He suddenly appeared anxious to leave and said, "Steven, I'm glad we had this little talk, but I must be going now."

Dillenbeck didn't realize it, but his reaction left Steven with something to think about.

Andrea, unlike Gina, was a very race conscious person, Afrocentric culturally and otherwise, and the idea of race mixing disturbed her. What Marybeth had implied made her angry and very disappointed in Steven, but she knew she had

Chapter 9

to hide her emotions from him. When she got back from the xerox room, she sat at her desk and shriveled at the thought of Steven and Marybeth being together that night. Just as tears started to come, Steven came out of his office and asked Andrea if she had the copies he needed.

She looked up at him with reddish, watered eyes and answered, "Right here, Steven."

He was alarmed when he saw tears about to fall and said with concern, "A-h-h . . . what's the matter, Andrea? What are you crying for?"

"Oh, it's nothing, Steven. Don't pay any attention to me. I just found something out."

"Well, it must be something serious for you to be in this state."

"No, really, Steven, everything's okay. I'm the kind of person who cries at the drop of a dime."

"Are you sure?"

"Yes, I'm sure. I'll be alright."

"Andrea, have you been talking to Beth?"

"Beth? I haven't seen her at all today. No, I haven't been talking to her."

"I just wondered," Steven said quietly.

Later that night at Marybeth's apartment, after Steven came in, she asked, "Can I get you something to drink?"

"Do you have any Pepsi?"

"Pepsi? I didn't mean soft drinks - I have vodka, blended whisky and some Scotch. Which do you prefer?"

"Do you have any ginger ale?"

"Yes."

"I'll just take a glass of that over ice. I don't drink hard stuff."

"Anything you want, Steven," Marybeth responded in a sultry voice, "Tonight, whatever you want is yours."

When she returned with the soda, she handed it to him and let her hand linger to caress his. She asked, "Are you hungry?"

"No, not very. I've had such a hectic day I don't think I would want any food on my stomach."

"Well, all you need is a little relaxation, Steven, and I can give you that if you'll let me."

Steven asked mischievously, "Martin Pollock would be horrified if he knew I was up here with you, wouldn't he?"

"Why do you ask that?"

"How long have you been working for him?"

"Now wait a minute, Steven, did you come up here to see me or ask me questions about my boss?"

"Oh, no - I'm just talking. But, I get the impression that he's a racist."

"Well, that he is. I've heard him use the "n" word on several occasions. Well, anyway, I don't want to talk about that. I'm going to make myself comfortable, and I'll be right back."

From where Steven was sitting on the couch, he noticed a picture on the mantle and went over to get a closer look. It was a picture of Gina and Marybeth with two white men at the beach. When Marybeth came out, she saw him gazing at the picture and said, "Something told me to put that picture face down - I should have paid attention to my instincts."

"Oh, no problem - who are the guys there?"

"One of them is my brother, Ted, and the other is a guy that Gina used to go with."

"How long ago was this taken?"

"Oh, about five years ago."

When Steven looked up, his attention was immediately distracted from the picture when he saw how Marybeth was dressed. She was wearing a negligee that looked to be made of very sheer, pure silk, and he could see every curvature of her body - it was obvious that she didn't have anything on underneath it.

"Come on, Steven. Come on over here. I want to help you relax a bit."

He crossed the room to her, and Marybeth reached up to him, saying softly, "Here, let's just take this tie off."

Steven stood still. Although their bodies weren't even touching, the sensuous fashion in which she leisurely loosened his tie and pulled it from him gave him a sharp thrill of anticipation. She then slowly unbuttoned his shirt and stripped him of it in the same tantalizing way. He couldn't wait to touch her. He put his hands on her waist. She asked teasingly, "Should I go any further?"

Steven didn't say anything; his hands traveled around her body, gently kneading and feeling, until he finally came to the little bow at the top of her negligee. He pulled at it very gradually until it came loose, and then he watched in fascination as the thin silk slipped away from her, leaving her quite naked. Marybeth unbuckled Steven's belt and he stepped away slightly, let his pants drop to the floor and stepped out of them. He pulled her back to him again, this time into a much closer embrace.

Marybeth was squirming now and murmured, "Oh, Steven, I can feel you. You really want me, don't you?"

Steven responded with a low-key "mm-hmm," a little reluctant to satisfy her ego or imply any commitment by admitting the strength of his desire.

His hands and eyes roamed freely over her until he had her almost begging. "Steven . . . please . . . please . . . take me to bed!" He picked her up in his arms and carried her into the bedroom.

Later that evening, as they were lying in bed, Steven thought it might be a good time to try again to get Marybeth to talk about Martin Pollock and asked, "How well did you know Martin Pollock, Junior?"

"Oh, pretty well."

"Did he and his father get along?"

"Well, most of the time when I heard them, they were arguing. There's not much that I can tell you, Steven - really."

"Well, tell me this then. When you heard these arguments, what were they mostly about?"

"Now, come on Steven - I don't want to talk about this any more."

"Just answer one question for me, Beth, and I'll leave you alone about it.

"You promise?"

"Scout's honor."

Marybeth sighed and said, "Go ahead, Steven. What is it?"

"How did Martin Junior's dad feel about his son's homosexuality?"

"Oh, that was a real sore spot in their relationship. Whenever that subject came up, they would almost come to blows. He hated him for it. And the day he found out Martin was seeing Jeffrey, he really went crazy - you know, 'cause Jeffrey was black and all."

Steven just said, "M-m-m, that's very interesting. But let me say this - I have an innocent man in jail. In the future, if there's any information you can give me that might be meaningful, I would really like your cooperation."

"Is that why you're here?"

"Yes and no, Beth."

Chapter 9

"Do you sleep with everyone who might help to clear your clients?"

"Don't start talking to me about morality . . . please."

"And just what do you mean by that?"

"Beth, I really don't want to argue with you. We both know why I'm here. I enjoyed myself with you tonight, and I hope you enjoyed me. But if there's information you could give me that would help Jeffrey Burroughs, I'll take it anyway I can get it."

"Okay, Steven. I guess I understand."

At that point, the phone rang, and Marybeth picked it up. "Hello. Who's this?"

"It's me, Beth, how're ya doin'?"

"Oh, Gina! How you feelin', Girlfriend? How's the bruises?"

"Much better. I'm coming to work tomorrow."

"I got someone here who's dying to talk to you."

Steven looked horrified and violently shook his head - no! His eyes were pleading with Marybeth not to go any further.

Gina asked, "Who, Girl?"

In reply, Marybeth shoved the phone toward Steven.

He held his hand over the receiver and whispered angrily to Marybeth, "You talk too much, you know that? Just tell her it's me," and handed the phone back to her.

Gina asked, "What is goin' on over there?"

"I'll give you three guesses who's here," Marybeth teased.

"I know; it's Steven, isn't it?"

"You got it . . . and so did I - right where it counts! And, Girl, let me tell ya' - you don't know what you're missin'!"

Although Gina claimed she didn't want Steven because of his color, she did revel in the fact that he admired her and now found herself feeling jealous that he was romancing her best friend. She told her, "Oh, he doesn't really want you - he's just using you to see how I'm going to take it."

"What's wrong with you, Girl? You sound like you're jealous."
"Jealous of what? I'm not jealous - you can have him. Have a ball! Maybe it'll get him off my back. Give him the phone - I want to say something to him."
Marybeth handed Steven the phone. "Here, she wants to speak to you."
Gina said, "Steven."
"Yes, I'm here."
"Why're you doing this to her? You know you don't care about her. You're just trying to make me jealous, aren't you?"
"How can I make someone jealous who doesn't care about me?"
Gina angrily hollered, "I hope you're having a ball, Buddy!" and slammed the phone down in Steven's ear.
Steven laid back on the bed and stared at the ceiling.
Marybeth asked, "What did she say?
"Oh . . . nothing."
"C'mon, Steven, what did she say?"
"She didn't say anything important." Steven had been thinking of what Marybeth had just done and said, "You know what, Beth, I bet you've chased a lot of people out of your life."
"You don't say! And what would you know about that, Counselor?"
"Well, you certainly can be vicious whan you want to be."
"Vicious . . . do you think I'm a vicious person?"
"No, personally I don't think you are; I think your actions are coming more from insecurity than anything else. But if one doesn't take the time to know you, then they'll only know you by your deeds."
"Give me an example - like what?"

Chapter 9

"I'm not putting you down, Beth - I'm just trying to give you some constructive criticism."

"I'm waiting, Mr. Constructive Criticism," Marybeth responded sarcastically.

"Well, for example, there's no need for you to agitate people the way you do. First it was Andrea, and now here you are, trying to upset your best friend, Gina."

"Oh, you don't understand Gina and me. We've been doin' this type of stuff to each other for a long time."

"Gina and you . . . Gina and you are good friends, and you've known each other for a while. People who are able to ignore your actions will eventually get to know you and get used to some of the bitchy things you say and do; but most are probably not that patient." Steven paused and then went on. "I'm going to ask you a question, Beth. When you and Gina first met, did you rub her the wrong way?"

Marybeth thought back to that time and told him, "You know, you're right, Steven. She didn't like me at all when we first met."

In her room at her mother's house, Gina was sitting crosslegged on the bed, quietly weeping. It was hard to tell if she was crying from anger or from jealousy after learning that Steven was with Marybeth. After a few minutes, she impulsively picked up the phone and dialed Bob Rosenberg's number. "Hello, Bob, this is Gina."

Before she could get a chance to say anything more, Bob immediately started apologizing to her. "Oh, Gina, I'm sorry - I'll do anything if you just come back. Please, please, Baby, just give me another chance, and I promise you things will be different."

"Wait, Bob. Will you hold on a minute and let me say something? I called you to tell you that I want to be with you tomorrow night."

"Sure, Baby, anywhere. Where do you want to go?"

"Oh, it doesn't make any difference. You can pick me up at work at five."

When she hung up, she felt annoyed at Bob - she hated the whining, pleading tone in his voice, but more than that, she knew that his apology was really worthless - that he was quite capable of doing the same thing again and again because of his extreme jealousy. She couldn't help briefly comparing him to Steven - a man who would never have beat her in the first place and certainly wouldn't be caught begging for her love, no matter how much he might care for her.

Chapter 10

The next morning, Steven left Marybeth's while she was still sleeping. When he got to his office, he was very surprised to see Gina there. Her bruises hadn't healed, but with a few cosmetics, she looked none the worse. She was dressed as provocatively as she had been before her father's death, wearing a tight, white sweater dress with the front buttons opened to the cleavage of her breasts and the hem of the dress riding up almost to her behind. When she looked up from her work, he quickly averted his eyes so that she wouldn't think he had been gawking at her.

As for Andrea, she was watching the both of them.

"Good morning, Ladies," Steven said. He stopped at Gina's desk. "How do you feel?"

She gave him a rigid "I'm okay."

Steven felt the coldness of her response and quickly went into his office. At this point, if there were even the smallest chance with her, he thought he had really blown it by sleeping with Marybeth. It might seem that Steven was masochistic or just plain stupid in still wanting to pursue a relationship with Gina, considering her attitude toward him, but the fact is, he was hopelessly infatuated. He called Gina on the intercom. "Gina, could you come in here for a minute, please?"

Gina got up and went in the office, with Andrea's eyes on her every movement. Before Steven could say what he wanted, Gina started right in on him. "I hope you haven't called me in here to talk about last night. I've heard all I want to hear."

"Gina, let's not go there, okay? You're on the job now. Damn, you've got a hell of an ego, woman. I called you in to tell you I want to add a lawyer to my staff. I'm interviewing someone named Arthur Gwaltney, and he'll be here about ten o'clock. As soon as he gets here, just send him in to me."

Gina lingered a moment in front of his desk, and Steven said, "That's all."

She walked to the door and then turned around, and, with her hands on her hips and her head dropped to one side, she gave Steven a stare.

Steven said, "Well?"

Gina turned and left. Despite Gina's distaste for black men, she was beginning to see Steven as a man of substance - someone who not only wanted to, but could, provide her with security for the rest of her life. Perhaps she was being foolish not to give him any consideration at all.

At ten o'clock sharp, a handsome African-American man, about six foot one, entered the office. He had the complexion of a brown paper bag and a thick moustache and was sharply dressed. Even with a suit on, you could tell he was a well-built, muscular man. He approached Gina and said, "I have an appointment with Steven Richards."

"Are you Arthur Gwaltney?"

"Yes, I am."

"He's waiting on you - you can go right in."

After he went into Steven's office, Gina said to Andrea, in a sarcastic tone, "It's getting pretty dark around here, isn't it?"

"What do you mean?"

"Oh, nothing, Honey. You wouldn't understand."

"I might. Try me - you never know."

"It's just that I'm not used to working around a lot of blacks."

Andrea gave her a hard stare and retorted hotly, "Well, maybe it will be beneficial to you!"

Chapter 10

Gina shrugged and said, "I knew you wouldn't understand," and returned to her work.

As lunchtime neared, Gina asked Andrea, "Do you want to have lunch with me?"

"Sure."

"Let's go somewhere different - that cafeteria food downstairs - I'm sick of it."

At noon, Marybeth came in, as usual, and asked Gina if she was ready to go to lunch. For the first time, Gina tried to avoid Marybeth.

"I'm not going out to lunch today, Beth. I've got a load of work, and I have to stay here."

Marybeth turned to Andrea. "What about you?"

"No, I can't; I've already made plans."

Marybeth went over to Gina, leaned over, and whispered in her ear, "You're not angry about last night, are you, Honey?"

Gina said, "Oh, Girl, get outta here - what you talkin' 'bout?"

"I don't know, Gina, I don't know - just asking. Okay, you guys. Tata, see you later."

Marybeth went to the ladies' room in the corridor, and when she came out, she saw Andrea and Gina standing together at the elevator with their coats on. She didn't call out to them; she just stood there looking hurt.

Andrea convinced Gina to go with her to an eating place called Delilah's, known for its delicious, African-American food. The two women had ordered their lunch and were waiting for it. Andrea asked, "Have you ever been here?"

"No, I haven't."

"Well, how do you like it?"

Gina sniffed, "Oh, it's okay. I prefer continental cuisine myself."

Andrea laughed and said, "That figures," and then changed the subject by asking, "Why did you lie to Beth that way, Gina?"

"Oh, I just didn't feel like having lunch with her today. Don't misunderstand - Beth and I are very good friends. I hope she never finds out, 'cause I'll have a hard time explaining it to her."

Andrea was puzzled and said, "But there must be some reason why you wanted to go to lunch with me and not have her present."

"Well, I'm a little angry with her right now."

"Would I be too nosy if I asked why?"

"I'd rather not discuss it. What I really want to talk about is Steven. I know how you feel about him, and I take it you know how he feels about me. As much as I hate to admit it, he's grown on me a little bit which I didn't expect to happen, but I want you to know that Steven and I would never be able to make it because of our differences."

"And what are your differences?"

"Primarily, I'm not interested in a relationship with a black man."

"You know, Gina, I've heard that mentioned as far as you're concerned, but I have a hard time relating to how you feel. I wouldn't want any kind of man but black. And if you say he's growing on you, what do you plan to do about that? And wasn't your father black, Gina? How did you feel about him?"

Andrea was the kind of person who was able to make people feel very comfortable around her, and Gina felt she could tell her about her relationship with her father. "Well, Andrea, this is something that I don't usually talk about to anyone, but my father loved me to death - he treated me like I was a piece of gold. In return, I gave him absolutely no love at all because of his color. When I was a kid, I used to run away from him in public and later, I just tried to deny his existence. I'm not proud of it, and it's caused me to have a really rotten relationship with my mother."

"Oh, Gina, I feel so bad - that's a horrible story. Gina, I don't mean to be pushy, but you still didn't answer my question. What do you plan to do about your feelings for Steven?"

"Oh, it'll probably pass, and that's why I'm talking to you. Andrea, you're a very attractive woman, and I think what makes Steven so crazy about me is the way I dress and look. Maybe if you were to dress and make up more like me, he'd be more attracted to you."

"Gina, I think you're selling yourself short. Steven isn't that superficial - I'm sure he sees more in you than how you look."

Just then the waiter came with their food, and they fell silent. Andrea took that time to reflect on Gina's statement that Steven was growing on her, and it made her feel afraid.

After the waiter left, Andrea couldn't help returning to the subject. "Gina, the feeling you have for him - what is it?"

"Well, the other night, we really came close to making love, but I pushed him away and was sort of sorry afterwards 'cause I think I really did want him."

Andrea said, "That must have been the night he and I went out together - he told me you'd had a fight."

"Oh, that's where he went, huh? To you."

Andrea sensed the annoyance in Gina's voice, and said, "Gina, I think there's more to the way you feel about him than you're willing to admit."

"No, no! It's not what you think."

"Oh, I believe it is, Gina. I feel about him the way he feels about you, and right now, I'm scared that you want him just as much as I do. I think the only thing that keeps you from running to his arms is your racist attitude toward your own people. You need to come to grips with that."

"I know that, and I'm trying to work on it," Gina said defensively.

Andrea pressed on. "I need to know something. I need to hear you admit how much you're attracted to Steven - whether it hurts me or not."

Again, Andrea's ability to set her at ease allowed Gina to answer honestly. She confessed, "I guess you're right, Andrea. I didn't realize it until last night, but I do care for him."

"What happened last night?"

"Well, there's a third party involved in this."

"Let me guess," Andrea said. "Beth, right?"

"Yes, that's where he spent the night last night."

"I thought so. He's developing a regular little harem, isn't he?"

"It sort of looks that way. Well, anyway, when I found out, I was very upset, and it made me realize my feelings for him. That's why I'm a little angry with Beth. But don't worry, I won't be a threat to you. It just would never work out with Steven . . . and besides . . . I'm back with Bob now."

Andrea drew in her breath sharply. "Oh, Gina, you're back with Bob! Why would you go back to somebody who beat you up?"

"No, things are going to be different. He's promised it's not going to happen again."

"Oh, my God, Gina, don't you know that's what those kind of men always say?"

"Well, that's the way it is. We belong together. Listen, we gotta get back now."

As they were getting their coats, Gina said, "Andrea, do you want to have some fun? Why don't I come in dressed real plain tomorrow, and you come in looking like me - just to see how he reacts to it?"

Andrea was shocked. "Oh, no, I wouldn't want to do that to him."

"Oh, Girl, lighten up a bit - we're just having a little fun!"

"You don't think he'll get angry?"

"So what if he does - what's he going to do, fire us?"

Andrea giggled, and Gina joined in until they were both laughing like schoolgirls.

When they got back to the firm, Marybeth was waiting for Gina in order to confront her. She had left her office door open so that she would see them when they passed by. As soon as she spotted them, she called out, "Gina! C'mere a minute."

Gina groaned, "Oh, no, maybe she knows. Go ahead, Andrea, I'll see you back in the office."

Gina went in to see Marybeth who pounced on her. "Would you mind telling me why you lied to me about lunch?"

Gina didn't have an immediate answer for her, and Marybeth went on to say, "Be truthful. I think you're upset with me about last night, aren't you?"

"Maybe a little."

Marybeth responded, "No, I think a lot. I don't see how you can act like that. You don't want him, but you don't want anybody else to have him either. Isn't that true?"

Gina seemed to still be at a loss for words, and just stood there taking the tonguelashing from Marybeth.

"Well, don't you have anything to say, Gina?"

"Beth, I don't know how to respond to you, but I do know that I got angry when I found out he went to bed with you."

"Well, you don't have to worry - it isn't me he wants anyway - spent the whole time mooning over your picture and worrying about your phone call. The sex was good, but his company wasn't. But he did say a couple of things that made me think about myself."

"Yeah, I know. He does seem to have that effect on people. Look, Beth, I know I was wrong. I just needed someone to blame, and you were in the way."

"I know, Honey, but you have to communicate with me, not lie to me - that really hurt me - but I know why, and I understand."

They hugged, and as Gina was about to leave, Marybeth blurted out, "Oh, Chil', who is that hunk in y'all's office? Is he new?"

"What you talkin' 'bout, Girl - what hunk?"

"You need to open your eyes, Honey. That man is all that!"

"Oh, you must mean that guy that Steven was interviewing. He's a lawyer - somebody named Gwaltney."

"You'll have to introduce me."

"You know I will."

When Gina got back to her desk, Andrea brought Arthur over to her and said, "Gina, Arthur's going to be part of our staff now."

Gina responded coldly. She barely looked at him and said, "Well, whatever."

Arthur looked rather hurt, but then shrugged his shoulders, and walked away.

Steven called out, "Gina, can I see you for a minute?" When Gina came in, Steven asked her, "I didn't hear what took place out there, but from what I saw, you appeared to be pretty short with Gwaltney. What was that all about?"

Chapter 10

"It wasn't about anything, Steven. I don't know what you're talking about."

"Let me say this, Gina. Gwaltney paid his dues, went to law school, passed the bar exam - just like a white man who wants to be an attorney. Now he's entered this firm and deserves to be treated like any of the other lawyers here. In this office, there's a chain of command: me, him, Andrea and you, in that order. And I'd like you to respect that order, and in turn, they are each supposed to treat you with respect."

Gina stood there, with tears coming from her eyes, and said, "Steven, I'm really trying, and maybe you shouldn't be so quick to jump on me."

Steven rose and came around his desk. "Oh, Gina, I didn't mean to make you feel bad. I just want a staff that functions well as a team." He took a tissue from the desk, and wiped the tears from her face. Gina fell into his arms, sobbing, "I'm so sorry I'm the way I am."

Steven held her tightly and said, "I am, too."

She suddenly realized that he was holding her, and she quickly stepped back. Their eyes met, and then Gina said, "Under the circumstances, I wish you'd take down that damn one-way mirror. I think it's an invasion of privacy - especially mine."

Steven pulled her back to him and began to kiss her. At first, Gina didn't resist; in fact, she encouraged him, but after a moment, she jerked away from him and angrily told him, "Don't get the wrong idea, Steven - I still feel the same way." Then she rushed out of the office.

When she came out, Andrea looked up and noticed that Gina had been crying. "What's the matter, Gina?"

"Oh, nothing, it's that damn Steven. He just won't stop criticizing me."

"About what?"

"He saw how I treated Gwaltney and gave me a hard time about it."

"Well, you were pretty awful to Arthur. And, Gina, you gotta remember - you treated him that way just because he was black!"

"Oh, I know - I can't help it - I guess I'm really an awful person."

The more time Andrea spent with Gina, the more she was growing to like her, and she said, "Oh, Gina, you're not an awful person - I know if you want to, you can be very kind and loving."

"Thanks, Andrea, for that vote of confidence. I needed that. Nobody has ever tried to take time to understand me the way you do."

"Well, Gina, I don't really understand you, but I am trying."

"Andrea, you're okay. I like you. I think you're a really wonderful person."

Andrea went back to her desk and thought to herself that she might actually be helping Gina become the ideal woman for Steven.

That same day, Dillenbeck came to see Steven. He looked curiously around the office, and then went to Gina's desk and said, "Tell Mr. Richards I want to see him."

"Yes, Sir, Mr. Dillenbeck."

In Steven's office, Dillenbeck commented, "Just a little piece of advice, Steven. I couldn't help but notice when I looked around your office out there - I don't see anything but black faces. You know, we wouldn't any charges of reverse discrimination coming down on us."

Steven responded, "Is that so? I thought I was doing us a favor by hiring a few blacks - to avoid any charge of real

Chapter 10

discrimination, you know. If you look through this firm, I think you'll find that there's a minimal number of African-Americans in it - perhaps you didn't realize that, Dan," he said in a tone of mild sarcasm.

Steven's intent was not lost on Dillenbeck, and he said quite honestly, "You know, Steven, I don't know what I'm going to do with you!"

Steven laughed, "Don't do nothin' - just let me do my thing! Speaking of doing my thing, I don't know what the one-way mirrors are for, but I don't want mine. I need someone to come in here and take it down and patch the hole up."

"Why do you want to do that?"

"I don't think it's fair to the employees to be watching them like that."

Dillenbeck said, "Well, it's your office, Steven, do what you want. Getting to the reason I'm here . . . uh . . . I'm beginning to be a little concerned about the Pollock case. I've been having some second thoughts."

"Why is it I knew you were going to say that?"

Dillenbeck went on, "Well, maybe it isn't appropriate for you to be representing Jeffrey Burroughs under the circumstances. Uh . . . you know, it's pretty hard on Pollock and all. What do you think?"

"I think it stinks."

"Now, now, it's nothing for you to get upset about - it was just a thought I wanted to run past you."

Steven probed. "Aside from Pollock, what is it, specifically, that bothers you about me being on this case?"

"Steven, my only interest is the firm. You know how the press is - they might get hold of it and try to exploit it - say we're experiencing internal strife."

"Well, Dan, I don't know about that, but if you guys were to vote to force me off this case, even if it meant taking a leave from the firm, I would still represent Burroughs - that's how strongly I believe in his innocence."

"Steven, I think you're just too sensitive. Nobody's talking about forcing you off the case."

"Well, what you call sensitive, I call being cautious, given the history of what my people have gone through in this country. Now don't misunderstand me, I'm not trying to attack you, but the first thing you did when you came in here was criticize me for the number of blacks in my office, when in reality the firm is almost entirely white - a fact that I never would have mentioned to you when I came here because that's the way things are, and I expect it. Do you understand what I'm trying to say, Dan?"

"Well, I guess so, but I didn't come in here to argue about social issues."

"But, Dan, social issues can't be avoided - they're part of our everyday existence, although you may not recognize them in the same way I do."

Dan let out a big sigh. "You're wearing me out, Steven - I gotta go. Maybe you can recommend a book that'll teach me how to approach you without offending you."

Dan got up to leave, and Steven said, "Just one more thing before you go. Jeffrey Burroughs told me that there was a problem which involved Martin and his father here at the firm - maybe something about money - would you happen to know anything about that?"

Dillenbeck looked startled, but just said, "I can't imagine."

"Oh, and another thing, I understand there was a meeting the other night of the senior partners and someone from the accounting firm. Again, with all due respect, shouldn't I have been included in such a meeting?"

"Steven, you got to understand - you're new here and we're used to meeting with just the three of us - it was an oversight on our part. You're absolutely right, and I can assure you it won't happen again."

Dillenbeck left, and Steven turned his chair to the window, propped his feet up on the sill, and gazed out over Philadelphia. In thinking about his conversation with Dillenbeck, he had the impression that something didn't ring true - the startled look Dan gave him when Pollock and money were mentioned - and the failure to include him in the meeting seemed like more than an oversight. Perhaps something was being kept from him. He thought to himself that since Andrew Talley was the one who brought him into the firm, maybe he could get some straight answers from him.

Steven wheeled around in his chair and asked Gina to get Talley on the phone. When Talley came on the line, Steven made arrangements to meet him for coffee the next morning.

When five o'clock rolled around, Gina came in and said, "Steven, I'm leaving now. Bob is waiting for me downstairs."

You could see the muscles in Steven's face tighten when he heard that, and he exclaimed, "Bob! Why are you telling me this?"

Even though she had no intention of changing her mind about going back to Bob, Gina wanted Steven to show her one more time how much he cared for her. In response to his question, she replied, "I don't know. I just thought maybe you should know that I'm going back with him."

Steven's voice was tense with emotion. "This doesn't make any sense. I don't understand why you're telling me this. Is it to make me angry or jealous or what? What are you trying to do to me?"

"I'm not trying to do anything to you - I just wanted you to know that it's okay between Bob and me again, and everything's going to be alright."

"Gina, that man is never going to have any respect for you, judging from what he's done to you, and I don't think that was the first time either. Right now, it doesn't matter whether it's me you're with; I just don't want to see you go back to someone who abuses you that way."

"You sound like my mother, Steven . . . please, I don't need a lecture right now. I have to go."

Gina left, and Steven went back to his desk and got the binoculars. He looked down into the street and saw Bob leaning on the fender of his car. He watched until Gina came out. Bob reached to kiss her, but Gina avoided his grasp and got in the car.

Steven banged his fist on the sill and said quite loudly, "Damn it! . . . Goddamn it!"

From the outer office, Andrea heard the distress in his voice and came in and saw him standing there, looking out the window. She asked, "Are you alright, Steven?"

He was startled by her voice. He felt ashamed and tried to compose himself. "Yes, Andrea, I'm fine," he answered.

She advanced toward him, saying, "Is there anything I can do?"

"No, everything's alright. I want to be alone."

Andrea left, thinking that Steven must have found out about Bob coming back into Gina's life.

After a while, Steven left the office, and when he arrived home, he played back the messages on his answering service. One of them was from his mother. "Steven . . . Son . . . it's your mother. Please call me as soon as you get in; it's very important."

He heard the stress in his mother's voice and called her right back. "Mom, I got your message. You sounded kind of upset."

"Oh, Steven, I want you to listen at something." She then played a message from her answering machine. "Tell your son to get off the Burroughs case, or he's going to be missing a parent" was the message, delivered by a male voice.

Steven was horrified. "Mom, whatever you do, don't erase that tape. I'm coming over to pick it up. Does Dad know about it?"

"'No, I didn't tell him; I didn't want to alarm him. What should I do if he calls again?"

"Just hang up. Mom, I'll be right over."

As soon as he hung up, Steven called Lieutenant Dickens. "Lieutenant, I think I've got something you'll want to hear. I wonder if you could meet me over at my mother's place in about an hour - it's not far from where you are."

Dickens responded, "This better be good, Richards; I was just getting ready to go home."

"Thanks a lot - I really appreciate it." He then gave Dickens his mother's address.

When Steven got to his parents' house, Dickens was waiting outside for him. They went in, and Steven introduced him to his mother.

Steven's mother, Anna Richards, was a beautiful stout woman with a complexion about the same shade as Steven's. She was a woman who always dressed in African garb with lots of beads around her neck and wrists. She wore a close-cut, natural hairdo like a lot of black women did in the sixties. In fact, that's the era she sprung from, and she had fond memories of that time. She often told Steven that blacks were too complaisant nowdays and had lost the will to take to the streets and fight for what they believed in. Sometimes Steven joked with her, calling her his sixties Mama.

Mrs. Richards played the tape for them.

"What do you think of that, Lieutenant?" Steven asked.

"What did you expect me to think of it?"

"To me, this tape indicates that Jeffrey is innocent - doesn't it to you?"

Dickens said, "No, not necessarily."

"Well, who but the killer would want me off the case so bad that they would threaten my parents?"

"I don't know, but it's going to take a lot more than this to clear Jeffrey, Steven. Someone that knows Jeffrey is guilty could be doing this as well - just to cast doubt, you know."

"I thought you said you believed he was innocent?"

"I do, Steven, but, believe me, this is just not enough."

Steven asked, "Would you like me to make a copy of the tape for you?"

"Yeah, you can give me one just in case it becomes relevant in the future. Steven, I've got to be getting along now - thanks for letting me hear it."

Steven went back into the house, and, although still very upset himself, he did his best to calm his mother.

Chapter 11

As planned, Steven met with Talley in the cafeteria the next morning.

"So, Steven, what did you want to see me about?"

"Well, before I go there, I want to tell you what happened last night." Steven told him about the threat to his parents.

Talley said, "This is serious, my friend. Have you decided what you're going to do about it?"

"Right now, Andy, I'm going to ignore it because I think it's just someone trying to scare me off, but it seems like the person making the call would need access to some detailed information about me in order to know where to reach my parents - especially since they have an unlisted phone. The only time I can remember using my mother's phone number is when I gave it to this firm to call in case of an emergency."

"Are you trying to say that it's someone here?"

"Well, what else am I to conclude? But getting to what I really wanted to talk to you about, I may be paranoid, but there's some things that have been going on that I'm a little confused about."

"Like what?"

"First, you told me about a meeting with the accountant, but no one told me when it was, and the meeting took place without me. Could you explain to me how that happened? Before you answer that, I think it's only fair to tell you that Dillenbeck has already given me a reason which I didn't find acceptable."

"In all fairness to me, what did he say?"

Steven smiled and replied, "That's a good lawyer's response."

"Well, to be truthful, Steven, I don't want to get into a lot of he-said, she-said stuff - I can tell you that it wasn't anything anti-Steven or anti-black - I don't want you to believe that."

"Well, let's get past that. I'm not concerned as long as it doesn't happen again. The other thing I wanted to ask you is whether you might know what Martin, Junior meant when he told Jeffrey that there was a problem between his father and him at the firm involving money."

Talley hesitated, thinking about the embezzlement which Rhyner had uncovered.

Steven said perceptively, "You see, Andy, that's the kind of stuff I'm talking about - that question seems to give everyone pause. I have a feeling that if I ask Grundage, he would respond in the same way. What's going on - is that what that meeting was about that I was conveniently left out of ?"

Talley thought to himself that he'd better be straightforward with Steven because if he found out from another source, it would certainly mar their relationship. He reluctantly said, "Steven, I have something to tell you, and for now, you mustn't reveal that you know anything about it. Our accountant says that there's about three hundred and sixty thousand dollars missing, and that's what the meeting was about. Right now we're trying to sort it out ourselves, rather than bring in an outside investigator. We talked about whether any of us was involved; personally, I can absolve myself as suspect, and I don't have reason to believe that it was Dillenbeck or Grundage."

"If Dillenbeck or Grundage were involved, do you think they would tell you?" Steven asked.

Chapter 11

"Well, I thought about that, but I've known these guys for quite a while, and there's never been the slightest hint of a problem of that sort in the past."

Steven said, "I believe there is something going on, Andy. So far, both times that I've met with Dillenbeck when Pollock was around, whenever I left the room, he always asked Pollock to stay behind. I don't know whether you noticed it or not. I think they're tight."

"Well, I used to think so, too, but then I heard them having a big blowout the other day."

"What do you mean - just what happened?"

Andrew told him about the incident in which Dillenbeck was shouting 'over my dead body' at Pollock.

Steven asked, "And what has Pollock contributed to believe that it would be appropriate to make him a senior partner?"

"I don't know - he hasn't been here that long - a lot of the other junior partners have been here a lot longer. And to be truthful, he hasn't been that productive as far as bringing in new business."

Steven said, "Maybe he feels he can make demands because he knows something. More than that, when I was questioning him about his son's murder, he was very uptight, and I got the feeling he was hiding something."

Andrew asked, "Are you saying that Pollock's death has something to do with the embezzlement?"

"I never mentioned that to you, but in order to ask that question, you must have made the connection."

Andrew nodded in silent agreement.

Steven moved closer to him. "Andy, can I count on you? We both have an interest in getting to the bottom of this. I've got an innocent man that I'm representing, and as partners we both have the firm's interest at heart. I'm asking that you keep your eyes and ears open, and maybe we can get some answers."

Talley said, "You got it, Steven. We'll talk again soon."

Up in Steven's office, Andrea and Gina had carried out their plan to change their appearances to see how Steven would respond.

Andrea was sitting at Gina's desk wearing a blonde wig with hair cascading in curls below her shoulders. She was heavily made up with pinkish eyeshadow, long, false eyelashes, and brilliant red lipstick. She had on a red blouse, sheer enough that you could clearly see the color of her bra underneath, and a micromini skirt which she had borrowed from her sister who was two sizes smaller and which left hardly anything to the imagination, panty line and all. The outfit was finished off with spike heels. In this clothing, it was evident that Andrea was every bit as shapely as Gina. In fact, coming in to work that morning she had received the same wolf calls that Gina received on a regular basis.

On the other hand, Gina, sitting at Andrea's desk, was not wearing a wig, and had drawn her natural hair into a bun in the back. She wore no make-up at all and had on plain shoes with one-inch heels and a beautiful, one-piece dress in an African print which covered her from the neck to almost her ankles.

Arthur Gwaltney had certainly noticed the difference in the two women from the day before and was completely mystified as to what was going on.

When Steven entered his office suite, he was still preoccupied by the conversation he had just had with Talley - so preoccupied that he walked right past Andrea sitting at Gina's desk without realizing who it was.

Chapter 11

After he disappeared into his office, the two women looked at each other and burst out laughing. Steven heard them and looked out through the one-way mirror and saw Andrea walk from Gina's desk over to hers and double over with laughter as she said to Gina, "Can you believe that - he didn't even notice!"

Puzzled by the two women's hilarity, Steven wondered, "Are they laughing at me?" and looked himself up and down to make sure that nothing was out of place. Still not realizing that a change had occurred, he went back to his desk and rang Gina's extension. In the outer office, when they heard the phone ring, Gina said to Andrea, "He's calling me! He's calling me - go get it - hurry up!" Andrea rushed back over to Gina's desk, picked up the phone and said, "Yes, Steven?"

"Yeah, Gina, will you come in her for a moment?"

When Andrea came in, her head down, he asked, "May I ask what the big joke is out there?"

Andrea looked up and said, "Good morning, Steven."

Steven realized immediately that he was the object of an elaborate prank. He stood, looked at her from head to toe, paused a moment, and then asked, "Andrea, what is this all about?"

Andrea could sense that Steven was not pleased with the escapade and shyly said, "Don't you like the way I look, Steven?"

He didn't answer her question, but asked his own. "Is this your idea or Gina's?"

Andrea replied, "The idea was both of ours."

"What result was it supposed to produce?"

"I don't know, Steven - we were just kidding. If I've offended you, I want this to end now, and I'm very sorry."

"No, it's not that simple, Andrea - you can't do this to me and then just want to forget it."

He got up and went to his door and called out, "Gina, please come in."

Gwaltney shook his head; he still looked perplexed as to what was taking place. He was beginning to think that maybe this firm was not as conservative as he had once thought.

Gina came in, and Steven asked her, "Can you explain what you two are doing a little better than Andrea just did?"

"What did Andrea say?"

"She didn't say anything useful. Maybe you can be more descriptive."

Andrea looked at Gina. "Gina, this isn't going too good. We might as well explain it to him."

"Oh, Steven, don't be such a damn stick-in-the-mud. We were just having a little fun with you - that's all! I told Andrea to dress like this in the hope that you might see how beautiful a woman she is."

"Oh, and that would just automatically take my attention off of you, is that right?"

Gina said, "Well, yeah, Steven, I guess that's right."

"Things are not that simple. I think the both of you know that. Andrea, you should never try to be something you are not. I like you the way you are."

Gina said, "C'mon, Steven, admit it - she looks great, doesn't she?"

"If you want me to be honest, she looks like a tart!"

At that, Andrea rushed out of the room, and Gina turned on Steven in a fury. "Oh, great, Steven - that was really great! That was the best thing you could say to her. She only did it to try and get your attention. Don't take it out on her - if you want someone to blame, it's me. I'm the one you're really angry with!"

"What do you expect me to do? You guys are playing with my feelings and expecting me to laugh and grin about it.

Chapter 11

Don't you understand what this stunt is really saying? There's two victims here - Andrea, for one, and myself, the other. You're the only one who doesn't stand to be hurt."

Gina said, "What is the joke saying, Steven?"

"I don't believe that you don't know the answer to that. The joke, as you call it, is saying that all you care about is getting me off your back - well, you've done that." For the second time since knowing Gina, Steven found himself saying, "From now on, there'll be nothing but business in this office. That's all, Gina."

Gina stormed out of Steven's office.

Arthur's curiosity was getting the best of him, and when Gina came out, he asked her, "Would it be too presumptuous of me to ask what's going on around here?"

Gina snapped at him. "Nigger shit, Arthur . . . just nigger shit!"

She then turned and asked Andrea, "Are we going to have lunch? I want to get out of here."

"No, I want to go home and change."

In his office, Steven thought to himself that Andrea had looked pretty sexy which made him wonder if that was the point that was being made - that he was only attracted to Gina because of her looks. And what was it about her looks that attracted him? Steven was a fairly perceptive person; now he asked himself, "Why am I so attracted to this woman who obviously doesn't want me and with whom I have very little in common? Is it her European looks that make me so crazy about her? Am I secretly infected with the same distaste for blackness - the same desire for assimilation as Gina?"

That night, in his hotel suite, what had happened at the office was still plaguing Steven. He felt that he had treated Andrea unfairly, and he called her at home. "Andrea, this is Steven. I would like to apologize for the awful things I said to you today - and I'd like to do it in person. Why don't I come over and pick you up?"

"Oh, it's that simple, Steven? You really think I'm so taken by you that all you have to do is call me, and I jump and go out with you?"

"No, Andrea, that's not the case at all. We can just sit in the car outside your house if you want. I just want to see you."

There was silence, and Steven said, "Andrea, are you there?"

"Yes, I'm here, Steven. We can talk outside the house."

"I'll be there in about fifteen minutes - I'll just blow the horn."

This time, Andrea did not rush to change her appearance for Steven. When he came, she just went out to the car in what she had been wearing, a pair of blue jeans and tee-shirt. When she got in the car, he asked her, "Why did you come out without a jacket? It's pretty cold out here."

"Oh, I'm alright. What did you want to talk about?"

Steven plunged right in. "Andrea, I really think you're a wonderful person. There's no woman in my life at this time, and if you can tolerate me, I'd like us to be closer friends. I think it might be very easy for me to eventually fall in love with you."

Andrea eyed him with suspicion. "What was it, Steven - was it the way I looked today, 'cause if it was you'll never see me like that again. You were right - I looked like something out of a peep show. And what about Gina? You told me you couldn't turn your feelings on and off anytime you felt like it."

"That's true, Andrea, but I think I learned something today. As confused as Gina's mind may be, I think she might be right - I might be attracted to her looks and not her character or personality. And if that were the case, and I were to win Gina over, I'd probably regret it for the rest of my life."

Andrea again fell silent, thinking about how badly she really wanted to be with Steven, and started to weaken. "What about in the office, Steven? That would be very hard with the three of us there. Every time you called her in your office for something, I would be jealous."

"Well, the way Gina feels about me, I don't think your jealousy would be warranted. Do you understand what I'm saying?"

"I understand, Steven, but I don't think you understand. Gina's coming from an irrational basis - she's made a commitment to herself that she isn't going to get involved with a black man. But that has nothing to do with how Gina really feels about you."

"What do you mean?"

Andrea let out a sigh. "Uh . . . yesterday at lunch when we thought up the idea to play our little trick on you . . . well, we also talked about some true feelings. Gina does care about you - I think more than she really knows."

"Did she say that out of her mouth or is that your interpretation?"

"No, Steven, she said, 'I do care for him.'"

"Regardless of what she said, Andrea, it's what's she's doing that bothers me. If being with a black man is so distasteful to her, then that's a problem for me. Anyway, I don't want to talk about her anymore. Let's talk about you and me."

"Steven, you're just angry now and need someone to talk to . . . and I'm here for that. I think you're just coming on to me because you think Gina doesn't want you, and I refuse to be caught up in the middle of a love triangle. In fact, I've been thinking that maybe it would be good if you gave me some time to find another job."

"Oh, no! Do you really feel that strongly about it?"

"Steven, I just can't stand to be in that office every day, feeling the way I do about you and knowing how you feel about Gina. Can't you understand that?"

"Yeah, I guess I can, Andrea. I'm just being selfish. I'll tell you what, take whatever time away from the office you need to look for a job, but I do hope that the situation might resolve itself in some way before you actually leave because I think we work well together." He gave her a fond look. "You know, I really like you - if you leave, can we still go out together sometimes?"

"I don't know. We'll see."

Steven reached over, turned Andrea toward him until they were facing, and held her firmly by the shoulders. He brought her close to him and kissed her hard on the mouth - not gently at all. Andrea initially tried to push him away, but as he persisted, she relented somewhat. As Steven felt her begin to relax in his arms, he no longer felt the need to be so forceful, and his kiss became softer and more sensual.

When he finally released her, she caught her breath and asked him, "Why do you do that, Steven? It's not fair to me."

"I don't know - it's kind of strange - I just really, really like kissing you!"

Andrea laughed at that, and they said goodnight.

After Steven got home and had poured himself his usual Pepsi over ice, he drank half of it, sitting on the couch and thinking about his conversation with Andrea, and then laid back against the pillows and drifted to sleep. About two hours later, the phone rang, startling him out of a deep sleep, and when he jumped up from the couch to answer it, the slurred voice of a female said, "Hello, is this Mr. Steven Richards?"

Chapter 11

Steven answered groggily, "Speaking."
"Well, Mr. Richards, I think I may have some pertinent information for you about the Burroughs case."
Steven was instantly alert. From her voice, he realized that she was quite drunk. He asked, "To whom am I speaking?"
"Who I am is not important - do you want to hear what I have to say or not?"
"Of course."
"It isn't something I want to talk about on the phone - I'll have to meet you somewhere - somewhere out of the way where I won't be seen."
"What do you suggest?"
"I'll be seated on a bench in the courtyard of the Rodin Museum at 22nd and the Parkway - tomorrow at three o'clock. Do you know where that is?"
"I'm quite familiar with the Rodin."
"I'll be in disguise because I don't want to be recognized."
"How will I know you?"
"I'll know you."

Chapter 12

The next day, Steven walked to the museum from his office. When he got inside the courtyard, he saw two people, a man sitting on a bench on one side of the courtyard, and a woman sitting on the extreme opposite side. The path was made of gravel and when you walked, you could hear the stones crunching beneath your feet. Because of the threat made against his parents, Steven cautiously walked toward where the woman was sitting. When he got about five feet from her, she said, in a low voice, "Mr. Richards? Have a seat."

Steven sat down beside her, and he could smell the reek of alcohol. He looked carefully at her in an effort to penetrate her disguise. It was obvious that she was wearing a wig, black in color. She was wearing very large dark glasses and a veil through which he could see signs of heavy makeup. The disguise was very good - almost as if a professional makeup artist had done it - and Steven felt that there was no way that he would be able to identify her out of her disguise. He asked, "Who are you?"

"I would rather not say. Let's leave it at that."

"What is it that you think you have which would be helpful to my client?"

"Well, for one, I know that your client is innocent."

"I know that, too, but I have to prove it."

"If I can learn to trust you, perhaps I'll supply you with the proof you need."

"Trust me to do what?"

"For one, not to try to find out who I am. I don't want to be called as a witness - I don't want anyone to know where you got the information or evidence."

Chapter 12

Steven was beginning to get anxious. "Well, you have my word on that, but what do you have for me?"

"As time goes by, you will see. If you are able to keep the fact that this meeting took place a secret, it will not be our last one."

Steven said, a bit impatiently, "I don't want to play a cat and mouse game with you. I've got a client suffering in prison for a murder he didn't commit - you either have something for me or you don't."

"Listen, Mr. Richards, if we're going to do this, we're going to do it my way. I have my reasons." She rose from the bench and said, "I'll be in touch with you."

"But one last thing - what do I call you?"

She replied, "Whatever you wish," and walked away.

As Steven left the courtyard, he paused a moment to look up at the statue out front and then thought to himself, "That's what I'll call her - the Thinker."

By the time Steven returned to his office, it was almost time to leave for the day. Gina couldn't help but notice that Steven was very high-spirited for some reason and asked, "What are you so happy about?"

He responded with great joy, "Gina, things are starting to look up around here!"

Steven was happy because his mystery lady, "The Thinker," was the break he had been looking for, and now it might only be a matter of time before Jeffrey would be free.

Just then there was a knock on Steven's door. It was Andrew Talley.

"Andy, my man, how are you? Do you have some good word for me?"

Like Gina, Talley picked up on Steven's mood as well and remarked, "My . . . you must have gotten out of bed on the right side this morning!"

"Yes, I think I did."

Then suddenly the expression on Talley's face changed when he said, "Well, Steven, I don't have much to report, but today when I went into Dan's office - Simon and Martin were there with him. I got the funniest feeling that I was interrupting something. As soon as I came in, a strange quiet fell over the room . . . I don't know, Steven, it could be me - maybe you've made me a bit paranoid. I've walked in on them plenty of times before, and the same atmosphere was probably there - but I paid no attention to it. Perhaps it wasn't anything."

"And maybe it was, Andy . . . maybe it was, you can never tell . . . and that's more reason why we have to pay close attention to everything that goes on around us."

"Well, I just thought I'd pass that by you, Steven. I'm headed home now. I think I'll stop for a drink on the way. Would you like to join me?"

"No, I don't drink, Andy."

"Oh, that's right, I keep forgetting that." Talley smiled and said, "You know, Steven, I wish I had your strength; I could probably save myself a lot of money. Well, goodnight, I'll see you in the morning."

After Talley left, Gina came into Steven's office.

"What is it, Gina?"

"Where's Andrea? She didn't come in today."

"Oh, I don't know - maybe she didn't feel too good or something."

"Steven, I want to ask you something. Are we gonna act like strangers to each other or be friends? You obviously did everything you could to avoid me today, and I don't want it to be like that."

Chapter 12

"Gina, I've decided to put you in the proper perspective as far as my love life is concerned, and right now you're on the back burner. If you should change your mind, I'll be here for you . . . if you don't take too long. And as time goes by, I'm sure I'll develop a more natural attitude toward you in the office."

Just at that moment, Marybeth came barging in. "Hi, y'all! What's goin' on in here?"

Steven was annoyed. "Beth, I don't appreciate you busting in my office that way. Would you do that to any of the other senior partners? I don't think so."

Gina defended her. "Steven, you know how Beth is - I don't think she meant any harm."

Marybeth spoke up. "Gina, I don't need you to defend me. I'm quite capable of doing that myself."

"Oh, shut up, Beth. I think we should leave now. And before we leave, I want you to apologize to him."

Marybeth said, in a sexy voice, "I'm sorry, Steven, I'll try not to do that ever again."

"That's alright, Beth."

"C'mon, Beth, let's go," Gina urged.

Marybeth purposely left her small handbag on Steven's desk and left with Gina. When they got out in the hall, she said, "Oh, Gina, wait a minute - I must have left my purse in Steven's office. I'll be right back." She ran back in, just as Steven was closing his door. "Oh, I think my handbag is on your desk. Could you let me in?" After she retrieved it, she asked him, "Why don't we hang out tonight? I think I have some information you might be interested in."

Steven thought for a moment and then said, "What the heck - I don't have anything to do."

Marybeth said, "Okay, I'll see you at my place at nine" and kissed Steven on the mouth.

Gina had doubled back to look for Marybeth and got there just in time to see them kiss. She was angered by what she saw and said sharply, "C'mon, Beth." She turned and started rapidly striding down the hall.

Marybeth came out and chased after her, calling, "Gina, wait for me, Girl. Where you rushin' off to?"

Gina snapped, "I'm in a hurry."

When Marybeth caught up to her, Gina said, "I got a feeling you left your purse there on purpose. What did you do, make a date with him?"

"So what if I did?"

"Well, the other day, you chewed me out for deceiving you - and here you are, doing the same thing to me."

"Gina, you're not going to let this man come between us, are you? I don't understand - you're living with Bob, and I have the feeling you don't want me to have anything to do with Steven."

"Girl, you can do what you want . . . I'm not your keeper."

"But I don't want you angry with me for seeing him . . . somebody you claim not to give a damn about."

Gina recognized how irrational her behavior must seem and apologized. "Oh, Beth, I'm sorry - I guess I haven't been myself lately."

"You can say that again! I think you might be falling for him . . . and I think you're beginning to wonder how the juice of the blackberry tastes!" Marybeth giggled at her own remark.

Gina said, "Oh, Girl, shut up . . . you crazy," and started laughing with her.

They both went down the hall, arm-in-arm, laughing hysterically.

Chapter 12

That night at Marybeth's apartment, it was nine fifteen, and Steven hadn't shown up yet. She had the table set with candlelight, a bottle of champagne chilling in an ice bucket, and a few hors d'oeuvres. She was pacing the floor and looking at her watch every minute. When the doorbell rang, she rushed to the buzz-in system. "Who is it?"

"It's me - Steven." She buzzed him in and ran to the closest mirror for last minute assurance. Even before he got there, she was standing in front of the door, staring at it, anxiously waiting for him to knock. When he did, she slung the door open and threw herself into his arms and kissed him.

"Oh, Steven, I'm so glad - I thought maybe you wouldn't show up 'cause of what I did today."

"What did you do?"

"Oh, you know, when I came into your office today without knocking."

"Beth, to tell you the truth, I didn't give it much thought afterwards."

She planted another kiss on him, but this time a much more passionate one. They stood there, kissing and groping at one another, with the door wide open, until Steven closed it with his foot. When they came up for breath, Beth grabbed him by the hand, pulling him further into her apartment and asking, "Would you like something to drink?"

"What do you have?"

"I have some champagne on ice."

"No, Beth, I don't drink alcohol - I thought I told you that. Would you happen to have any Pepsi?"

"Sure, but it might be a little flat - it's been opened and sitting in the fridge for a while."

"That's okay, I'll take it."

When Marybeth walked away from Steven, he couldn't help noticing the way her jeans fit so tightly around her well-shaped body. They were so tight, if she were in silhouette, you'd think she was stark naked. He kept on watching her, and just before she entered the kitchen, she turned and posed, putting her left hand up on the door frame and the other on her hip and giving him a mischievous smile.

Steven just shook his head and went to sit on the couch.

As soon as Marybeth came out of the kitchen, she handed him the soda, sat down beside him, and in seconds she was all over him again. He was not quite ready for what she wanted and jokingly remarked, "Whoa, whoa . . . hold on a minute there, Beth - if you keep this up, you're gonna make me think you only want me for my body."

"Well, maybe that is all I want from you. After all, you don't take me seriously, do you?"

"I take everybody seriously."

"Some more seriously than others - right?"

Steven groaned. "What do you mean by that, Beth?"

"Oh, you know what I'm talkin' 'bout."

Steven ignored her remark and said, "Beth, I don't understand you - what do you want? I'm here tonight . . . who's going to be here tomorrow night . . . and the night after? Isn't there anyone that you really care about or want to commit yourself to?"

Marybeth smiled, pointed at him, and said, "You! Can't you tell?"

"If you had me, I don't think I'd satisfy you for long. I think your insecurity drives you to keep running to the next man."

"You don't mind saying insulting things to me, do you, Steven? Why do you want to spoil the night like this?"

"I don't mean to. I'm just a forthright person - I believe in telling it like I see it."

"Well, I know you didn't come up here to preach to me, did you? You sound like my goddamned father."

Chapter 12

Steven laughed, "Oh, I'm glad I'm not your father!"

Marybeth laughed, too, and then said in a serious way, "Steven, can I ask you something? If it weren't for Gina, would you look at me differently?"

"Gina has nothing to do with the way I see you, Beth. To be truthful, when I think of making a commitment, I think of a black woman."

"Geez, Steven, you're as bad as Gina!"

"No, there's a big difference. I want to stay in my race; Gina wants to go outside of hers - just like you. You're more like Gina than I am."

Marybeth seemed sincere when she responded, "Well, I understand how you feel, Steven - I really do."

He changed the subject and asked, "What about this information you have for me?"

"Steven, you have to promise me you won't tell anybody where you got this from."

"I promise."

"Well, first of all, I remembered something - about a week before the murder, Mr. Dillenbeck came to see Mr. Pollock. Well, you know how loud old DB is, and I heard him say to Martin something like, 'He's your son - find a way to shut him up.' I didn't think anything of it at the time, but now after what's happened, maybe it means something."

Steven said, "Well, Beth, 'shut him up' doesn't necessarily mean murder him! I don't know - it's something to think about - that's for sure. Was there anything else?"

"Only one other thing - the other day, I heard Martin on the phone say: 'I can't believe you think I would have anything to do with the death of my own son'."

"Very interesting - but who was he talking to?"

"I don't know."

"Aren't you his secretary - wouldn't the call have come through you?"

"No, I'd been out of the office when I came in and heard it."

"Good . . . that's some pretty good information, Beth. I'd appreciate if you'd keep your eyes and ears open."

Marybeth moved closer again to Steven and put her hand on his inner thigh. She started stroking him, saying, "Business is over - it's time to play!" Just then, the phone rang. Marybeth said, "Oh, damn it!" and picked it up. "Hello . . . Hello?" There was no answer, but no dial tone either. "Who is this?" No answer. She slammed the phone down, but then hit Star 69. The voice who said "hello" was Gina's, and Beth quietly hung up. She didn't say anything to Steven.

About mid-morning at the office the next day, the phone rang, and Gina picked it up. A woman's voice said, "I wanna speak to Steven Richards."

Gina said, "Who's calling, please?"

"Never mind who's calling; just tell him I have some more information for him."

"I'm sorry, but I have to let him know who is calling."

"Young lady, this is a very important phone call, and if he doesn't get it, you probably won't have your job."

"Hold on, I'll discuss this with Mr. Richards."

Gina put her on hold and called Steven. "There's someone on the line, Steven, who insists on speaking to you but won't give her name. She threatened my job if I didn't give you the call. Do you want to talk to her?"

"Yes, I'll talk to her."

When the call was put through to Steven, Gina never hung up. He realized it right away and told Gina, "That'll be all. Hang up." When he heard the click, he asked, "Who is this?" and discovered that it was the Thinker, who said, "I want to

Chapter 12

meet you in the same place at three o'clock. I have some information I believe you'll be interested in hearing."

Steven said, "I'll be there."

After he hung up, he called Gina into his office and asked curiously, "Why did you stay on the line like that?"

"Oh, I was doing something and didn't realize that I hadn't broken the connection."

Steven looked suspiciously at her and said, "I don't know, Gina."

In a cutesy voice, Gina asked, "Who's the mystery lady?"

"Gina, I hope we're not going to have a problem with you scrutinizing my calls this way. Do you understand?"

"Yes, Steven, I understand. But off the record, I think you're getting to be quite a ladies' man."

He ignored the remark and told her that he would be leaving the office a little before three.

Then Gina asked, "Where's Andrea? Is she alright?"

"Oh, I gave Andrea a little time off to find another job."

"What? Whose idea was that?"

"I'm afraid it was hers."

"Was it because of me?"

"There's that ego, working overtime again, Gina. But this time, you're right. She feels that it's impossible to work effectively . . . considering the situation."

"Gee, she must really have it bad if she would give up her job because of it. Steven, can I say something to you as a friend?"

"Shoot."

"I think you're pretty stupid. You know, Andrea's really crazy about you, and I think she's a very nice person. Why are you letting her get away from you this way?"

"Well, that's my business, Gina, and I want this conversation to end."

"Have it your way," Gina responded and left the room.

As planned, Steven met the Thinker at the museum. As soon as he sat down on the bench with her, he could tell she had been drinking. By now, he had concluded that she was an alcoholic. He told her, "Since you won't give me your name, I've had to give you one. I refer to you as the Thinker."

"Well, whatever."

"Look, why don't we just stop playing this game. Who are you, and what relationship do you have to the people in this case?"

"Look, Buddy, I'm calling the shots here. Now, you can take it or leave it."

"Well, maybe I'll leave it because I don't have time to play this cat and mouse game with you. I think you need me as much as I need you. It's obvious that you want whoever did it to be brought to justice, and you need me to do that. If you have information which can speed up my efforts, tell me now. I'm not going to let you dangle me on a string this way." At that point, Steven got up and started to walk away.

"Mr. Richards . . . uh . . . don't go yet. Don't be so hasty. Come back and sit down. My, they say you people are very high strung, but I didn't know you were this bad!"

Steven ignored her racist remark and said, "You said you had some information for me. Are you going to tell me or not?"

"Well, the murderer works at your firm. That's as much as I can give you right now."

"To be truthful with you, Thinker, I was beginning to come to that conclusion myself."

"Now you know it for sure."

"Are you sure that's all you want to tell me?"

"Yes, I'm quite sure."

Chapter 12

"You know how to reach me if you have anything else. And one last thing, the next time we meet, I'd appreciate it if you would come sober."

The Thinker was horrified that he would have the nerve to say something like that to her and just glared angrily at him.

Steven walked away, thinking to himself that speaking his mind to her had put him in a better position to get what he wanted from her.

Chapter 13

Two weeks had passed and even though Steven's feelings about Gina hadn't changed, he was getting used to the idea that they were not the world's most compatible couple. Although he thought often about what Andrea had told him about Gina really caring for him, he couldn't see much evidence of it in Gina's behavior toward him.

Andrea had found a new job with another law firm, but she and Steven were still communicating with one another by phone on occasion.

Steven had become suspicious that Martin Pollock had killed his own son, but all he could do was sit on what little information the Thinker had given him, since he certainly couldn't accuse him unless he could prove it.

Talley had been out of town, and, upon his return, he came to visit Steven who greeted him with, "Andy, what's up, Man?"

"Same-o same-o. What's going on with you?"

"Well, I'll tell you, Andy, I think I'm finally making some headway on the Burroughs case."

"Good, I'm glad to hear that, Steven. What kind of headway?"

"Well, for one . . . and you've got to keep this to yourself, Andy, because my source has promised to cut me off if I divulge any of the information I'm getting . . . you know what I mean, buddy?"

"Sure, Steven, you can trust me. Go ahead, I'm listening."

"See, there's this woman that I meet in the park, at her whim. I believe she knows everything about the case, including who the murderer is, but won't tell me. She prefers to leak the information to me little bits at a time, and I get the feeling that she's familiar with people in this firm."

"But, Steven, when you meet with her, doesn't she look familiar to you at all?"

"No, she's in disguise with a veil over her face. She wants to stay anonymous - I guess for reasons of her own."

"Can you tell what nationality she is - white, black, hispanic, or what?"

"I'm pretty sure she's white, but there's one thing about her that annoys me, Man."

"What's that?"

"Every time we meet, she's drunk. I mean stinking, sloppy drunk - that odor, I can't stand it. I had to tell her, the next time, don't bother to come if she wasn't sober."

While Steven talked, Talley was thinking hard about who the Thinker could possibly be. He suddenly snapped his fingers and said, "Wait a minute, Steven, this is just a wild guess, but maybe you've been meeting with Martin Pollock's wife, Jody. Everybody in the firm knows she's a lush. . . personally, I've never seen her sober."

"You know what? I don't know why, but that crossed my mind a couple of times, but I dismissed it. I didn't know Mrs. Pollock drank a lot." Steven rubbed his chin with his hand and looked thoughtful. "You know, I believe you may be right, and if it is her, then I'm sure Pollock is my man." Steven jumped up from his desk, excited, and extended his hand and said, "Andy, give me five, Man . . . you are fantastic! I'm sure you're right!"

"But, how are you gonna get her to cooperate with you?" Talley asked. "You may still need her to testify."

"If she doesn't want to cooperate with me, I think I can work around that . . . but, we'll see."

"What do you think? Should we go and see Dan about this?"

"I don't think we should at this point. I wouldn't want to jeopardize Mrs. Pollock in any way. And as it is, I'm beginning to wonder a little about Dan and Simon."

After Talley left the office, Gina knocked and came in. Steven looked up, smiled and said, "Yes, Gina, what is it?"

"Oh, I just wanted to know if you wanted me to go through these applications for Andrea's job."

"Just leave them on my desk, and I'll have a decision by morning."

"What's the matter, Steven? You don't trust me to choose the best qualified?"

"Well, let me see . . . there are two black applicants and one white. I think if I let you choose . . . somehow or other, the white one will win out. No, I guess I don't trust you, Gina."

"You have a very low opinion of me, don't you, Steven? It really cuts deep sometimes, you know. I told you I was trying, but you won't give me a chance."

"I'm sorry, Gina, I never mean to hurt you. I guess it's just my way of lashing out at you for the hurt you've caused me since I've known you."

"But you can't blame me for that. I've never given you any reason to believe that you and I could ever make it."

"You're right, Gina, you haven't. I'll tell you what - you go ahead and choose the applicants you think are most suitable, and then I'll pick from them."

Steven got up and came around to the front of his desk, backed up against it, and sat up on the edge with his legs spread wide apart. The easy grin on his face and the way he was sitting, with his trousers drawn tight against his opened thighs, made him look very sexy, and Gina found herself eyeing him with great interest. She wondered, "Does he always look this good, and I just haven't noticed before? Is he deliberately trying to turn me on?" If he was, he was quite successful, because in a second, Gina had come over to him and planted herself between his legs.

As she did, Steven's arms went around her, and he whispered fiercely, "Gina, no matter how hard you try to fight it, I know you love me." He bent over and kissed her on the lips.

Gina's whole body came alive at his touch, and she eagerly began to kiss him back. There they were, kissing, grinding and groping for at least a minute. When they did finally come up for air, Gina spoke breathlessly. "I don't know if you can call it love or not, but I do know that I am very much attracted to you, Steven. I also know that it will never work between us."

"Why not?"

"For the reasons I gave you before."

"But, Gina, as reasons, they're not good enough. If you're attracted to me the way I am to you, then what you're doing doesn't make any sense."

Gina laid her head on his chest, started to sob quietly and said, "I'm sorry, Steven, please forgive me. It would make me very happy if I only knew that you understood enough to forgive me."

"I wouldn't have to forgive you, Gina, if you wouldn't do it."

"Steven, can we talk about this at your place tonight?"

He was so elated by her words that he didn't question her motives and just asked, "What time?"

"I'll be there at nine."

"What about Bob?"

"Oh, don't worry about him."

"I won't be made a fool of, Gina! If you're not there by nine, I won't wait for you. I'll find something else to do."

"Steven, will you stop worrying? I'll be there . . . honest, I will."

When Gina went back to her desk, the phone was ringing. "Hello, Gina, this is Andrea. Howya' doin'?"
"Oh, Andrea, it's good to hear from you. We have to get together some time, Girl."
"Yeah, that'll be great . . . hey, Gina, is Steven in?"
"Yes, he's here. Did you want me to get him for you?"
"Would you please?"
Gina put her on hold and called Steven. "Andrea's on the line."
Gina really wanted to listen in on them, but she remembered that Steven had caught her the last time she tried to do that, and she decided against it.
Steven said, "Andrea, are you there?"
"Yes, I'm here."
"How are you?"
"I'm fine . . . I know this is short notice - but, I was . . . wondering if you would like to have dinner with me tonight?" Steven started to say something, but Andrea kept on talking. "I'll understand if you've made previous plans."
"Oh, Andrea, I would love to, but I do have other plans." At that point, Steven saw the light on his phone flashing, indicating that someone was on the line. He asked her, "Will you hold a minute, Andrea? I have another call." He put her on hold and answered the other line, "Hello, Richards here."
The call was not long, and Steven went back to continue talking to Andrea. "Hello, Andrea, are you still there?" There was no answer. He repeated, "Andrea . . . Andrea, are you there?" He muttered to himself, "Oh, God, what did I do now?" He tried calling her back, but got a busy signal.

Chapter 13

That night at Steven's suite, he was pacing the floor, waiting for Gina to arrive. He looked at his watch and saw that it was only seven-thirty and said to himself, "An hour and a half - damn, that's a long time . . . listen at me . . . I'm acting like a love-sick teenager . . . get hold of yourself, Man - you're losing it!"

To pass the time, he decided to resume his call with Andrea.

When she answered the phone, Steven asked, "Andrea, are you angry with me?"

"No, of course not, Steven."

"Then why did you hang up today?"

"Oh, I don't know. I just had a feeling it was the wrong time to be bothering you."

"If you mean you thought I was busy, then you're right. But, guess what, I think I know who Martin Pollock's murderer is."

"Oh, Steven, that's great!"

Through their occasional phone calls, Steven and Andrea had become pretty good friends over the last couple of weeks. If you didn't know better you would have thought they were the perfect couple. They ended up talking for almost an hour, and although Steven had been anxiously waiting to see Gina, by the end of his conversation with Andrea, he was feeling relaxed and enjoying himself.

In the meanwhile, as Gina was leaving her apartment and getting into her car, Bob Rosenberg was coming down her street and spotted her. Deeply suspicious of her, he ran back to his car and followed her. When she ended up at the Four Seasons Hotel, he went in behind her and watched her speak briefly to the desk clerk and then get on the elevator.

Bob went over to the clerk and, flashing a badge from his employment, asked, "That woman who just left here - what suite number is she going to?"

The clerk was inexperienced and readily told him the number of Steven's suite.

Bob warned him, "Don't let him know I'm here. Do you understand?"

"Yes, Sir," the man said in a frightened voice.

Bob saw an elevator door open up, and he rushed over and jumped in.

When Gina got off the elevator, the first thing she saw at a distance down the hall was Steven standing outside of his door waiting for her. At first she started toward him at a normal pace, but the closer she got, the more excited she became, and started to speed up her stride. It wasn't long before she was running to him. When she got there, she cried out, "Oh, Steven . . . oh, Steven . . . why did I wait so long? Why did I wait so long?"

Steven put his arms around her and held her as tight as he could, whispering, "I don't know, Gina. I don't know . . . "

By this time, Bob had gotten off the elevator at Steven's floor. Right away he saw Gina and someone he was sure was Steven, locked in an embrace. He was afraid of Steven, so to keep from being seen, he quickly stepped back into the elevator archway. He stood there watching them until they disappeared into Steven's suite. Angry and despondent, Bob pushed the button for down, went to the lobby and left the building. He sat in his car outside the hotel for a long time before he eventually drove away.

Chapter 13

In the apartment, Steven asked, "Can I get you anything, Gina?"

"I'll have what you're having."

"But I'm just having a Pepsi . . . are you sure that's strong enough for you?"

"I'm quite sure."

Steven went to fetch the drinks and returned as rapidly as he could. He stood there in the doorway of the kitchen, with the drinks in his hands, looking at her, thinking how beautiful she was sitting there, with her legs crossed, one arm resting on the back of the couch, the other gracefully dangling in her lap. She was wearing a black leather, micromini skirt which left exposed the entire length of her beautiful, bare legs. Steven stared, hoping that she would shift position, and he might be able to see some secret part of her.

After a moment, he went in and put the drinks down on the coffeetable. He sat down beside her, pulled her to him, and they kissed. Even though Gina was responding passionately, and Steven was very excited, he stopped short to ask, "Gina, why are we here . . . or better yet, why are you here?"

"Steven, please, let's not spoil the evening by asking me a lot of questions about my reasons. I just want to enjoy you tonight. I owe it to myself and most of all I owe it to you."

Steven stiffened and exclaimed, "Owe it to me? Gina, you don't owe me anything. Anything I get from you, I get it because you want me to have it, not because you owe me!"

Gina could see she had said the wrong thing, so she clutched him to her tightly, and before she could get out all the words of "I'm sorry, Steven," she was fervently kissing him. He made a feeble attempt to break loose from her, but before he knew it, he was helplessly locked in her embrace, reeling with desire. She gradually broke the kiss, and her lips, nibbling all the time, slowly worked their way to his ear. She whispered to him, "Steven, I do love you . . . I really do love you, and I want tonight to be a night that I'll always remember for as long as I live."

Steven took Gina by the hand and led her into his bedroom. She excused herself and went into the adjoining bathroom. When she came out, she saw that he had turned the lights out and pulled up the blinds. His suite was situated in such a way that the glow from the moonlight outside the window gave the room a soft, romantic ambiance. "Oh, Steven, this is so beautiful . . . I borrowed your robe. I hope you don't mind?"

He didn't say anything, and all Gina could see was a dark, shadowy figure sitting on the side of the bed.

She said to him, "Steven, why are you being so mysterious?"

His only response was, "Come here, Sweetheart . . . come here."

Gina walked slowly over to him, and he took her by the waist and pulled her to him. She tangled her fingers in his hair, and Steven opened her robe and rubbed his face against her belly. Gina leaned over him, and began to run her fingers down the length of his back. When she did, she realized that he was completely naked. "Why, Steven . . . you don't have anything on!"

Steven pulled her down on the bed, turned her on her back, and mounted her, and then took her, slow and easy. And that was about how it went all that night . . . slow and easy.

That same night, a far different sexual act was taking place. Jeffrey had been having a rough time in prison. At times, he had even seriously contemplated suicide. It all started with a lot of teasing from the other inmates about his homosexuality. This escalated into actual physical abuse, and then it went so far as to the guards letting certain inmates into his cell to rape him late at night.

This particular night, Jeffrey swore he wasn't going to let it happen again. He was sitting in his cell, afraid to go to sleep because he knew they would be back again . . . but, tonight he believed he was ready for them. He had taken a spoon from the dining hall and painstakingly sharpened it into a crude weapon. Soon, just like clockwork, he heard their footsteps approaching. When they got there, he saw one guard and five inmates with their faces partially covered. Jeffrey thought to himself, "They're gonna kill me tonight!" As the guard opened the door, Jeffrey waved the sharpened spoon at them and hollered out, "I'm gonna kill somebody - stay away from me! Leave me alone . . . please . . . go away!"

One guy went for the spoon and grabbed it, yelling, "What the fuck you gon' do wit dat, bitch?"

Another said, "Shit, Man, lem-me go first - this motherfucker look g-o-o-o-d!"

The five men quickly overwhelmed him and had their way. Jeffrey's screams echoed throughout the cellblock, and one of them sneered, "You can scream all you want, Sucker, ain't nobody gon' pay no 'tention to ya."

The morning after, Jeffrey called his father, "Dad, you gotta get me out of here. I can't take it any longer."

"What's the matter, Son? What are they doing to you?"

"You don't understand - I gotta get out of here!"

"Calm down, Son, and tell me what's wrong."

"I don't know how to tell you this . . . I, uh . . . uh . . . I'm being sexually abused - in other words, raped - regularly. I've even thought about killing myself - I wasn't going to tell you, but I can't take this. You've got to call Steven and see if he can get me out of here - or at least get me into isolation."

"Oh, my God, Son. What next? And that notion about suicide - just forget about that! I'll call Steven right away."

"Dad, don't tell Mom."

"Don't worry about that, Son, I won't. I'll be up to see you today. Stay strong."

The same morning about six o'clock, Steven was sound asleep, and Gina was in the living room having a cup of coffee, thinking about the night before. Steven had been different from the men she had been with before him. He had seemed more concerned about her satisfaction than his own . . . and he had really taken his time, paying attention to the little details of lovemaking. The men in the past, for the most part, had been the wham-bam, thank-you-ma'am type. Yes, he certainly was the best she'd ever had, and she couldn't help wondering, "Are all black men like this?"

But more than just thinking about Steven as a sexual partner, Gina now realized that she was very much in love with him. After sitting a while more, she couldn't wait to see him again and went into the bedroom to wake him. "Steven, it's time you got up - it's getting late."

She watched in fascination as he stirred and luxuriously stretched his full length, his naked body dark and sensual against the pale sheets. He got up and went into the bathroom without dressing, stopping first for a minute to hold her close against him.

When he came out, Gina had breakfast just about ready for him, and she asked, "How do you like your eggs?"

"Over light." Then he exclaimed, "Oh, my God, I feel like a king . . . you'd better watch it - you're gonna spoil me if you're not careful." He eased up behind her and kissed her at the base of her neck.

Chapter 13

She turned to him and said in a whisper, "I still love you... do you still love me?"

"Why would you ask a silly question like that? You know very well that I do."

"Oh, no, I don't. You know how men are."

"No, I don't. Tell me."

"Well, you know, they believe we're all different until they get what they want, and all of a sudden we're all the same."

"Well, I'll tell you, Gina, I've never heard it put quite that way before, but I know in my case, that's not true."

After they ate, Steven told her, "I really enjoyed myself with you last night. It wasn't just the sex - I know it wasn't, I could tell."

Gina smiled lovingly at him and said, "Yes, Steven, you're right. It meant more to me than you'll ever know."

After they gazed into each others' eyes for a moment, Steven blurted out, "Why don't you come and stay here with me?"

Gina's response came quickly. "Oh, no! I couldn't do that."

"Why not?"

"I just couldn't."

"It's him, isn't it?"

"C'mon, Steven, please - no pressure, okay? Besides, I'm not with him anymore. In fact, I have my own place now!"

"Oh! I didn't know that. Congratulations! When did this take place?"

"I don't want to talk about this."

Steven was so pleased to hear that Gina had left Bob, he decided not to press her any further and said, "Okay, Gina, we can talk about it some other time. Let's get out of here; it's getting late."

Gina hesitated a moment and said, "You go ahead. I have something to take care of. I'll be along later."

Steven didn't like the way that sounded. He squinted one eye and gave her a troubled look.

She asked, "Why are you looking at me that way?"

There was a moment of silence before he spoke. Then he said, "Gina, I have to say this, even at the risk of sounding paranoid. I think the reason why you don't want to leave this building with me is because you're afraid people will see us together . . . and get the right idea. Isn't that so?"

She just stood there speechless, as if he had read her mind. Steven could see that the question couldn't be answered honestly and eased the tension by saying, "That's okay, Gina - you don't have to answer that." He put on his suit jacket and, as he was walking out the door, said, "I'll see you at the office."

On his way into work, Steven kept thinking of Gina. It was obvious that her attitude toward black men went far deeper than he could ever imagine. What had he gotten himself into?

Chapter 14

As soon as Steven arrived at his office, Arthur Gwaltney gave him several messages. "Mr. Burroughs called and said that it was very urgent that you get back to him as soon as possible, and some lady who said her name was 'Thinker' called and that she would call you back. Talley was in and said he wants to see you sometime today. He too said it was important."

Steven called Burroughs first. "Hello, Ozzie, this is Steven. You called?"

"Oh, yes, Steven - how're things coming along?" Burroughs asked anxiously.

"Well, Ozzie, I tell you, I don't want to build up your hopes, but everything is going quite well. Keep your fingers crossed - I might be able to get Jeffrey out of there pretty soon."

"Oh, Steven, I hope so, because each time I talk to him, he seems more depressed than the last."

"Are they treating him alright?"

Not knowing just how to say what was on his mind, Burroughs hesitated and then reluctantly said, "Well, Steven, he says he's being raped by the other inmates."

"Being raped! Jesus Christ!"

"Yeah - and he asked me to see if you could get him put in isolation - that way they wouldn't be able to get to him. I tell you, Steven, when my boy gets out of there, somebody's really gonna pay for this. I mean it!"

"I understand, Ozzie, and I don't blame you."

"I don't care what it takes, Steven; you've got to do something."

"Okay, Ozzie, I can't promise anything, but let me get to work on it. I'll let you know as soon as I know something." Steven got hold of the judge who was presiding over the case and explained the situation to him. He told him that he knew Burroughs didn't do it, and, at this point, it was just a matter of proving it. It wasn't easy to convince him, but after some smooth talking on Steven's part, the judge gave in and said he would arrange for Jeffrey to be put in isolation, but he couldn't promise for how long. Steven knew that he would have to do something to move the case along much more quickly.

As he was about to call Ozzie to let him know, another call came through to him; it was the Thinker. "Mr. Richards, can we meet again? I have something more to report to you."

"Yes, we may, but if I find that you've been drinking, I'm telling you - I'll turn around and walk away. Do we understand each other?" Steven felt pretty confident and in charge of the situation now and said, "We'll meet tomorrow at our usual time."

The Thinker, subdued and overwhelmed by Steven's air of authority said softly, and with a hint of sarcasm, "Whatever you say, Sir!"

He hung up just as Gina came in the office. "Steven, is there anything you need before I start the work that's on my desk?"

"I want you to edit this deposition."

"How soon do you need it?"

"By noon, if that's possible."

Gina wanted to know if he was upset with her, but didn't know how to bring the subject up. Steven saw that she was bothered and asked, "What's on your mind, Baby . . . this morning - is that what's bothering you?"

Chapter 14

"Yes, as a matter of fact it is, Steven. I didn't mean to hurt your feelings this morning, but what you have to understand is - in all my life, no black man has ever so much as touched me, let alone shared the type of intimacy you and I have. Do you understand? I used to run from my father as a child because I was ashamed of his color. You can't expect me to just change overnight!"

"I don't know, Gina . . . I don't know. It's not anything I can imagine getting used to. But let's put it aside for now. We're going to have to stop bringing our personal problems to the office - okay? Right now, it's urgent that I concentrate on the Burroughs case."

"Sure, Steven, you're right - I was thinking the same thing. After a while, our business will be all over the darn firm."

"Gina, before you go, do you want to come over tonight?"

"Oh, Steven, I was hoping you'd ask me that. Of course I do."

When Gina came back to her desk, she saw Beth talking to Arthur Gwaltney. Marybeth looked up and saw her. "Hey, Girlfriend - whatcha doin'?"

"No, the question should be, what are you doing?"

"Oh, I was just keeping Arthur company until you came out of Steven's office."

"Yeah, I'll bet," Gina responded with a big smile.

"Well, I didn't wanna barge in on you guys like I did before - you know how he is about that. So where you been, Girl? I haven't seen you in a couple of days."

"You must not have been looking very hard 'cause I been right here."

"Have you and Bob broke up again?"

"Yes, but what made you ask?"

"Well, I called his place this morning looking for you, and he told me to tell you he saw who you were with last night and that you'd better watch your back. I'm telling you, Gina - you better be careful of that man - he sounded pretty serious to me."

"To hell with him, Beth. I'm sick of his crap. All I have to do is stay ten minutes longer at the drug store than he thinks I should, and that's enough for him to go through one of his jealous rages and accuse me of the pharmacist, the cashier and any man that came within ten feet of me. I was really tired of that dumb shit - I can do better than that!"

Beth was elated by Gina's passionate desire to rid herself of Bob and said, "Yes-s-s! You go 'head, Girl - I hear ya! It's about time - now maybe you can start enjoying yourself again." Beth paused for a moment and said, "By the way, Gina, just where were you last night?"

"Why do I believe you already know the answer to that question, Beth? If he saw me, I'm sure he told you who I was with . . . I was with Steven. Now . . . you've heard me say it. Are you satisfied?"

"Well, I did kinda want him for myself . . . but . . . it wouldn't have worked anyway. So, come on, Girl, tell me."

"Tell you what?"

"Well, you know . . . after all that playing hard to get, was he worth it?"

"Why are you asking me? You should know . . . you were there before I was."

"Yeah, I sure was, Gina . . . and I can testify, he sure knows how to please . . . but do I sense a little hostility in your voice?"

"Yes, you do."

"Girl, you got it bad! You should see the way you're lookin' at me. If your eyes were daggers, I'd be dead!"

"Oh, Beth, I'm sorry. I guess I just hate thinking of anyone else being with him. I'm crazy about him . . . and nobody ever made me feel the way he did last night."

"Sweetie, if you really feel that way about Steven, you don't have to worry about me. I'll stay clear of him."

"Beth, I appreciate that, but I guess it really doesn't make any difference. You know how I am, and that's not gonna change no time soon. Do you know what I did this morning? I made up an excuse not to come to work with him, and he read right through it. He knew it was because I didn't want to be seen with him. I never felt more ashamed in my life. Beth, it was awful!"

"But, Gina, if you love him the way you say, I don't understand why you would act like that. Steven's a good catch . . . and if I was you, I wouldn't let him get away. Love is hard to find in this world today, Honey, and if it comes your way, you better grab it. Love is everything, Baby. Believe me, it is."

"It may be for you, Beth, but, for me . . . well, I'm afraid it may not be enough."

"So what're you gonna do, Honey? Just see him at night and hope no one sees you? And what about right here on the job? How're you gonna handle that?"

"I don't know, Beth. He'll bring it up tonight . . . I know he will. C'mon, Beth, get out of here. I gotta get to work."

Later in the morning, Steven returned the call from Talley, and they agreed to meet at Gaines Restaurant, a very popular, cafeteria-style place in the center of the city. When they got there, Steven looked at how crowded it was and said, "I don't know, Man, is it worth it? By the time we get anything to eat here, it'll be time to go back to work." But the food was so good, with such generous portions, that it was hard for anyone to walk away. It was one of the last eateries left in the

Philadelphia area that reminded you of the way things used to be. Just looking at the servers alone, in their tall white hats standing over the steam table with spoon in hand, waiting for you to make up your mind, made you hungry and anxious to be served. Everything looked so good - beef stew, chopped sirloin steak, fried and baked chicken, chops smothered in gravy and onions, and every kind of vegetable you could imagine.

When it was their turn to order, Steven asked for the chopped sirloin, and Talley had the smothered chops. After a moment or two of searching for an empty table, they finally settled down to enjoy their lunch. Steven spoke first, "So, Andy, my friend, what is it you wanted to talk about?"

"Steven, right now, I'm pretty hungry . . . so let's eat and talk afterwards," Talley told him bluntly.

"I agree, m' man . . . let's eat." And that they did.

Talley commented after they finished, "Damn, that food was good!"

Steven quickly affirmed, "You got that right, Buddy! Whenever I get to missing my mom's home cookin', I come right here. But, Andy, you sound like somebody that's not used to good home cookin'."

"You're right! All I get from Allison at home is nuked food . . . microwaved - you know what I mean?"

"Well, now that you know about this place, maybe you could bring your wife here. She might get the hint."

"Naw, I doubt it. She spends too much time on the tennis court."

"All right, Andy, so much for that. Let's get down to business - whatcha got for me?"

"Well, you know, Steven, I think you're right about one thing. Martin Pollock must have something on Dan and

Chapter 14

Simon. Or maybe the three of them are in cahoots as far as the missing money is concerned."

"Why do you say that?"

"Do you know what they tried to do? They tried to talk me into making Pollock a senior partner . . . and when I refused, they gave me a pretty hard time. Why, it was only last week that Dan was telling Martin the only way he could be a partner was over his dead body."

"Was Pollock there?"

"No. I did ask them if it was an official meeting of the senior partners, and they said yes, but made me promise not to tell you because of the high sensitivity of the issue."

"Oh, they did, huh?"

"Yeah, but Steven . . . for now, that's okay . . . can't you see that with you there, it would only tend to inhibit them from speaking openly? This way it will appear that I'm in agreement with the idea of keeping you in the dark about things - no pun intended, Buddy. You know what I mean?"

"Yeah, I know, I know. You do have a point there, so let's leave it like that for now."

The two men talked for a few minutes more before Talley looked at his watch and said, "Steven, it's getting late; I have a lot of work today."

"Yeah, me, too . . . lets get out of here."

When Steven got back to the office, he asked Gina, "Could you do me a favor? I have to meet someone at three o'clock. Don't let me be late, okay?"

"Sure thing, Steven."

Later that afternoon, Steven looked at his watch and thought, "Damn, time flies . . . I'd better get ready and go."

Just as he was putting his suit jacket on, Gina came in and said, "Oh, I was just coming in to tell you - it's almost three."

"Yeah, I know. I'm on my way."

As he was about to walk out the door, she stopped him and said, "Steven, just in case you don't get back to the office before I leave today, we're having dinner at my mother's tonight."

"Sure, Gina, but the next time I would appreciate it if you'd first let me know what my plans are gonna be."

"Oh, Steven, don't be so huffy - I didn't mean any harm. I just thought it would be nice if we had a change of venue tonight."

Steven leaned over and kissed her gently on the cheek and said, "That's okay, Baby. We're getting to know each other - that's what's important. And besides, I'd love to meet your mother. What time?"

"Any time after six."

As planned, Steven went to the Rodin Museum, but the Thinker hadn't shown up yet. He sat on a concrete bench, pulled some papers out of his briefcase and started to go over them, but he couldn't concentrate. The sexual assaults on Jeffrey had given Steven a sharp sense of urgency about the case. He felt he just had to make something happen. How long would Jeffrey be able to stay in isolation? And even in isolation, prison was a place where anything might happen. He began to be worried that the Thinker wouldn't show up. Maybe he had been too forceful with her.

After about five minutes had gone by, he checked the time and looked toward the entrance to the courtyard, and there she was, standing there all dressed in black with a black veil draped over her face, looking as if she had just come from her son's gravesite. She was drunk as a fish out of water, looking around without a clue as to where she was. Steven just shook his head and muttered to himself, "If it weren't for Jeffrey, I'd just get up and leave here right now before she noticed me."

Chapter 14 167

But today, he needed results, and he planned to really put the pressure on her. He got her attention by raising his hand in the air, waving it, at the same time, calling, "Over here - I'm over here."

When she saw him, she tried to straighten her composure but found it quite impossible. She stumbled over to him and, with a lethargic slur to her speech, said, "Oh, Mr. Richards, you're so dark, I couldn't see you."

Again, Steven chose to ignore the racial remark and said to her, "So, Mrs. Jody Pollock, what do you have for me today?" By identifying her, Steven was taking the risk that she'd run away, but Jeffrey's situation made him ready to gamble.

Mrs. Pollock stopped dead in her tracks. "What did you call me?" she asked in a stern and angry voice. It seemed as if she had sobered up immediately when he called her by her name.

"That's right, I called you Mrs. Pollock. It's time to stop playing games. Jeffrey Burroughs is an innocent man, and if you know who did it, you have to tell me. You have to free yourself of this terrible burden you're carrying."

She sat down beside him and started to sob. Steven was surprised at how quickly she had folded. He wanted to comfort her, but was very uncomfortable with the notion. She looked up at him and asked him, "How did you know . . . how did you find out?"

"Well, Mrs. Pollock, first of all, I believe your husband is guilty of murdering his own son. And I was talking to someone who knows you and your husband, and they told me that you did a lot of drinking . . . so, I put two and two together and thought, the one who would be able to divulge such esoteric information about the case would have to be someone very close to the murderer . . . as well as to the victim. And I came up with a grieving mother . . . which is what you seem to be."

She had stopped crying by now and told him, "I can help you, Mr. Richards, but I won't testify against him."

"You don't have to, Mrs. Pollock. Maybe we can do this without ever having to see a courtroom. Let me ask you, do you know for sure that he killed your son?"

"Do I? I have what he wore that day - covered with blood, which I'm sure is my son's. He doesn't know I have the clothes - I saw him bury them that same night in our backyard, and I dug them back up."

"Do you know what his motive could have been for killing him?"

"Well . . . they argued all the time . . . but, about a week before my son . . . uh . . . died . . . he and my husband had a terrible quarrel. My husband was saying some really nasty things about Jeffrey - that black friend of his - well, not that nasty - just calling him a nigger and stuff like that - and my son got real mad and said he knew about some money missing from the firm and that he was going to turn them in - I don't know who he meant by them, but my husband just went crazy - said he would kill him if he did that." She then lowered her voice to a whisper and said, "I don't know whether you know it or not, but . . . my son was a homosexual."

Steven found himself whispering back at her, "Yes, I know, Ma'am. "

"Well, that made my husband real crazy, too."

They talked for a few minutes more, and then Steven said, "Tell me, is it possible I can get hold of those clothes?"

"Sure, they're in my trunk so he won't find them. If you walk me to my car, you can have them."

Once they got to her car, she opened the trunk and pulled out a stuffed brown paper bag. She handed it over to him and said, "Mr. Richards, try not to be judgmental of him. I'm sure it was an accident. Maybe my husband panicked and tried to cover it up. I don't think he would ever have purposely killed our son."

Steven felt pretty sure that she knew that her husband was capable of having deliberately murdered his son, but that she didn't want him to think of her as someone who would stay married to such an awful person.

"Well, Mrs. Pollock, if that makes you feel better and eases the pain, then I can understand why you choose to take that position . . . but I think your husband's a cold-blooded killer. Does he have any idea that you know what he did?"

"Well, I called him one day at work, and I did imply it, but he denied it, and I didn't say anything more." Steven remembered that Marybeth had told him about overhearing a conversation like that.

Steven warned her, "If I were you, I would cut down on the drinking - you might just say something to him that would put yourself in danger. You've been a great help to me - and more especially to an innocent man." He handed her his card and said, "If you want to tell me anything else or if you need me, just give me a call."

As he drove away from the Rodin Museum, Steven checked the time. It was after five, and he thought that if he went to the office first and then home to freshen up, he would be late getting to Gina's mother's house for dinner so he drove straight to the Four Seasons. When he walked into the lobby and headed for the elevator, he heard someone calling him. "Steven!" He turned around and saw that it was Andrea.

"Oh, Andrea, what are you doing here?"

"I was just driving by coming from work and thought I would stop in to see how you were doing - I enjoy our phone conversations, but there's nothing like seeing you in person!"

"I know, Andrea - it's just that I've been so busy lately."

"Are you busy now?"

Steven didn't know how to answer her and said, "Uh . . . well . . . I . . ."

She cut in on him. "Oh, that's okay, Steven. You don't have to explain. That's what I get for coming unannounced. I'll catch you another time - if that's alright with you?"

"That's fine with me, Andrea - you know that. As a matter of fact, I'm going up to change. Why don't you come on up and keep me company? I'm only gonna be a couple of minutes, and then we can leave together."

"No, Steven, I couldn't. Now I feel like an intruder."

"Oh, Andrea, that's crazy - come on up."

"Are you sure you don't mind?"

"Of course not. Come on."

"Okay, okay, you've convinced me."

On the elevator, Andrea said to him, "Steven, I've really missed you!"

"I've missed you, too, Andrea. Right now, I've got a whole lot of things coming at me at once, and I have to prioritize them. Do you understand?"

"Aren't I one of those things to be put in its proper perspective?"

Steven laughed and said fondly. "Oh, Andrea, I know you won't believe me, but yes, you are."

On impulse, she reached up and pulled Steven close to her, inviting him to kiss her. Steven wasted no time accommodating her. Their embrace became so intense that when the elevator stopped, someone got on and back off without them even noticing. When it stopped on Steven's floor, they were still locked in a kiss of oblivion. Andrea broke the tie and, giggling, said, "We have to get off now, or we'll be right back down in the lobby!" and then said, "I do hope that kiss moves me higher on your scale of priorities!"

Steven hugged her and said, "I told you once before you have a real good sense of humor." They went down the hall laughing together.

In the suite, Steven was in the bedroom changing clothes when the phone rang. Andrea called to him. "Do you want me to get that?"

He quickly thought, "That might be Gina," and hollered out to Andrea, "That's okay - I'll get it."

Just as he thought, it was Gina who said, "Steven, are you coming over here or what? It's after six, and we're waiting on you."

"I'm on my way out the door. I'm coming."

When Steven came into the living room, the look on his face was one of discomfort, and it was apparent to Andrea, who of course noticed everything about him. She assumed the call had been from Gina, but didn't say anything to him. They left the suite and went down in the elevator; because of the phone call, there was a tension between them now which made the ride down seem very long. When they finally arrived at the lobby and went out the front door, Steven turned to her and said, "Good night, Andrea. I'll be seein' you."

Andrea said, "That was Gina, wasn't it?"

"Yes," Steven replied.

Andrea solemnly said, "Goodnight, Steven," and they parted.

On his way to the car, Steven thought, "Damn, that woman has bad timing."

Chapter 15

At Gina's mother's house, Gina was upstairs in her old room. Her mother, Florence, called, "Gina, what are you doing up there - that young man is gonna be here soon, and I want you to be down here to let him in."

"Mom! Why can't you let him in? This is your house, isn't it?"

"No, Gina! I would prefer it if you were down here to receive him - please."

In the past, when Gina had been living at home with her parents, whenever she had male company over, they were always white boys. Although her parents had treated them civilly, they had not approved. But now, Mrs. Epps was even more disapproving of her daughter's rejection of her own kind, after the way she had treated her father on his deathbed. She simply did not want to answer the door to another one of Gina's white boyfriends. On the other hand, Gina was looking forward to her mother's meeting Steven. She hadn't told her that he was black and knew it would be a big surprise.

Knowing what her mother was probably thinking, she yelled out, "Okay, Mother, I'll be down."

After a few minutes, the doorbell rang. As soon as Florence heard it, she headed toward the kitchen. As Gina came running down the steps, she saw the kitchen door swinging. She paused a moment on the bottom step; smiling, she shook her head and continued to the door and opened it. With a big grin, she called out, "Steven!" Right away, she realized she was losing her cool. After all, she was supposed to be angry with him for being late. She changed her tone and said, "So, you finally got here, huh?"

Chapter 15

"I'm sorry, Gina. It was unavoidable. The meeting I had took longer than I thought it would. I hope you're not going to stay angry with me. This is the night I'm supposed to meet your mother, and we have to show her what a loving couple we are."

With that, he drew a smile from her, and she put her arms around him, and they kissed.

Mrs. Epps was curious about the silence from the living room and peeped out. She did a doubletake when she saw that Steven was a black man - not only was he a black man, he was a very dark one. She let the door go and went back into the kitchen, saying to herself, "Well, Suh . . . I never thought I'd see the day!"

At that point, Gina called, "Mom, would you come in here a minute - I want you to meet somebody!"

When Mrs. Epps came in, she stood there spellbound, staring at Steven. She looked so long and hard at him, Steven had to ask, "What's the matter? Is something wrong?"

"No, Son . . . at last, something is right." She turned to Gina and said, "Gina, your father would be very proud of you, Honey; I only wish he was here to see this."

"Mother, this is Steven Richards, my boss. Steven, this is my mom."

Mrs. Epps said, "You children sit down. Dinner will be ready in about ten minutes." As she returned to the kitchen, she said under her breath, "Praise the Lord! God has been good to my child!"

Steven hadn't noticed it when he first came in, but Gina was not dressed in her usual sexy fashion. She was dressed the way she was on the day that she and Andrea played their trick on Steven - very conservatively. Now he looked her up and down and asked, "Why are you dressed that way?"

Gina could not tell from the tone in his voice whether he approved or disapproved of the way she looked. "What's the matter - you don't like it?" she asked.

"Oh, yeah . . . you look great, Baby. I was just asking. Tell me, did you dress like this for me?"

"What do you think?"

Steven hesitated and then teasingly said, "Well. . . let me see . . ."

Gina interrupted, saying, "Of course I did, Silly!"

"What's next? Andrea isn't gonna show up looking like you, is she?"

They both laughed and were about to sit down when her mother called, "Gina, come in here and help me put the food on the table." Gina excused herself and went in the kitchen just as her mother was coming out with a bowl of steaming, hot broccoli, saying, "Honey, bring that macaroni and pot roast in for me, will ya?"

Florence used the opportunity of being alone with Steven to say, "Son, I don't know what you did to her, but she's changed. I've never seen her like this before . . . and the way she's dressed . . . well, whatever you're doing, keep on doing it."

"Well, Mrs. Epps, it's a start."

Just then Gina came in and said, "Are you guys talking about me?"

"Yes, I was just telling Steven how nice and radiant you look tonight."

"Well, Mom, it's not how I look, it's how I feel . . . and it's Steven who makes me feel that way. What do you think of him, Mom? Isn't he a real hunk?"

"Oh, Gina, I wouldn't put it quite that way. But, I think Steven is very nice, along with being a handsome young man."

"I knew you would, Mom . . . I knew you would like him!"

"More than you'll ever know, Sweetheart."

Steven was starting to feel a little uncomfortable with all the compliments he was getting from Gina and her mother. He decided to cut them short and said, "It's the food that looks pretty good around here, and I'm getting hungry - may we eat now?"

After they ate, Steven and Gina went to the living room. Mrs. Epps came in and said, "Children, I'm tired now, so I think I'll call it a night. Steven, it was very nice meeting you."

"Mrs. Epps, I've been looking forward to this day . . . believe me, the pleasure is all mine."

"It's so nice of you to say so, Son . . . oh, and, Gina, don't forget to put out the lights. Goodnight, now!"

"Sure, Mom, and thanks for dinner . . . and for treating Steven so nice." She turned to him and said, "My mother said that because she still thinks I'm irresponsible. When I was younger, she and dad were always hollering at me for not turning the lights out whenever I left a room."

Steven smiled but almost immediately afterwards became solemn.

Gina noticed and asked, "What's wrong, Honey?"

"Oh, I was just thinking - I'm gonna have a big day tomorrow."

"Why do you say that?"

"Well, Gina, you have to promise me that you won't open up your mouth to anyone about this."

"I promise - and I'll seal it like this," she said, leaning over and giving him a kiss.

"Wow . . . for some more of that, I'll tell you anything you want to know."

"Oh, come on, Steven, stop jiving around and tell me."
"Okay, Baby. You see, I know now for sure that Martin Pollock killed his son, and I have to make sure the next move I make is the right one."
"If I were you I wouldn't worry about it. You're a clever and intelligent man, and I know you'll do the right thing."
They talked for a little while longer about the case, and then Steven asked, "Are you ready to go home, Gina?"
"Where's home?"
"Well . . . back to your apartment?"
"No, I want to stay with you tonight."
"I'd be delighted."

The first thing next morning, Steven went to see Talley and told him about the meeting with Martin's wife and the evidence she had given him.
"What's your next move?" Andrew asked.
"I think the first thing I should do is call Lieutenant Dickens. I want my client out of jail as soon as possible. I hope Pollock owns up to this crime 'cause that'll certainly make things easier for everyone involved."
"Yes, it sure would."
"Andy, let me ask you this: do you think Dillenbeck and Grundage are in on this - or know anything about it?"
"Well, Steven, there's one way to find out - just come right out and ask them."
"Yeah, like they're gonna admit it, huh? Come on, give me a break."
"But, I think it's time that you at least tell them what you know about Pollock and talk to them about the embezzlement.
"That's a good idea, except for one thing. If I go to them alone, they may react a little differently than if both of us

were to confront them - it would show sort of a united front. Y'understand what I'm saying?"

"Oh, I don't know, Steven."

"What's wrong?"

"I don't know - I just don't like it."

"Wait a minute, here, Andy - what am I hearing? I thought we were working together on this thing . . . well, are we?"

"Yeah, Steven, but ever since I left law school, my one dream was to be a full partner in a prestigious firm such as this one. And just when I think I'm well on my way, something like this happens. Everything I've ever worked for seems to be falling apart right before my eyes."

"Well, I'll tell you, Andy, I understand how you feel, but this firm is going to hell in a handbasket, and it's up to you and me to save it. And if we don't, it certainly won't be considered prestigious any more. I don't think you want to sit by and let that happen - do ya?"

"No, definitely not."

"Well, then, I think we should call a meeting of the four of us and thrash it out . . . really, that just makes good sense to me."

After some thought, Andrew agreed with Steven and said, "Go ahead, call Dillenbeck - I'm with you."

Steven didn't waste any time; he went right to the phone and called. "Dan, an urgent matter has just come up so if you don't mind, I would like for the four of us to get together and talk."

"What's it in reference to?"

"Dan, at this point, I'd rather not say."

"Are you talking about getting together today?"

"Well, Andrew and I think this is a matter of urgency, so the sooner the better."

There was a moment of silence. Then Dan spoke, "How's four this afternoon?"

"Sounds great - we'll see you then."

As soon as Steven hung up, he dialed Lieutenant Dickens.

"Lieutenant Sean Dickens here, how can I help you?"

"Oh, Lieutenant, this is Steven Richards."

"Oh, yeah . . . howya' doin' there, Richards? What can I do for you?"

"I have something for you that'll break the Burroughs case wide open."

"Yeah . . . whatcha got?"

"I don't have much time. I have to be somewhere at four. If possible, I'd like to shoot over there right now and turn it over to you."

"Well, I don't have much time either. I hope this isn't something like that phone call someone made to your parents; that one took us nowhere. Come on over, and don't break any traffic laws on the way."

"Thanks. I'll be there shortly."

After Talley left Steven, Dillenbeck saw him walking back to his office and asked, "Could I see you a minute, Andy?"

Talley went to Dan's office with him. Dan said, "Andy, I'll cut to the chase. What is this that you and Steven want to meet about?"

"Come on, Dan. I was there when Steven told you on the phone he would rather wait to tell you the details. It wouldn't be right for me to discuss it now. I want to wait for the meeting."

Dillenbeck was irate. "Andy, this is bullshit! We've been partners for more than eight years, and you mean to tell me you're gonna consider that man before me? What I'd like to

Chapter 15

know is where in the hell does your allegiance lie? That's why Simon and I brought you on board in the first place, because what we thought we had in you was a man of unquestionable loyalty. And now this!"

"I'm not considering him more than you, Dan; it's just a matter of respect. I respect the man."

Dan was not satisfied. "Well, I don't know what you guys have up your sleeve, but I don't like conspiracies, and that's what this sounds like to me."

"Come on, Dan, please. Nobody's conspiring against anyone. If anything, we might have some answers to what's been going on around here lately."

Dan shouted, "What's been going on! What do you mean what's been going on?"

"Dan, I've gotta go . . . you're not in the mood for talking now - all you wanna do is holler. I'll see you later."

Talley's walking out on him made Dan even more furious. He yelled at the top of his voice, "Andy, come back here . . . don't you dare walk out on me like that. Did you forget who I am? I built this firm - and it's about time people around here start recognizing that!"

Talley continued walking away as Dillenbeck stood there screaming at him.

By now, Steven had gotten to the police station and was in Dickens' office. He put the brown bag on Dickens' desk. "It's all in here."

Dickens stood up, started to open the bag, at the same time saying, "What's all in here?" By the time he unrolled the top of the bag, he could smell the blood. He held his nose, looked in and said, "What the hell is this, Steven? What are you trying to do? Kill me?"

"It's the clothes Martin Pollock wore when he murdered his son."

"How do you know this?"

"I got it straight from an excellent source - his wife."

Steven then told Lieutenant Dickens about the meetings between Mrs. Pollock and him and about Pollock's relationship with his son.

Dickens laughed. "Well, glory be! You've been a pretty busy little elf, haven't you? What are you trying to do, knock me out of a job?"

"Naw, you can have your job. I don't like police work. I wouldn't ever want to be in a position of having to kill someone . . . although you guys seem to thrive off it."

Dickens frowned and said, "I don't know what you mean by that. We're not always right, but we do the best we can."

"Yeah, I know, I know. I don't want to talk about that. I should tell you - there's a problem with this evidence."

"Oh, yeah, what's that?" Dickens asked.

"She said she wouldn't testify against him."

"We'll worry about that when the time comes. Right now what I want to do is get some DNA testing on the clothing. Depending on the results, I'll haul Pollock in here to see what he has to say."

"Couldn't you bring him in now before you get the results?"

"You wouldn't make a very good cop after all. Right now, it wouldn't be smart to let him know he's a possible suspect."

"Well, is there any way this evidence might convince you to let Jeffrey out?"

"No, Jeffrey stays in custody until we've made the case against someone else."

"One more thing, Lieutenant. I don't think she realizes it, but I think Mrs. Pollock's life may be in danger. If he finds out that she's the one who led us to him, he might try to kill

Chapter 15

her as well. If this guy has the chutzpah to kill his own son, he wouldn't have any problem knocking off his wife."

"There you go again, Richards . . . trying to do my job for me."

"Well, think about what I said - and will you promise to call me as soon as you get the results from the DNA test?"

"The sooner you get out of here, the faster I can get started on this. I'll let you know as soon as I know."

Chapter 16

Steven left the station feeling good about how things were going. On the way back, he called Ozzie Burroughs on the car phone and shared the news with him. Then he looked at his watch and saw that he only had twenty minutes to get back to the firm for the meeting, and he sped up a bit.

When he got there and was in the outer offices of Dillenbeck's suite, he heard an angry Dan speaking very loudly to Simon. Steven couldn't quite make out what he was saying, but as soon as he entered the room, it fell silent.

It was not exactly four, and Talley had not yet gotten there. Dan said, "Steven, we've been waiting on you. Now, what is it that's so important that you would call us together like this?"

"Where's Andy?" Steven asked.

"Oh, he'll be along in a few minutes. If you don't mind, I'd like to start without him . . . I'm in pretty much of a rush."

"I'd just as soon wait on Andy, Dan. For what has to be said here, I think all of us should be present."

Dan tried his best to hide the anger he felt for the mutual respect Steven and Talley had been exhibiting. His jaws tightened, he gritted his teeth and, in a rigid voice, said, "Boy, you two are really something, aren't you?"

Steven asked innocently, "What do you mean by that, Dan?"

"You know just . . . "

Before Dan could finish his response, Talley walked in. "Gentlemen, I hope I haven't held things up."

Simon chimed in at this point. "No, not really, Andy. Dan and Steven are just venting their spleens a little. There's been a lot of tension building around here lately."

Chapter 16

"Okay, let's cut the bull crap," Dan said. "What is this meeting all about?"

Steven and Talley took a quick glance at each other before Steven said, "Alright, Dan, I'm gonna try and lay this right on the line. In the interest of all of us, I think we should try and be as civil as we can. We have a serious problem and going at each others' throats is not going to help."

Dan cut him off. "Get to the point, Steven . . . we didn't come here to hear you preach a Sunday morning sermon . . . get on with it."

Steven gave Dan a hard look and then said, "I've found out that Martin Pollock murdered his son."

Dan jumped up from his seat. "Goddamn it, Steven, I've had just about enough of your arrogant behavior. You may be a partner on paper, but you're no longer a partner at heart in this firm."

Simon said, "Calm down, Dan - what are you getting so upset about?

"Calm down, my ass . . . I'm gettin' sick and tired of his shit."

Talley joined in. "Dan, I don't understand. What are you afraid of?"

"I'm not afraid of a goddamn thing."

Talley pushed on. "Then why are you acting this way?"

"Who is he to come in here and accuse one of our own of murder? Questioning Pollock is one thing - this is something else!"

Talley replied, "Now, wait just a minute, Dan - I happen to know it's true so I think you should hear him out."

Simon agreed. "Yeah, Dan, Andy's right. What's wrong with hearing him out?"

Dan stood looking out the window with his back to them. After several minutes of thought, he turned back to Steven and reluctantly said, "Steven, you'll have to understand that

I'm a very highstrung person, and I go off at the least little thing. So, if you'll allow me?" Dan held out his hand. "Let's put this behind us and get down to business."

Steven shook his hand and said, "That's okay. I understand."

Dan went on, "Now, if I'm not mistaken, I think we left off where you were accusing Martin Pollock of murder. So go on . . . please."

"That's right, Dan, and as we speak, the police are actively investigating the evidence against him."

"How did you find this out?" Simon asked.

Talley answered before Steven could. "His wife told Steven, and she also led us to believe the murder was related in some way to the embezzlement."

Immediately after Talley mentioned embezzling, Steven couldn't help noticing the way Dan's and Simon's eyes met ever so briefly.

The meeting was not really productive. Dan and Simon characterized Martin's wife as a liar and a sick woman and were not convinced of Pollock's guilt. When asked about the embezzlement, they again denied any involvement.

When Talley and Steven left, Steven said, "I wish you hadn't told them the role that Martin's wife is playing in this."

"Why not?"

"Well, I didn't want them to know that. It might really jeopardize her."

In the meanwhile, in Steven's office, Marybeth had stopped in to see Gina. While they were talking, the phone rang. When Gina picked it up, a voice on the other end said, "Remember what I told you - your love belongs to me . . . and only me . . . and before I'll let you live in peace with someone

Chapter 16

else, I'll kill you first. Remember . . . you're dead, Gina! It's just a matter of time. You're fuckin' dead!"

When Gina hung up, Marybeth knew something was wrong and asked, "What's the matter, Sweetie?"

"Oh, just another crank call. Sometimes I get them all day long here. You'd think people had something better to do with their lives, I swear!"

"Come on, Gina, this is Beth you're talkin' to - that was more than just a crank call. I saw that look on your face - who was that?"

I told you nobody, Beth . . . now, drop it, will ya?"

"I'm not gonna drop it. You either tell me, or I'll tell Steven about it."

"Come on, Beth, I can handle this by myself. Stay out of it - please."

Beth knew who made the call but wanted to hear Gina admit it and pressed on. "If something should happen to you, God forbid, I want to at least have some idea as to what direction to send the police. Y'know what I'm sayin', Honey?"

"Okay, okay, Beth - for God's sake - please - you know who it is - it's Bob. Now will ya cut it short?"

"Goddamn it, I knew it, Gina. That bastard's gonna hurt you one of these days - I'm telling you."

At Beth's words, Gina broke down and started to cry. "Beth, I don't what to do! He won't leave me alone . . . this is the fifth time he's called, threatening to kill me, and it's starting to get to me now."

"Well, why don't you go to the police? Or tell Steven?"

"Telling the police won't do any good; you know how they are. They'll just tell me there's nothing they can do until he actually does it. And I'm afraid to go to Steven. He'd go off on that man, and I wouldn't want to be responsible for that. Anyway, I think Bob will eventually get over me - at least, I hope he will."

"Take it from me, Sweetie - his kind never do."

As Steven was returning to his office suite, he met up with Arthur Gwaltney in the hall and inquired about a case Arthur was handling. "How'd it go in court today, Art?"

"Oh, not so good. A major witness for the prosecution didn't show up, so they called for a postponement. Y'know, that really pissed me off 'cause I think we could've won that case today."

"Well, Art, look on the bright side of it. All a postponement means is that you haven't lost your case yet. And remember this - any time a hostile witness doesn't show up in court, it strengthens the defense's case. Plus, it gives you more time to interact with your client, which enables you to better defend him. Besides, if you could've won today, you can win anytime!"

Arthur gave Steven a big grin and said in jest, "I don't know whether to call that kind of talk wisdom or just optimism, but from now on, I think I'll try and incorporate it into my way of thinking . . . I love it!"

Steven patted Arthur on the back and said cheerfully, "That's the spirit, m'man . . . that's the spirit!" He knew he had just made Arthur feel much better about himself - and made a day that he might have considered to be just a waste of time, a day of triumph. They walked back to the office together.

As soon as Gina saw Steven come in with Arthur, she whispered to Beth, "Please don't say anything to him about Bob!"

Beth responded, "Not unless you want me to, Honey."

Gina tried to look as unconcerned as possible as Steven approached them, but he was a little suspicious - not so much as to what they had been talking about, but as to why they started speaking in a whisper as soon as they saw him. He asked her if there was anything wrong.

"Oh, nothing," she answered.

"Are you sure?"

"Quite sure."

Now that Gina had claimed Steven, Marybeth had started looking around for a likely candidate for a serious relationship - a new concept for her and one that had come in part from Steven's criticism of her promiscuity. So while Gina and Steven were talking, Marybeth was doing her best to charm Arthur Gwaltney. It wasn't difficult. Arthur was not very worldly. Having spent the last few years hitting the books and working to get through law school and prepare for the bar exam, there had been little time for the opposite sex. Now he stood blushing and shifting from one foot to the other, while Marybeth smiled up at him provocatively, touched his arm as she spoke, reached up to straighten his tie - all the little flirtacious gestures that she knew how to do so well. Arthur was no match for her, and it was obvious that he was rapidly succumbing to her charms.

Suddenly, there was a disturbance in the hall. Everyone stopped what they were doing and rushed to the door to see what was wrong. It soon became clear. Four police officers appeared, escorting Martin Pollock in handcuffs to the elevator - one on each arm, one behind him and one in front. As Pollock passed by Steven's office, he gave Steven a sneering look and mumbled under his breath, "You black ass motherfucker!"

Gina asked, "What did he say?"

"You don't want to know," Steven answered.

At the opposite end of the hall, Steven saw Dillenbeck, Grundage and Lieutenant Dickens talking. Just as he was about to go back into his office, Dickens called, "Richards, can I talk to you for a moment?"

Steven summoned him with his hand to come to his office.

When Dickens got there, Steven asked him, "I take it you got the test results back?"

"Oh, no, not yet."

Steven was surprised. "Then what reason did you have to pick up Pollock?"

"We really just came to ask him some questions, but he gave us such a hard time we decided to take him in. He actually did us a favor. Now I can get him away from his wife for a little while at least, and maybe I can get a voice print to match against that tape you gave me - you know - when your parents were threatened."

Later, at the police station, during interrogation, Dickens asked Pollock, "Why did you give us such a hard time? Your lack of cooperation makes us very suspicious."

Pollock answered belligerently, "Why would you want to question me about anything?"

Dickens said, "Well, it's about your son who was murdered."

"My son's murderer is locked up. What would you need to know from me? Why don't you ask that fuckin' faggot?"

"Oh, is that the way you choose to address him - that fuckin' faggot? Is that also how you characterized your son?"

"What's this all about anyway? I wish you would tell me what you're driving at."

"Well, for one, we'd like to know where you were at the time of the murder."

"Am I being accused of something here?"

"You're making it hard on yourself, Mr. Pollock. Just answer the question - please?"

"I was at work, of course."

"Can anybody corroborate that? Did you have any meetings with anyone there that day?"

"Sure, if I'm not mistaken, I was in Dan Dillenbeck's office right about the time my son was murdered."

"And I'm sure Mr. Dillenbeck will verify that, right?"

"Well, why wouldn't he? . . . Wait a minute. I don't like the way this is going. You either charge me with something, or I'm walking out of here."

"Well, I'm afraid it's not as simple as that, Mr. Pollock. You see, we have reason to believe that you had something to do with your son's murder."

Pollock said, "I want my phone call."

Dickens went to the door and hollered, "Somebody get me a phone in here!"

A sergeant brought a phone and handed it to Pollock who started to dial but when he saw that Dickens was not leaving the room, said, "If you don't mind, Lieutenant, this is personal."

"By all means," Dickens said and left.

As soon as he was sure that Dickens was out of earshot, Pollock dialed Dan Dillenbeck's office. "Dan! This is Pollock. You know where I'm at. You've got to get me the hell out of here. These bastards are trying to accuse me of murdering my own son."

"Don't worry about it, Martin. You won't spend another hour there. Our man is already on his way down there."

By four o'clock that afternoon, Martin Pollock was walking out of the precinct doors. Dickens was not able to hold him because he couldn't obtain the lab report on the bloody clothes for at least another forty-eight hours, and that was too long to hold Pollock without charging him. He did, however, get the voice print he wanted.

When Pollock got back to his office, he was almost immediately joined there by Dillenbeck and Grundage. Pollock called Marybeth on the intercom and told her he didn't want to be disturbed.

"Yes, Sir," she responded.

Pollock was agitated and carelessly left the intercom open. Marybeth had been about to hang up when she realized that she could hear what was being said in Pollock's office, starting with Dan asking, "What the hell was that all about, Martin? Why do they believe you killed your son - do they have any proof?"

"What proof? I didn't do it. I didn't have anything to do with the death of my son."

"Well, Steven and Andy said your wife supplied them with information that would lead the police to you as a prime suspect."

When Martin heard this, his face turned beet red, and he began to shake with rage.

Grundage pressed him, asking, "Is there any truth to this at all?"

Martin hesitated in answering him, and Dan said, "Martin, I want you to be perfectly honest with us, and I promise you - nothing you say to us will leave this room. I'm asking you again . . . did you have anything to do with your son's murder?"

In Pollock's outer office, Marybeth had continued to listen in, quiet as a mouse and curious as a cat, and now eagerly awaited Pollock's answer. She was not disappointed.

Pollock replied to Dan, "Well . . . you knew he was threatening to expose us. It was you guys who said I had to find a way to keep him quiet."

"So you killed him?" Grundage said in a shocked voice.

"I had to - don't you understand? He would've blown the whole thing."

Grundage said, "Jesus Christ, Martin, we didn't mean for you to kill him . . . your own son!"

"That nigger-lovin' queer wasn't my son. He lost that right a long time ago."

Dan exploded. "Pollock, you murdering little shit! You're in a real mess now. What do you expect us to do?"

"I expect you guys to get me out of this. We're all in this together. I told that detective I was in your office at the time of the murder."

Grundage jumped to his feet. "Listen, Martin, we didn't murder your son. You did. That's something you'll have to answer to all alone. Dan, I want no part of this bullshit . . . just count me out." He headed for the door.

Martin called out, "Wait a minute, Simon, don't be so hasty. If you guys think I'm going down the drain by myself, you'd better think twice. Remember, embezzling that money for Brolin was your idea!"

Dillenbeck shouted, "We'll put on a defense for you, but you can forget about using me as an alibi." He motioned to Grundage to follow him, and they hurriedly left Pollock's office.

Senator Thaddeus Brolin was a conservative politician with ties to such groups as the Aryan nation and the Ku Klux Klan. Grundage and Dillenbeck had wanted to make a large, and illegal, contribution to his campaign, partly because they supported his conservative philosophy, but primarily because they wanted the legal business he would send their way. Talley had objected vehemently to the idea of contributing to someone like Brolin, so the other partners had resorted to embezzling the funds needed for the contribution; they had involved Martin Pollock, because they knew he was an avid supporter of Brolin's racist views, and he was better situated to carry out the various transactions needed for the embezzlement. As a result of the contribution, the firm had received a significant amount of business from the Senator.

When they were back in Dillenbeck's office, Grundage said, "Damn it, Dan, I should have went along with Andy. We should never have backed Brolin's campaign with the firm's money."

Dillenbeck responded, "No, what we shouldn't have done is involve a crazy, murdering bastard like Pollock - first he put the Brolin scheme in writing - a damn memo, for Christ's sake - then he leaves it around where his son gets hold of it - and he handles that little problem by going completely nuts and killing him!"

Grundage added, "Not to mention trying to extort a partnership out of us to keep quiet about something he was involved in, too! The guy's a real lunatic!"

In the meanwhile, Steven was waiting for Lieutenant Dickens to return a call he had put in to him. When he called back, Steven said, "Oh, Dickens, I'm glad you got back to me. I noticed that Pollock is in his office. How did he get back here so fast? What happened? . . . You didn't have enough to hold him?"

Chapter 16

"I'm afraid not, Steven. We had to let him go. We're still waiting on the test results from the clothing and the voice match."

"Well, I think you should stake out his house. That man is gonna go after his wife as sure as my name is what it is."

"I'm ahead of you this time, Steven. As soon as he left headquarters here, I sent a unit over there."

"Does she know they're there?"

"No, but if he makes any attempt to harm her, my men will be right on him."

"Oh, in other words, you're using her as bait?"

"Well, I guess you can say that."

"Lieutenant, I feel responsible for that lady. I could never forgive myself if something were to happen to her. I have to go now. I'll see ya'."

Dickens felt that Steven might be thinking about interfering with police work and told him sternly, "Steven, stay out of this . . . stay away from that house, I'm warning you."

Steven said, "Yeah, okay, I hear you," and hung up.

Steven immediately called Marybeth and asked her, "Do you have Martin's home number?"

"Oh, Steven, I was just coming over there. Do I have something to tell you!"

"Beth, I don't have time for gossip now. I need his number."

"I'll bring it over to you."

In a matter of seconds, Marybeth rushed in to Steven's suite. She called to Gina, "C'mon, Girl, follow me!" and continued into Steven's office.

"Beth, do you have the number?" Steven asked anxiously.

"Yes, but first I gotta tell you - this is really important." Marybeth then proceeded to tell Steven everything she had heard Pollock and the others talking about.

Steven listened intently to her story and then asked, "Is Pollock still there?"

"No, he left in a hurry."

"My God, now that he knows his wife is involved, it's even more urgent that I get hold of her!"

Marybeth handed the number to Steven and he dialed it. "Mrs. Pollock, this is Steven Richards. I think you should get out of there. Your husband knows that you supplied me with evidence. He's probably on his way home."

It was immediately obvious that Mrs. Pollock was very drunk. In a slurred voice, she whined, "Wh-a-a-t? You promised me, Mistuh Richards. You promised me he would never find out. Now what the hell am I gonna do? He'll kill me!"

"It's important that you leave the house now, Mrs. Pollock. I'll tell you what - I'll meet you at the museum, and we'll get you to a safe place. Leave now!"

Chapter 17

Pollock headed straight home from the office. As he was coming down his street, he saw his wife backing out of their driveway, and he quickly pulled over and parked, ducking down in the front seat so as not to be seen. The two officers who were supposed to be watching Mrs. Pollock were busy talking and weren't looking in the direction of the driveway, which enabled her to slip by them. Unaware of her husband's presence, she went swerving down the street drunkenly, almost hitting every parked car she passed, including Pollock's. He made a quick u-turn and began to follow her. As drunk as she was, one would find it hard to believe that she could even drive, but she made it to the museum. When she pulled up in front of it and stopped, she didn't realize she couldn't park because it was rush hour. All she could hear was the honking of horns. She pulled off again and went around the corner and parked on a side street. She got out and headed straight for the courtyard where she and Steven always met.

Pollock pulled up shortly afterwards. When he came into the courtyard, he saw her sitting there with her head down, staring at the ground. He looked around to see if anyone else was there, and when he saw that the area was empty, he walked slowly over to her. She didn't hear or notice him until he was standing right in front of her. When she saw his feet, she was filled with dread, fearing that it was her husband, not Steven. She brought her head up slowly until she was looking him right in the eyes. "Martin . . . what . . . what are you doing here? How did . . . ?"

He didn't let her finish. "Shut up, Bitch . . . never mind that! What did you tell the fuckin' police about me? . . . huh? . . . what did you tell 'em? Goddamn it - I wanna know!"

Ms. Pollock was really afraid, but the alcohol she had consumed earlier that day helped build her nerve. Since he now knew that she knew what he had done, she felt compelled to let him know how she felt about it and said, "Martin, you bastard, you . . . you killed our son! I've known it from the beginning. I saw you bury those clothes in the yard. And do you know what I did, you son of a bitch? Huh? Do ya? I went right out there the next morning, dug 'em up and hid 'em, and now the police have 'em. I was afraid to say anything to you 'cause I thought you'd kill me too. Now, I don't give a damn! And ya know what else, Martin? . . . I hope they lock you up, and you never see the light of day again as long as you live!"

Pollock stood there staring at her with squinted eyes, his temple and jaws throbbing, his face a livid red. The look in his eyes told her that he did not intend to let her live another minute.

At the same time Pollock was following his wife to the museum, Steven was hastily preparing to leave the office. Gina was very concerned. "Steven, I'm comin' with you!"

"Gina, I would prefer you didn't come . . . please - stay here! Mrs. Pollock doesn't want to be seen by anyone."

Gina instinctively felt there was going to be trouble and insisted, saying, "I don't care about that. I'm going with you."

"Okay, Gina, I don't have time to argue with you. If you're coming, close up the office right now. I've gotta get the hell out of here."

Marybeth tried to tag along, but Steven was firm. "Beth, you cannot go, and that's final."

Chapter 17

Back at the museum, Mrs. Pollock rose unsteadily to her feet and made an attempt to get away from Pollock. As she did, he grabbed her by the arm and snatched her back to him so that he was behind her with his arm around her throat. That's when she screamed. He then put his other hand at her mouth to quiet her and began choking her. Mrs. Pollock squirmed, wiggled and kicked, fighting for her life until she miraculously got away from him. She ran, screaming, "Help . . . help! Somebody help me - he's trying to kill me!"

Steven and Gina had just pulled up and were out of the car headed for the courtyard. They heard her screams, and Steven shouted, "Go back . . . go back, Gina! Go back to the car and call the police!"

"But, Steven, what about . . .?"

"Do as I say, Gina - now! Call the police!"

Mrs. Pollock came jolting out of an opening in the hedges that acted as a fence around the perimeter of the museum property. She ran right into Steven's arms. "Mr. Richards! Please help me . . . don't let him kill me!" Just then, Pollock came charging out of the courtyard but stopped dead in his tracks when he saw Steven with his wife. He stood there a moment, trying to decide what to do. His car was right beyond where Steven was standing.

"All right, Pollock." Steven shouted. "It's all over. You might as well turn yourself in." Pollock suddenly broke out into a run. When Steven saw he was headed right for them, he grabbed Mrs. Pollock and they both stepped aside. Then Steven remembered that Gina was with the car, and that's where Pollock was headed. Steven immediately took off after him, but Gina was the last thing on Pollock's mind. He jumped in his car and sped off.

Gina got out of the car and said, "The police are on their way. I was so afraid - I thought he was coming after me!"

"I did too, Baby . . . that scared the hell out of me."

Mrs. Pollock joined them and said with a slur, "I wanna thank you, young man, for savin' my life, 'cause he was hell bent on takin' it."

"Well, Mrs. Pollock, I just thank God we got here in time."

Just then, the Philadelphia police drove up, along with Lieutenant Dickens who jumped out of an unmarked car and headed straight for Steven. "Damn it, Richards, what in the hell's going on here? I told you not to meddle in this."

Mrs. Pollock didn't waste any time coming to Steven's defense. "Just a minute, young man. I think you should apologize! If it hadn't been for Mr. Richards here, I might be dead now."

The scare Mrs. Pollock had experienced had just about sobered her up, and she was quite coherent when she explained to Lieutenant Dickens what had taken place.

Dickens believed that Steven had interfered with his plan to capture Pollock. He looked at Steven suspiciously, and Steven shrugged his shoulders as if to say, "You heard what the lady said."

Dickens wasn't satisfied, but went on. "Well, anyway, Richards, we got the DNA tests back a little sooner than we expected, and they're proof positive that it's Martin Pollock Junior's blood on the clothing. Not only that, Pollock's voice is a match to your tape."

Steven quickly asked, "At this point, I don't see my client as a suspect anymore. So will you please let him go now?"

"Yeah, we can let him go. Right now, what I want to do is catch up with Pollock before he tries to leave the area."

"I don't think he's going anywhere because I believe he's determined to kill his wife. She's not safe until we get him off the streets."

Chapter 17

"Yeah, you might be right about that, Steven. Well, we sure won't catch him standing around here like this."

That evening, Steven and Gina delivered Jeffrey Burroughs to his parents. When his mother opened the door and saw her son, she inhaled sharply and then stood there speechless with her hands covering her mouth. Ozzie Burroughs joined them in a threesome hug, accompanied by tears. When they finished, they turned to Steven. Helen grabbed him and gave him a tight squeeze and said, "Mr. Richards, you are a wonderful man, and I'll never forget what you've done for my son."

Ozzie took his turn and said, "I couldn't have said it better, Steven. You've put our lives back together again, and I'll never be able to thank you enough for it."

Gina just watched, teary-eyed, thinking how great a person Steven was - especially the way he had never for a moment doubted Jeffrey's innocence. At this moment, she was very proud of him and even more proud that she was his woman.

That night, as predicted by Dickens, Pollock showed up at his house to make another attempt on his wife's life - not to shut her up - it was too late for that - his motive was simple revenge because of her betrayal of him. Mrs. Pollock had been taken to a safe place, but the police were waiting for him, and he was apprehended and charged with the murder of his son.

The next day on the job, Steven got a message from Dillenbeck's office that there would be a meeting at one o'clock that day. He immediately called Talley. "Hi, Andy. Do you know about the meeting today?"

"Yeah, I was just getting ready to call you. What do you think?"

"I'll tell you, Andy, I think the shit's gonna' hit the fan today. You know Pollock was captured last night."

"Yeah, I heard."

"And that's not all." Steven then told Talley what Marybeth had overheard Dillenbeck, Grundage and Pollock talking about. Talley filled him in on the history of his opposition to the Brolin contribution.

"We really have to confront them now, Andy. Are you with me on this?"

"Well, Steven, we've come this far with it - we might as well stick it out together the rest of the way."

"Good, that's what I wanted to hear!"

"But, Steven, I just can't believe that I could've been so naive as to let them pull the wool over my eyes that way."

"Aw, don't worry about it, Andy. It happens to the best of us."

At one o'clock, the four of them were in Dillenbeck's office. Dan didn't know how to start the meeting because of the sensitive nature of why he had called them together, so he put the burden on the others by asking, "Well, Gentlemen, does anybody know why I called this meeting?"

There was a moment of silence before Steven spoke up. "Well, I don't know what's on your mind, but, for me, there's a lot of things that have to be cleared up around here. First let me start by asking, is it the intention of the firm to defend Pollock?"

Grundage replied, "It's not only our intention to do so; it's our duty. He's one of the family."

"But it's a cut and dried case," Steven protested. "He is in fact guilty of the crime, and there is no indication to the contrary."

"That doesn't mean that he doesn't deserve the best defense that we can give him," Grundage said.

The more Talley thought about how they had deceived him, the angrier he got, which caused him to speak out. "Let's stop bullshitting each other here. The real reason why you guys want to defend Pollock is because he has you by the balls. Isn't that so?"

Dan jumped out of his seat, in his usual fashion, and shouted, "What the hell you mean by that nasty remark, Andy?"

Talley told him, "Sit down, Dan. At this point, I'm not interested in or afraid of your bully tactics. We have to get to the heart of this matter, and I'm for whatever it takes to bring it out into the open."

Dan stood there speechless and then surprised everyone by sitting back down as Andy had requested. It was as if he knew the time of reckoning had come.

"Bring what out into the open, Andy?" Grundage asked.

Talley said, "Don't play stupid, Simon. You know precisely what I'm talking about - the money you guys embezzled to support that racist creep, Senator Brolin. Pollock knows about it, and you've promised to defend him to keep him quiet."

Grundage said, "Where did you come up with that cock and bull story?"

Talley responded, "We know it to be a fact, and it would be better if you would stop denying it so that we can deal with the matter of saving this firm. Pollock committed a heinous crime, and I think we should let him go down the drain and go from there. Gentlemen . . . that's where I stand."

Dan and Simon looked at each other, and that's when Steven thought he saw a weakening in the two men and said, "To be truthful, I think Pollock is going to spill the beans anyway, so what you should do is beat him to the punch. I know I've only been here a short time, but my primary interest now is saving the firm. There's two possibilities - one, we can bring Rhyner in . . . be up front with him . . . let him know exactly what happened and see if he'll go along with trying to hide the loss. Personally, I don't think he'll go for that. Or two, you guys can own up to what's been done - and that would mean being willing to pay any consequences there might be, including jail time. I can assure you that Andy and I would have the firm intact upon your return." Steven felt pretty smug in his position and asked them, "Would you guys like some time to think about that?"

Grundage said, "Yeah, we do need some time to talk about it. Whadaya say, Dan?"

Dan was not quite ready to admit to any wrongdoing, especially to Steven, but he did want to be alone with Simon to talk it over. With a grim face, he said, "Yeah . . . I guess so."

"Okay," Steven said. "Andy and I will come back in half an hour and see what you have to say."

"Sure, sure . . . leave us now, willya?" Dan said impatiently.

After Steven and Andy left, Dan said to Simon in a low growl, "That black son of a bitch came in here and has just about taken over the fuckin' place, hasn't he? I don't like this goddamn shit! Isn't there some other way to handle this without having to answer to that fuckin' bastard? This shit ain't right - I don't like the situation we're in and moreover, I don't like him!"

Chapter 17

Simon responded, "Dan, Dan, please . . . get yourself together. This isn't the time to be expressing your personal feelings toward Steven. He's right . . . it's all over . . . we're in a serious bind here. The way I figure it, I think our first option should be to offer to pay the money back through our personal funds - that's if we can get Irving Rhyner to overlook what he's found in the books."

As they talked, the time passed very quickly and before they knew it, Steven and Talley were back in Dan's office. Steven started with, "Well, Gentlemen, what'll it be?"

Dan was so disturbed by Steven's arrogant attitude that he said, "I'm not interested in hearing any more of your sanctimonious shit. Whatever Simon says, I'll go along with it." He stomped out of the room.

"Tell me, Simon, does he really hate me that much?" Steven asked.

"Oh, I don't know . . . when things don't go his way, he's pretty hard to get along with. Other than that, he's really a nice guy once you get to know him."

Steven remarked sarcastically, "Is that so?"

Talley spoke out. "Simon, I think it's imperative that you know that Steven and I are not your enemies. We're all on the same team here. This is out in the open now, and the only way to solve it is to stick together. Can we at least agree on that much?"

Simon agreed and then went on to explain to Steven and Talley how he and Dan planned to handle the crisis they now faced. Steven asked, "But what if Rhyner doesn't want to overlook what he's uncovered - you'll then be faced with the consequences of option number two."

"We really don't have much of a choice, now do we?" Grundage responded grimly.

"Well, if you want to look on the bright side," Steven remarked, "along with being one of the most prestigious firms in Philadelphia, it's also very locked in politically - and I'm sure that'll help a lot. Anyway, I believe our next move should be to get hold of Irving Rhyner as soon as possible. Andy, do you want to take care of that?"

"Sure, I'll get on it right away."

"Okay, let's get to work," Steven said, while reaching out to shake Simon's hand. Simon just looked at him momentarily and then extended his hand also. Steven, although not at all puzzled by his hesitance, mischievously asked, "Why the hesitation, my good man?" Steven saw that Simon was groping for an answer to his question, and because he didn't want to hear some bullshit answer from him, decided to spare him the agony of coming up with one by saying, "Never mind, Man - you don't have to answer that. Believe me . . . I understand . . . I really do!"

Later that day after the staff went home, the four of them met with Irving Rhyner. When Dan started to explain the facts, Simon remembered how it went with Dan and Irving before and thought it would be best if he did the talking. He cut in on Dan, saying, "Wait a minute . . . hold it - hold it, Dan, I'll explain. What he's trying to say, Irv . . . we were wondering, if the missing money is returned, would you omit any mention of it from your report?"

Irving replied, "Where did the money disappear to in the first place?"

Grundage said, "To be very candid with you, Irv, Dan and I used the money to make a campaign contribution which Talley didn't know anything about. He only found out when you brought it up, and, of course, Steven wasn't even here at the time."

Irving thought for a moment and then said, "You have to understand what you're asking me to do - my involvement in this could come to light, and I can't afford to put my business on the line to save you guys. I'm sorry; I really feel bad about it, but I have to report this to the authorities."

At that, Dan banged his fist on the desk and shouted, "Fuck him . . . let him go ahead - don't beg him for shit. Don't beg him for a goddamn thing! As of now, Rhyner, you no longer have this account. I don't know about you guys, but as far as I'm concerned, this meeting is over. I'm hungry . . . let's get the hell out of here. You comin', Simon?"

Two weeks passed during which Dillenbeck and Grundage underwent investigation by the authorities. Pollock confessed, and it was learned that the day of the murder, he had been leaving the country club after meeting there with a client when he saw Jeffrey and his son pull into the parking lot. He had followed them back into the club. When the opportunity presented itself, he had brutally stabbed his son to death, completely satisfied that Jeffrey would be blamed.

Chapter 18

One evening, Steven had stayed late to catch up on some work, and as he was leaving the building, he heard a voice calling him from a car across the street. "Steven - over here!"

He saw that it was Andrea and walked over to her. "Andrea, what are you doing here?"

"What do you think I'm doing here? I came to see you."

"But how long have you been waiting? I might never have come out!"

Andrea didn't want him to know to what lengths she had been willing to go for the chance to see him, so she answered, "Oh, I haven't been waiting that long," even though she had been sitting outside his office building for almost two hours.

Steven walked around the other side of the car and slid in beside her and kissed her on the cheek. At the touch of his lips, Andrea's hand involuntarily moved to his face in a soft caress, and then she dropped her hand quickly back to her lap.

She asked, "How've you been, Steven?"

"Oh, as well as can be expected."

"And Gina?"

"She's fine, too . . . I guess."

"What do you mean, you guess? She's either okay or she's not. Which is it?"

"To tell you the truth, Andrea, I don't want to talk about Gina right now. Let's talk about you - how've you been, and are you seeing anyone?"

"Yeah, I've met this really nice guy named Bill - we go out once in a while."

Although Steven sensed Andrea was lying about seeing someone, he still felt a twinge of jealousy at the idea of it. He said, "Oh, really? That's great. Tell me - is it serious?"

Andrea stared at Steven contemptuously because she believed that he should know how much she cared for him and that no other relationship could be serious to her. She responded to him curtly. "What do you think?"

"Did I say something wrong, Andrea?"

"Oh, forget it, Steven. You didn't say anything wrong."

"This isn't going too well, is it?" Steven asked.

"No, it's not."

"Well, let me start again. Andrea, you really look great!"

She laughed. "Oh, thank you, Steven."

Then he said, "Now what do we do?"

"Do you want to go get a cup of coffee?"

"Sure, why not?"

While they were drinking their coffee at a cafe around the corner, Andrea said, "You know, Steven, Gina was my friend, too, and I really would like to know how she's doing. I wouldn't want us to sit here and pretend she doesn't exist."

"Oh, she exists alright. As a matter of fact, sometimes I think that's all Gina and I do - merely exist."

"What do you mean by that?"

"Well, Andrea, I'll tell ya . . . I don't know about Gina and me. I believe she loves me . . . I mean, really loves me, but sometimes . . . I don't know . . . I get the feeling that . . . well, she still hasn't come to grips with the fact that I'm a black man."

"What's she doing now that gives you that impression?"

"Well, for one, I feel she's very uncomfortable being with me in public. For an example, if we're out at a restaurant or something - when we're finished eating and ready to leave, she always makes sure that we're not seen walking out of the place together by asking me to go get the car and she'll meet me at the curb. She denies it, of course."

For a moment Andrea looked somber and then spoke emotionally. "Oh, Steven . . . dear Steven . . . she's gonna hurt you as sure as I'm breathing. She's gonna hurt you, I can feel it. Don't misunderstand my motives - please - I'm not saying this because of my personal feeling for you, but as a friend who sincerely cares."

"No, I don't think she can hurt me, Andrea. I know how she is, and because of that my guard is always up. "

"Steven, if I must say so, that doesn't sound like the Steven Richards I know. You're much too intelligent a man to talk that way. It sounds like you're just making up excuses for putting up with the situation."

Steven felt that Andrea was right, but wasn't in the mood to hear the truth and snapped in a low voice so as not to be heard. "Alright, Andrea, that's enough! I don't want to hear any more about Gina - and I mean it!"

The two of them just sat in silence, sipping at what were by now cold cups of coffee until Steven inched his hand slowly across the small, cafe-style table where they were sitting, took her hand in his, and said quietly, "I'm sorry, Andrea. I shouldn't have talked to you that way."

"No, Steven, I'm the one who should be sorry, for trying to pry into your personal life that way . . . I'm sorry - really I am."

"Well, we were both wrong. Let's leave it at that, okay?"

Andrea looked into Steven's eyes and said to him, "Steven, will you take me somewhere so we can be alone - please? I feel that if I don't sleep with you tonight, the opportunity will never present itself again."

Steven hesitated a moment. "What about Gina?" he responded. "You know how I . . ."

Chapter 18

She cut him off before he could get it all out. "Didn't you say you didn't want to talk about her anymore? . . . Well, neither do I!"

Steven smiled at her and said, "Have it your way, Sweetheart."

Just before they got up to leave, Andrea said jokingly, "I'm going to the powder room; I'll meet you at the curb!"

They laughed and walked away, holding hands.

When they got to Andrea's car, Steven said, "I'll drive, if you don't mind."

"What's the matter - are you afraid of my driving?"

"Well, don't take it personally, but I don't trust anybody's driving but my own."

"I'll just ignore that remark." Andrea responded. "Now, if you don't mind me asking, Steven, where are we going?"

"Oh, some place nice and quiet where we won't be disturbed."

"Oh, yeah? And what's the name of this nice and quiet place you're taking me to?"

"The Blue Moon Hotel," he answered, "It's really the only place we can go on such short notice. Have you ever heard of it?"

"Sure, of course I have. What do you think I am - some greenhorn that doesn't know anything about Philadelphia - the city I was raised in?"

"Well, let me ask you this . . . since you know so much about it, have you ever been there?"

Andrea looked at him to see if he was joking or what. When she saw a slight smile on his face, she smiled back at him, at the same time gently elbowing him in the side, saying, "Hey, you . . . what kind of woman do you think I am, anyway?"

Steven laughed and said, "Oh, I don't know . . . what kind are you?"

They had to stop at a traffic light and for a moment, their eyes held each other in a lustful stare until Steven thought he felt someone else staring at him. He turned to see if his feeling was real, and, sure enough, it was. There, in the car beside him, was Marybeth Turner!

"Hi, Steven," she said, "Who's that in the car with you?" Steven was blocking her view, and she couldn't see that it was Andrea.

Andrea, remembering the incident at Steven's office, when Beth had done her best to make her jealous, didn't make any attempt to hide; she leaned forward so that Beth could get a clear view of her.

When Beth saw her, she said in a very surprised voice, "Oh, Andrea . . . it's you! How are you?"

"Fine, and yourself?" Andrea answered, smiling brightly, while Steven just sat there with his mouth wide open.

The light turned green and as Beth took off, she hollered out, "Steven, close your mouth before something flies in it!"

Andrea thought that this was the worst thing that could have happened. Steven was obviously upset, and she thought the rest of the night would be ruined. She tried to console him by placing her hand at the back of his neck and rubbing it gently, asking, "Are you okay, Steven?"

"Yeah, I'll be alright . . . just let me be for a moment."

Steven was quiet during the rest of the trip, and Andrea didn't dare bother him for fear that he might change his mind about the evening and take her home.

When they reached the hotel, Steven didn't notice it but Andrea suddenly became rather shy and stayed in the background while Steven went to the desk clerk to get a

Chapter 18

room. He believed that she was right beside him, but soon realized she wasn't. The clerk noticed him looking for her and said, "If you're looking for your friend, Buddy, she's over there." Steven then turned in the direction the clerk was pointing.

This was a first-time experience for Andrea, and when she saw both men looking at her, she clutched her handbag close to her body and held her head down in shame. She thought the man at the desk must know that they could only be there for one reason, and this made her feel very cheap, so cheap that she imagined that the desk clerk was undressing her with his eyes and that somehow Steven was involved in it some way or another.

The clerk told Steven, "You got a shy one there, Boy. You better catch her - she's getting away from you."

Andrea had started to walk away, and Steven chased after her. "Andrea . . . Andrea, wait a minute . . . what's wrong?" He caught up to her in the vestibule of the building, turned her around and said, "I thought this was what you wanted! Why are you running off like this?"

"Oh, Steven, I'm sorry . . . I didn't know it was gonna be like this!"

"Like what?"

"I feel so cheap - and the way that man looked at me, I could feel his eyes burning right through my clothing."

Steven asked with grave concern, "Andrea - you really haven't ever been in a place like this, have you?"

"No, I haven't."

He pulled her to him, put his arms around her and said, "Well, I'll tell you - right now it's all we've got - we're not likely to find a room anywhere else. So let's go upstairs, and I promise you'll feel much better once we're in our room."

This night with Steven meant a lot to Andrea and after some thought, she gave in to him. As they walked to the elevator, she made sure she was on the side of Steven that hid her from the clerk. She took a quick peek, and he was watching them just as she expected, looking at her as if to say, "And another one bites the dust!"

Once in the room, just as Steven had told her, Andrea felt much more relaxed. She commented, "Oh! I'm very surprised at how nice and well-kept it is."

Steven didn't respond to her, but just threw himself back-first on the bed. He was having mixed feelings about the events of the evening. He had not forgotten about Marybeth seeing them and knew she would take it right back to Gina.

Andrea came over and sat down on the bed with him. "You were right," she said, "I feel much better now. That's what I like about you - you seem to know how people are gonna feel before they do." Steven's eyes were shut. She leaned over him and kissed him softly on the lips. He gave a tired sigh, and she told him, "Steven, I know how rough your day must have been. I'll just rub your head and don't feel bad if you fall asleep."

Steven luxuriated in the feeling of her fingers moving through his hair, massaging his scalp, and he soon fell fast asleep. Andrea thought he would sleep more comfortably if she took off his shirt and trousers, and she managed to do so without thoroughly waking him. She was enjoying the quiet intimacy of the moment, not daring to think about when the evening would finally come to an end, and they would have to leave this room they were sharing together. After a couple of hours, Steven stirred and moaned in his sleep and then awoke with a start. "Andrea, it's you! I was just dreaming that you and I were making love."

Chapter 18

Andrea took a quick glance. His undershorts could not conceal the fact that he had an erection, and Andrea laughed and said, "So I see!"

Steven groaned and rolled over close to her. "I'll tell you what - make my dream come true."

Andrea asked coyly, "And in this dream, were you wearing a condom?"

Steven gave her a teasing look. "Why do you ask?"

"Well, if we're going to be intimate, I'm afraid I have to insist that you wear a condom."

"I always do," Steven replied seriously. "Now, why don't you get undressed . . . while I watch! Okay?"

Andrea blushed very deeply, but responded to what she considered a daring challenge by getting up from the bed and moving to the middle of the dimly lit room.

Steven said, "Wait, maybe I can find some music to put you in the mood. He tuned the dial on the radio supplied with the room until he luckily came upon Marvin Gaye's *Sexual Healing*. Andrea began a rhythmic bump and grind to the soulful sound of the music while Steven watched intently. Never missing a beat, she danced seductively to a chair in a corner of the room, put her foot up on it, and began to peel her stockings from her lovely, long legs. Then she unbuttoned her dress in a tantalizing, very leisurely fashion and let it fall from her body, leaving her standing in just her half-slip and bra. By now, Steven was fully aroused and watched in fascination as she slowly pulled down just one of her bra straps and showed him a softly rounded, brown breast which she then held and caressed ever so lightly. When she did that, Steven felt that he had waited an eternity for her and, moving to her swiftly, he gathered her in his arms and brought her to the bed where he laid her down. He put his hand under her slip and was surprised to discover that she wasn't wearing any panties; when he felt her, she seemed very ready to receive him. He didn't want to wait any longer - he wanted her right away and plunged into her with emphatic strokes. To his great surprise, he was met with very resistant flesh and a sharp cry from Andrea, and he stopped almost at once and whispered, "Andrea, relax and open up a little, Baby. I don't want to tear into you. Is something wrong?"

Andrea didn't answer right away and then reluctantly murmured, "Steven, I've never been with a man in this way before. I didn't know it would be so obvious."

Steven was stunned. "My God, you mean you're a virgin?"

Andrea whispered, "Yes," under her breath.

"You sure had me fooled, Baby . . . the way you stripped off your clothes - I thought you were an old pro!"

"I was just trying to impress you, Steven. Please . . . take it easy with me."

He spoke softly to her, "Don't worry, Sweetheart . . . I won't hurt you."

Steven reveled in the fact that he was the first for Andrea, and spent the rest of the long night skillfully, but gently, acquainting her with sensual pleasures. Andrea was happy to be in his arms and responded eagerly to his every caress, his every innovation. When they weren't making love, they talked quietly, discovering parts of each other's minds they had not known before. Toward dawn, after a last erotic encounter, followed by a drowsy, somewhat muddled conversation, they finally drifted into sleep, their bodies close and warm.

Sun streaming in the room eventually woke them. Steven turned to Andrea and said sleepily, "You weren't wearing any panties - when you came to get me last night, was it your intention to seduce me?"

Chapter 18

She smiled sadly. "You're right, Steven, it was . . . and now I regretfully say, this chapter is finally over in my life. You've gotten what you wanted, and I've . . . I don't know . . . somehow , I don't think I've . . . well, forget it, I don't think you'd understand anyway!"

"Now hold on here, Andrea. What is it that I wouldn't understand? Didn't you enjoy what we shared last night?"

Andrea threw the sheets back, revealing her stark nakedness, jumped out of bed, grabbed her clothing, and told him, as she hurriedly dressed, "You see there - I told you you wouldn't understand! . . . Tell me this, would you, Steven? Why do men always think it's the physical part of a relationship that matters more than what a man and a woman might feel for each other? You know - when I first met you, I thought you were different - you were the man of my dreams, the man I've been saving myself for all this time. You wanna know why? I remember the times when I was practically throwing myself at you, and you rejected me. Well, to me, that meant you were a pretty special guy; you didn't just want me for my body. All of my life I felt like the only thing I ever meant to a man was how fast he could get in my pants. But now I don't think you're any different than the rest of these jerks out here. After you've tried the merchandise, all you can think to ask me is, did I enjoy it? Yes, I enjoyed it, but only for one reason . . . it was with you - someone I care dearly about, that's why I enjoyed it."

Steven let Andrea go on uninterrupted until there was a pause in her ranting and then asked, "Are you finished?"

"Yes, I am," she answered angrily.

"Now it's my turn. But first let me ask you this question - what in the hell could I have possibly done to you that would cause you to tear into me that way?"

"I don't know, Steven - I guess . . ."

Steven cut her off in midsentence. "Well, I'll tell you what I think, Andrea. You're just angry with me because of something you've done that you couldn't take back if you wanted to. And you have no right to accuse me of using you as a sexual object when that's precisely what you had in mind. By getting me into bed you thought that would give me some kind of barometer to compare your sexual performance to Gina's - if you were better, I might leave her. Isn't that so?"

Andrea didn't answer, so he went on, "Remember, Sweetheart, you wanted this as much as I did. Now don't you think it's unfair to try and put all the blame on me? I'm not sorry that it happened, so don't try to make me feel guilty about something that you initiated. We both did what we wanted to do. And whether you believe it or not, I was also with someone that I cared for very much last night."

Andrea knew that he was absolutely right in his assessment of her motives, but she had lashed out at him irrationally because, after having spent the night with him, she couldn't bear the thought of him going back to Gina. After a moment, she went back over to the bed and sat down beside him and laid her head on his chest. "Steven, if I could help it, I wouldn't love you this way. You're right - we were both consenting adults, and I did enjoy you ever so much."

Steven kissed her tenderly.

Chapter 19

When Steven got into work that morning, he headed for the snack bar. From the doorway, he saw Gina and Marybeth having their usual coffee and doughnuts. He murmured to himself, "Ah, shit," figuring that Marybeth was probably telling it all. He decided to pass up his coffee and go straight to the office.

Marybeth hadn't wasted any time bringing up what she had seen the night before.

"Guess who I saw last night, Sweetie!"

"Oh, Beth, you always get in the first word." Gina complained. "Let me go first this time? Besides, it sounds like what you have to say is fascinating. What I have to tell you is horrible, so let's get mine out of the way."

"Okay, Honey, go ahead."

"Well, Bob has gone raving mad, Beth. He broke into my apartment last night and trashed it!"

"Were you there when this happened?"

"No, damn it. Actually, it's a good damn thing I wasn't - I probably wouldn't be here talking to you now. He's been calling me every night and leaving threatening messages on my answering service. But this is the first time he's ever gone this far . . . breaking into my place like that! I feel so violated! You know what I'm sayin', Beth? This is getting out of hand . . . he's really gone crazy. And he left this note on my bed, telling me that my days were numbered."

"Girl, I told you . . . you better tell Steven, or at least take that note to the police. I don't want to find you on some slab in the city morgue, Gina . . . please. Get some help before it's too late."

"I will, Beth. You don't have to worry about me. Now what is it that was so important you had to tell me?"

"Girlfriend, to be truthful with you, after what you just told me, I don't think you wanna hear what I have to say."

"Now, you know me better than that, Beth! If you think I'm gonna allow you to arouse my curiosity that way and then back off... well... you've got another thought comin'! Now what is it you have to tell me?"

"I hope you're up for this, Honey."

"Will you go ahead and say what you have to say, Girl?"

"Okay, Gina. Do you know where Steven was last night?"

"No, I wasn't over at his place. I don't know where he was. Why?"

"I saw him with an old friend of ours - Andrea - that used to work in your office?"

Gina and Beth didn't usually have any secrets from each other, but for some reason Gina didn't want Beth to know she was disturbed, so she said, "So what - they're friends. Don't try to make anything out of that."

"Well, I saw them about ten o'clock last night. And the way they were lookin' at each other led me to believe that there was more going on than you may want to think about. Do you have that much confidence in Steven?"

"Yes, I do, Beth. Now I don't want to talk about that anymore."

"Suit yourself, Honey. I'm just trying to be the friend that I am."

"C'mon, let's get out of here, Beth. It's getting late - we don't want to miss that elevator!"

When Gina got to the office, she went straight to her desk and buzzed Steven on the intercom. "What is it, Gina?"

Chapter 19

"Can I talk to you for a moment?"

"Sure, come on in, Sweetheart," and said to himself, "Uh-oh - here we go!"

Gina went in and came right to the point. "Where were you last night, Steven?"

"I ran into Andrea Hall, and we went and had a bite to eat. Why? You must have been talking to Beth."

"Yes, I was. She said she saw you and Andrea - and it was pretty late at night."

"Well, it was late, Gina. I don't know whether I like the way this is going - am I being accused of something?"

"Look, Steven, I know how Andrea feels about you - the woman is madly in love with you, so I think that's reason enough for me to be concerned."

"Oh, I don't think she was or is in love with me. We're just good friends . . . that's all, Baby - believe me."

"Yes, she is. We used to talk about you all the time, and she's definitely in love with you . . . as I'm sure you know."

"Well, there wasn't nothin' to it as far as I was concerned. We just got something to eat, and afterwards she took me back to my car, and I went home."

"But Marybeth said you were making goo-goo eyes at each other."

"You know, you may think that Beth is a nice person, but she can stir up a lot of trouble if you let her. Just by the mere fact that she would use a term like goo-goo eyes should tell you something about the woman's mentality."

"Steven, first of all, that wasn't the term she used - that's the way I put it. And there's no reason for you to talk about her that way. She's my best friend and I would like you to respect that - please."

"I'm sorry, Baby, but the woman rubs me the wrong way sometimes - you know what I'm sayin'?"

"No, I don't know what you're saying. Tell me, was she rubbing you the wrong way when you went to bed with her? Was she?"

Steven was quiet, and Gina went on. "Steven, I want you to be honest with me. Is anything going on between you and Andrea? If so, I need to know."

Gina sounded very demanding, and Steven felt that if he told her the truth, he would lose her. He wasn't ready for that, and so he tried to appease her. "Gina, after all the trouble that I've gone through to get you, how could you believe that I'd want to throw it away so quickly? Come here, Baby."

Gina, although still annoyed, couldn't resist his charm, and came over to him. He took her in his arms and told her, "It's you that I need, Sweetheart. If you don't know that by now, we're both in trouble." Then he pulled her closer and kissed her.

Gina gave in to his embrace and after a moment or two broke the kiss and pressed her lips to his ear, whispering, "I love you, Steven - and just the idea of you being with another woman upsets me terribly." Then she suddenly placed her two hands on his chest and, while still held in his embrace pushed away from him, and with a slight smile, said, "My, how things have changed. It wasn't so long ago that you were the one who was chasing me, and now who's doing the chasing?"

"Don't look at it that way, Baby - just look at it that you have come to know what I knew all the while . . . that you and I were destined to be together, and nothing in this world could have prevented it."

"Oh, Steven, what a beautiful thing to say . . . and just think, I almost let you get away!"

"Come on, now, we have to stick to our rules."

"And what rules are they?"

Steven gave her a smile. "You know... strictly business in the office and all pleasures left for home."

"Oh, yeah, I forgot - we did say that, didn't we?"

As Gina started to leave, Steven stopped her, saying, "Oh, and before I forget, Honey, there's gonna be a legal defense fund-raiser for Dillenbeck and Grundage this coming Saturday at the Bellevue. There'll be a lot of big mucka-de-mucks there so, when you get the time, why don't you go and get something real nice to wear." He handed her his VISA and said, "I want my baby to be the queen of the ball. And me? I'll be the envy of every man in the place."

"Should I concern myself with cost?"

"No, Sweetheart... do your thing! Now, let's get to work."

After Gina left his office, Steven leaned back in his chair, put his feet up on his desk, hands behind his head, and started to think about his encounter with Andrea the previous night. Steven was somewhat confused by now. Before, he was so infatuated by Gina that he didn't see Andrea as a rival to her, but since last night, it seemed that Andrea had accomplished exactly what he had accused her of trying to do - she had given him something to compare to Gina. He couldn't get Andrea out of his mind.

After a few minutes of thinking about her, the phone rang. It was Gina. "Steven, Mr. Talley is on the line."

"Hi, Andy - what's going on?"

"Well, Rhyner didn't waste any time... the feds were here today."

"What?"

"Yeah, they handed Dan and Simon summons for grand jury."

"No shit! They're not being arrested, are they?"

"No, they just served them with the papers. And guess what, Steven?"

"I'm listening."
"Dan wants you to serve as his counsel."
"Are you serious?"
"Yeah, I know . . . but I'm only delivering the message."
"You gotta' be kiddin' - as much as that man hates me? And can you beat that? He didn't even have the balls to ask me himself. Anyway, I don't think I would be able to represent the man properly."
"Yes, you can, Steven. That's why Dan asked for you, because he knows that regardless of what his feelings are for you, you're a good lawyer and you won't let that interfere with defending him to the best of your ability."
"A-h-h, I don't know, Andy - I have to think about it."
"Okay, I'll tell him what you said. Talk to you later."
Steven had second thoughts and caught Andy before he hung up. "Andy . . . tell him . . . if he wants me as his counsel, to come and ask me."

The rest of the day passed without event. At five o'clock, Gina peeped her head into Steven's office and said, "I'm leaving now, Honey, and Mom wants us for dinner tonight at seven - is that alright with you?"
"Ah, c'mon, Baby, I thought I asked you not to make plans for me that way."
"I'm sorry, Steven, but it wasn't my fault. Mom just called me about an hour ago and asked us over."
"Okay, I'll meet you there at seven."

Steven was a half hour late getting to Gina's mother's house. When Gina answered the door, she was annoyed. "Steven, where have you been? Why are you always late? We've been waiting almost an hour for you."

"It has not been an hour. You said seven . . . it's now seven-thirty - that's a half hour. Now, Gina, don't make a big deal out of it!" He kissed her and said, "I'm hungry . . . is dinner ready?"

Gina laughed and said, "Oh, Steven, I don't know what I'm gonna do with you."

After eating, they all went into the living room. Gina asked in a happy, but somewhat anxious, voice, "Steven, would you like to meet my father?"

"Yes, but . . ."

She whisked out of the room and up the stairs before he could finish what he was saying.

Steven looked at Florence, Gina's mother, and shrugged his shoulders. Florence had been wanting to talk to Steven and thought this was as good a time as any and started in. "I don't know what you've done to my daughter, but she seems to be a changed person."

Steven wanted her to go on talking, thinking that she might reveal something about Gina that would help him to better understand her, so he encouraged her by asking, "What do you mean, a changed person . . . what kind of person was she before?"

"Well, Son, I don't know whether or not you and her have ever discussed this, but Gina has a lot of problems."

Just at that moment, Gina had started down the steps. When she heard her mother talking to Steven about her, she stopped dead in her tracks, put the family photo album she had gone to get for Steven to see on the top step, and listened while Florence went on. "You see, even though it's obvious she's a black woman, she's always had a problem admitting it. The darker a black person is, the more she dislikes them. Her father was a real dark-skinned man and . . ."

Gina didn't want her to go any further. She came down the steps, saying, "Mother . . . please . . . Steven's heard all of this before . . . I'm sure he doesn't want to hear it again!"

"I don't think it's no more than right for him to know exactly what he's getting into with you, Gina."

"He already knows, Mom - I've told him everything!"

"Did you tell him what happened at the hospital . . . huh? Did you?"

"Steven, I think it's time we left now. I can't take this any longer - let's get the hell out of here!"

"That's right, Gina, go ahead and run!" Mrs. Epps shouted. "Run from the truth . . . you'll be running for the rest of your life, Baby!"

Gina rushed out of the house with Steven and slammed the door behind her, cursing, "Shit! Goddamn it!"

She hurried ahead of him on her way to the car, and he called out to her, "Hey, Sweetheart, remember me? . . . Wait up - I think I'm going your way!"

Gina stopped, patting her foot rapidly on the ground. When he caught up to her, he saw that she was crying. He took her into his arms, saying in soothing tones, "That's okay, Baby, that's okay. You just go ahead and cry."

Gina's only response to him was, "Oh, Steven . . . will she ever forgive me? . . . will she?"

He just held her and consoled her, "Get it out of your system, Honey. Crying is good for the soul."

Gina's mother was looking out of the window, and she too was crying while watching the scene on the sidewalk.

Steven then whispered, "I don't think you should be alone tonight, Sweetheart - come and stay at my place."

At that request, she clutched him tightly - so tight that Steven had to say, "Hold it, Baby. Hold on - you're gonna'

Chapter 19

squeeze me to death!" He had to pry her away from him, saying, "Let's go home, Honey."

When they pulled up to the Four Seasons, the valet took Steven's car. As they were walking into the building, Gina suddenly felt funny. She felt as if she were being watched by someone. She turned to look over her shoulder, and, across the street from the hotel, was a small sports car that looked like Bob Rosenberg's. She wasn't sure whether it was he or not, but it gave her a really eerie feeling, and she sped up.

Steven noticed and said, "What's wrong with you? You look as if you've just seen a ghost."

"Not really. I just got a sudden chill."

Steven smiled and joked, "Well, in that case, let's hurry up and get upstairs so I can remedy that!"

As soon as they arrived in the suite, Gina rushed over to the window and peeped out to see if the car was still there.

Steven was not paying much attention, but he did notice her looking out the window and asked, as he walked toward her, "What are you looking at? Is there something wrong?"

"No, I thought I saw someone I knew, that's all."

"From way up here?" he asked. He shook his head and said, "M-m-m - I don't know about you, Girl!"

It was a good thing the car left before Steven got to the window because he too would surely have recognized it.

After they had settled in, with Steven sitting at the end of the couch and Gina lying on her back with her head in his lap, he thought by now she had calmed down enough to talk about the argument she had with her mother and cautiously inquired, "What was your mother talking about when she asked you if you had told me about what happened at the hospital?"

"Please, Steven, I don't want to talk about that right now."

"Alright, Baby, whatever you say." Steven paused for a moment and then decided to try and approach the subject from another angle by saying, "Well, if you don't want to talk about that, then maybe you can tell me why you asked me if I wanted to meet your father when you know he's dead?"

Gina looked up at him suspiciously, smiled and said, "You think you're pretty slick, don't you, Steven? You think by getting me to talk about my father, I might say something in reference to what my mother and I were arguing about."

Steven laughed and said, "A-a-h, I like that in a woman."

"You like what, Smartie?"

"Perceptiveness." They both smiled, their eyes met and Steven bent his head down and started kissing her. His hands immediately began to move over her body, but Gina seemed distracted. She broke their embrace suddenly, got up, went over to her purse, and pulled out a photoholder, brought it back to Steven and pointed to one of the photographs. "That's my father!" she exclaimed with tears in her eyes.

Steven asked, "Are you ready to talk about him now?"

She sat back down beside him. "I guess so," she reluctantly responded. "But there isn't very much to tell. As you can see, he was a very dark-skinned man, and you know how I feel about that."

Steven answered gloomily, "Yeah, I do know how you feel about that. And I'm sure there was more to him than just being dark-skinned, Gina. Anyway, what happened that upset your mother so?"

"Well, like I told you before, I used to deny that he was my father. Whenever I saw him in public, I always found a reason to run and hide from him. But I did that right up to the day he died, and that's why Mama is so angry with me. I guess she thought the least I could do was accept him as my father during his last minutes on this earth. Instead, when I went to see him in the hospital, I gave the lady at the desk a fictitious name because I didn't want anyone there to know that black man was my father."

Steven was silent for a while and then said, "Well, I'm sure your father must have known that you really did love him."

"No, he didn't, Steven. I never showed him in any way that I felt anything for him at all."

"You know, Gina, you don't always have to say it or show it for someone to know that you love them - just as I knew you were attracted to me before you were willing to admit it. And while we're on the subject, how long are you going to be ashamed to be seen with me?"

She looked him straight in the eyes and said, "Steven, I don't think I can answer that - I just know that I love you. Isn't that all that matters?"

"No, Gina, that's not all that matters," he snapped at her. "You either love someone or you don't, and if you do . . . well, contrary to popular belief, love usually comes unconditionally."

"That's right, Steven, go ahead - rub it in. You sound just like my mother with the preaching bit . . . well, find yourself another parishioner, 'cause I don't feel like hearing nobody's sermon."

She rushed into the bedroom, slamming the door behind her, just as angry as she could be. Steven stayed out on the couch for a while, again thinking that the relationship would never work because of the way she was. The idea of going through the same thing her father went through didn't sound very attractive to him. But Steven soon brushed his thoughts off and went into the bedroom, too. The room was very dark and as Steven undressed, he assumed Gina to be asleep. He slipped in beside her, trying not to disturb her, and as they lay back-to-back, Gina, who was not asleep at all, opened her eyes. She made a complete turn so that she was facing the same way he was and said softly, "Steven, are you angry with me?"

"No, Baby, I thought you were angry with me!"

She put her face against his back, kissing it, and her arms around his waist, and that's the way they fell asleep that night.

Chapter 20

When Steven woke up the next morning, Gina had already gone to work, leaving a note that read, "I'll see you on the job, Sweetheart. I love you."

Again, he couldn't think of any reason why she would leave so early except to avoid being seen with him. Although he was never really sure, she had him to the point now that he couldn't tell if she was trying to avoid him or not. In fact, Gina was very subtle with it and had such well-thought-out, elaborate schemes that Steven felt paranoid at times for even thinking it.

Just when he was about to leave for work, the phone rang. "Hello, Steven. This is Beth. If Gina's there, don't let on it's me - okay, Honey?"

"Go ahead, Beth, you can talk; she's already left."

"You've got to promise me you won't tell I told you this."

"Well, that depends on what it is you have to say."

"For Chrissake . . . don't you ever stop being a lawyer, Steven?"

"I guess not, Beth - now what is it?"

"I'm afraid for Gina, Steven. Bob is seriously stalking her and threatened her life. He even trashed her apartment. She told me not to say anything to you about it, but I don't think she understands the potential danger of this man. Isn't there something you can do? You gotta help her."

"Calm down, Beth . . . I'm sure something can be done. What about a restraining order?"

"I already asked her to do that, and she said she didn't want to."

"Well, where does he live, Beth?"

"Steven, to be honest with you, right now I really couldn't tell you."

"Okay, Beth, thanks for calling me. I'll take care of it from here. I won't mention your name unless I have to. Talk to ya' later . . . oh, and Beth, everyone should have at least one friend like you."

After Steven hung up, he couldn't hold back the anger he felt for Bob. Gritting his teeth until you could see his jaw pulsating, he clenched his fists so tightly that his fingernails broke the skin in the palm of his hands and drew blood. He yelled out, "Goddamn that bastard - I'll kill him . . . I'll kill him!"

After his anger subsided somewhat, he decided to call Dickens. "Lieutenant, I wonder if you could do me a favor?"

"Sure, Richards, as long as it doesn't cost me anything."

Steven told him the story and asked him if he could get a restraining order against Bob. Dickens laughed heartily, but Steven was not in the mood for jokes of any sort and anxiously demanded, "What's the matter - what are you laughing at?"

"Ah, Richards, I'm sorry if I seem to be taking this too lightly for you, but for a while there I was worried about you being a better detective than I -- now I think I'm a better lawyer than you! I'm sure you know that only the plaintiff can take out a restraining order, and it has to be obtained from the court, not the police. A sigh of relief, at last my job is safe!"

Steven knew that under normal circumstances he wouldn't have ignored these simple legal facts, so he just laughed and said, "Oh, you know what? You're right!"

"So, there's nothing that can be done unless she's willing to swear out a complaint against this Bozo."

"Alright, thanks a lot. I'll work it out."

Steven went to work, and as he passed through the firm on the way to his office, he was aware of the excited hum from everyone who was anticipating the big fund-raising party for Dillenbeck and Grundage the next night and talking about the arrangements for it. It was almost as if they had forgotten the serious events which had led up to the need for such an affair. His preoccupation with Bob Rosenberg had made him almost forget about the party, and now he said to himself, "Oh, that's right - I wonder if Gina got something to wear." He entered his office and asked Gina to come see him. "Did you get yourself something for the party tomorrow?"

"No, I didn't have time," Gina replied. "I had planned on going after I got off work today."

"Well, why don't you go now? We can handle things here. Make sure you get something really stunning - after all, it is a thousand-dollar-a-plate dinner."

"Why, Steven, who are you buying this dress for - me or you?"

"I'm surprised you would ask that, Gina. As socially conscious as you are, I would think that you would want the best." Steven sounded irritated.

"And what's that supposed to mean?"

"Oh, forget it, Gina. I don't want to get into that."

"You're in a pretty bad mood this morning, aren't you?"

"No, not really."

"No, Steven, I think you are. Something's on your mind - what is it?"

"Okay, Gina, if you really want to know, why did you leave so early this morning?"

"Well, I couldn't sleep, so I just decided to get up and start the day."

"Let me ask you, Gina - is that really the reason or maybe you didn't want us to be seen coming into work together?"

"Oh, is that what's bugging you again? Damn it, Steven, if this relationship is going to work, you have to show a little trust!"

"Alright, Gina, okay. Maybe you're right."

"Thanks for nothing, Steven." On her way out, Gina slammed the door behind her.

Lunchtime had rolled around, and Gina had not returned to the office yet. Steven began to be concerned, especially remembering what Beth had told him about Rosenberg. As he was leaving for lunch, he ran into Andrew Talley. "What do you say, Steven - how 'bout some lunch?"

"No, thanks. I've got something to take care of right now."

He had decided to look for Gina, rather than eat. He thought she might be at Lily Ryder's since it was one of the most expensive stores in town and relatively close to the office. He walked over to Rittenhouse Square and went into the store, wandering through the glittering showrooms looking for her. Steven was no stranger to the store, having purchased a few items himself there in the past. He knew that the most exclusive section was on the third floor. A small elevator took him there, and he stepped off into the hushed, plush atmosphere of the elegant salon. Off to the right, he glimpsed her. The salon manager was hovering over her attentively, rubbing his hands, while a saleswoman knelt at Gina's feet, adjusting the hem of a pale, shimmering gown. Impulsively, Steven decided that this was a good time to find out if Gina would purposely avoid him in a situation like this - one in which she was surrounded by the trappings of white society. He worked his way across the room and then strolled past her without looking at her - close enough that he was sure she could not help but see him. He heard no cry of

Chapter 20

recognition - instead he turned and saw her lift her skirts and make a hasty retreat to the fitting room, with her attendants trailing behind her, hurrying to keep up.

In that instant, Steven knew his affair with Gina was over - that he could never allow himself to live with someone who was obviously so ashamed of what he was . . . and more than that, of what she was. And he couldn't imagine her ever changing - not even in a lifetime.

Steven left the store abruptly and returned to the office. He had decided not to say anything right away about the incident. When Gina came in, he just told her that he was leaving the office early and that he would see her at the apartment later.

After he had gone, Gina began to worry about whether or not he knew she had seen him at Lily Ryder's. That evening, when she came in the apartment, she called, "Steven, it's me - Honey, are you here?"

There was no answer. She walked through the apartment looking for him, and when she entered the bedroom, she found him lying on the bed, fully clothed, staring up at the ceiling. "Do you want me to fix you something to eat?" she asked, a little anxiously.

"No, thanks. I'm not hungry."

Gina left the room, went into the bathroom, looked in the mirror and said to herself, "Damn it, Gina, I think you blew it this time. He must have seen me run from him - why would he be acting this way? Or is he still angry with me about this morning?" She left the bathroom and paced the living room floor for a few minutes, trying to think of a way to approach him. In the course of her pacing, she turned back to the bedroom, and there was Steven, standing in the doorway . . . just looking at her. She gasped, "Oh!" And then she asked, "How long have you been watching me?"

"Not long," was Steven's reply.

She quickly came close and pressed herself against him, but his lack of response made her pull slowly away. She asked in a cunning, sweet voice, "Were you at Lily Ryder's today?" Before he could respond, she said, "I thought I saw you, but when I came out of the dressing room, you were gone!"

"Is that so? As a matter of fact, I did see you - running to the dressing room after you saw me. Gina, we both know how you feel. You've never denied it, and there's no sense in denying it now. You don't want to be seen in certain places with me. I care about you too much to have sex as our only reason for being together. I want all the things that come along with being in love with a woman. I want to take you places - I want to buy you things - I want to be seen with you! Don't misconstrue my hurt for anger - I've just come to the realization that this relationship will not work for either one of us."

Gina was shaking with fright, but looked him dead in the eyes and said, with tears streaming down her face, "Okay, Steven, I did see you. I got nervous and did the wrong thing. All I can say is that I promise you it'll never happen again. I do love you, and I don't want what we have to be destroyed by my craziness."

"But that's just it, Gina. We don't have anything. What do you want me to do? I won't play the role your father played. And the way I see it, that's where we're headed."

Gina grabbed him close and sobbed, "Oh, please, Steven, don't let it end this way. Give me another chance! I really, really love you."

Steven hated to hear her beg. He tried to soften the impact of how he felt by saying, "Gina, right now we need some space between us to find out where things really stand."

Chapter 20

However, Gina sensed that Steven intended a permanent separation, and her fear turned to rage. She stormed, "I wish you'd never walked in that fuckin' office in the first place, and I wouldn't have fallen in love with you. Why did you have to come there? Damn you, Steven, you black bastard, I love you! Don't you understand that? Isn't that what you wanted?"

Steven responded calmly to her outburst. "Gina, I'm truly sorry that things turned out the way they did. Right now, I need to get away. You can stay here tonight, if you want, but I prefer to stay somewhere else."

In desperation, Gina screamed, "If you leave me, I'll go back to Bob!"

"Gina, I would advise against that - the man is going to hurt you, believe me - but of course all I can do is advise you."

"But what about the party?" Gina wailed.

"Ah! Do you want to go there with me or do you want me to meet you there after it's started?" Steven asked sarcastically.

"You can come pick me up, and we'll go together."

"I don't think so."

As he turned and walked toward the door, Gina grabbed up the box from Lily Ryder's and threw it at him, just grazing the side of his head. Steven turned and looked at her and said, "Yeah, I love you, too, Gina."

A short time after Steven had left, the phone rang, and Gina answered it in an abrupt voice, "Hello!"

On the other end, a voice said, "Is that you, Gina?"

"Who wants to know?" Gina demanded.

"It's Andrea. Is everything okay? You sound upset."

"Everything is not okay, and I am upset."

"I'm sorry - maybe I should call back another time."

Gina was annoyed by the call; it seemed as if Andrea was always in the shadows - sort of like an understudy, waiting for Gina to make the slightest mistake so that she could step in. She asked, not so cordially, "Andrea, did you call for me or for Steven?"

"Well, I actually needed to talk to Steven. I wanted his advice about a case I'm researching."

Gina was suspicious of her intentions and said, "Andrea, I don't know why, but for some reason, I knew you weren't quite out of the picture yet."

"Maybe I really should call back another time, Gina."

Gina sighed. "Oh, Andrea, I'm sorry for being so nasty. Steven and I just had a falling out, and he stormed out of here a few minutes ago. I don't know where he's off to. Will you forgive me?"

"No problem. Don't worry about it."

"Andrea, I do like you so much. We have to get together for lunch sometime."

"I'd love it," Andrea responded.

When Andrea hung up, she immediately called Steven on his car phone and was pleasantly surprised to hear him answer. "Oh, Steven, I guess I should consider myself lucky to catch you. I just called the apartment, and Gina told me you weren't there."

"I'm glad you called, Andrea. I was thinking about giving you a ring tonight. Can we get together?"

"Oh, yes!"

"Where are you?"

"I'm at home."

"I'll be right over."

Chapter 20

Andrea didn't know what to expect. Ever since she had spent the night with Steven, she had been in turmoil - sometimes hopeful, thinking Steven would eventually leave Gina, and sometimes despondent, believing that she would never feel his touch again.

When he arrived, Andrea invited him in, and they went out on the back porch. Steven slumped down on the porch swing, gave a big sigh, and put his elbows on his knees and his head in his hands.

Andrea immediately went to stand beside him and started to run her fingers through his hair, saying sympathetically, "Oh, poor Steven. What's the matter, Baby?"

"I can't take her any longer. It's not working out between us."

"I knew something was wrong. When I called the apartment, Gina was very angry. She even tried to blame me at first. Do you feel like talking about it?"

"I don't care," Steven said dully, and he described the events of the day.

Andrea thought for a moment and then said, "And I guess you're here 'cause I always seem to be the bouncing board whenever you and Gina have a falling out."

Steven jumped up from the swing. "I think I'll leave. I don't need that, Andrea. That's not why I came here."

Andrea was beginning to feel more confident in her relationship with Steven, and now instead of apologizing as she might have in the past, she snapped, "Steven, sit back down! Don't be so sensitive. We'll talk about something else."

He reluctantly returned to the swing, and this time she sat down beside him. "I miss you, Steven."

"Well, believe it or not, I miss you, too."

"How's everything at the firm - what's up with Dillenbeck and Grundage?"

"Oh, don't mention them - between that and Gina, I feel like I'm about to lose my mind. But we're throwing a big bash for them tomorrow night at the Bellevue - a fund raiser for their defense."

"Are you going to be there?"

"Are you kidding? I'm part of the team that put it together. Oh, incidentally, I won't be taking Gina - I know it's short notice, but would you like to accompany me?"

Andrea smiled broadly and said enthusiastically, "Of course, Steven. It sounds fascinating. What shall I wear?"

Steven laughed. "Whatever you do, don't come looking the way you did that day you and Gina switched places!"

"Oh, please, don't remind me."

"I was just kidding, Andrea. It's a dressy affair, but I wouldn't care what you wore."

"Steven, on a serious note, should I get my hopes up?"

"Get your hopes up for what?"

"Is it really over for good this time with you and Gina?"

"Well, this has been coming for a while, Andrea. Gina and I haven't been getting along at all - the only thing we enjoyed doing together was sex, and I'd be pretty shallow if I didn't want more than that. So . . . I guess my answer is yes, I think I've finally come to my senses. I don't think Gina and I will be seeing each other as lovers anymore. She might not even want to work for me."

Andrea seemed satisfied with his answer.

Chapter 21

The next night, the ballroom of the Bellevue Hotel was filled to capacity with the most important figures from the legal world of Philadelphia, as well as numerous well-known politicians and businessmen - most of them like-minded people, anxious to show their support for Dillenbeck and Grundage in their battle with the federal justice system. After most of the guests had arrived, Marybeth made her entrance on the arm of a beaming Arthur Gwaltney which raised quite a few eyebrows, not only because they were a mixed couple, but because Marybeth's gown was quite flashy - a bright orange and pink number with plunging back and neck and a skirt slit to the waist. But the couple who created the greatest stir that evening was Steven and Andrea. Andrea looked so elegant - dressed in a simple, deep green velvet dress which revealed very little of her body, but subtly suggested the richness of her figure. Steven was his handsome, assured self, resplendent in black tie.

When they came in, Marybeth was shocked and couldn't take her eyes off them. She knew nothing of Steven's separation from Gina and rushed over, dragging Arthur behind her. "Steven, Andrea, how nice to see you. Where's Gina?"

Steven responded. "Beth, by now I thought you would have heard."

"Heard what?"

"Gina didn't tell you? Well, as of last night, we're no longer together."

Although Marybeth was talking to Steven, her eyes were on Andrea, looking her up and down, in a rather belligerent way, as she bluntly asked him, "Why not?"

Steven simply said, "Beth, let's not go there," and turned his attention to Arthur, complimenting him on what he was wearing.

Marybeth then pushed herself on Steven, asking him to dance. He reluctantly consented after which Andrea and Arthur exchanged a glance. Arthur shrugged his shoulders and said, "Why not?" and they joined Marybeth and Steven on the dancefloor.

As they were dancing, Dillenbeck passed them with his wife and called out, "Great turnout, Steven! What do you think?"

"Yes, it seems to be going well."

There was a flight of about five steps leading down into the ballroom, which made it easy to see anyone coming in. While Steven was dancing, he turned Marybeth in a spin which left him facing the entrance stairs. And who should be there on the top step as big as day but Gina . . . with Bob Rosenberg at her side . . . and wearing the beautiful dress which Steven had bought her! Andrea noticed her at the same time as Steven and couldn't help but feel a twinge of insecurity. When Marybeth turned to see what had caught Steven's attention, she saw Gina and Bob. She gasped and then asked snidely, "Now, what are you going to do, Mr. Richards?"

"I don't know about you, Beth, but I'm not going to do anything."

Marybeth couldn't wait for the dance to end. She broke loose from Steven and ran to greet Gina on the stairs. Rolling her eyes at Bob, she embraced Gina, saying, "Girl, I'm so glad you got here. I'm sorry to hear about you and Steven. I really thought he was the man for you!"

Chapter 21

Bob looked at Marybeth with pure hatred. She grabbed Gina by the hand and pulled her down into the ballroom, leaving Bob standing there while the two of them went off into the crowd.

At the first opportunity, Gina sought out Steven. She found him seated at a table with Andrea. "Hi, Andrea. Hi, Steven - surprised to see me?"

"Gina, I'm not surprised at anything you would do. You're a remarkable woman."

"You see there, Andrea. He knows just how to make a woman feel good. That's why I love him so much. And, Andrea, you look beautiful tonight - I love your dress."

At that moment, Talley appeared and said to Steven, "Can I speak to you for a minute?"

When Steven went off with him, Gina turned to Andrea and said, "What is it with you, Andrea? I don't understand it; every time he and I have a little argument, he runs to you. Could you explain that to me?"

"Well, Gina, I don't think you should blame me for the problems that you and Steven have. I think because of the way you are, you're going to lose him, if you haven't already. And, yes, if you don't see the value in him, I do, and I'll always be there for him."

"Did he tell you that?"

"Tell me what?"

"That I've already lost him?"

"Well, I think you should find that out from Steven. You know, Gina, I think your love for him is just as strong as mine, but there's a difference - I could never be ashamed of him. How could you love a man so much and treat him the way you do?"

Aware of the truth in what Andrea was saying, Gina just looked away momentarily and then decided to drop all pretense and said sorrowfully, "Andrea, I believe Steven and I have had our last argument - this time, I think I've really lost him. Besides, you're probably better for him than I am anyway."

Just then, Gina looked over Andrea's shoulder and noticed that Steven's conversation with Talley had ended. Jumping at the chance to be with him, she gave an airy wave of her hand and told Andrea, "But, that's not why I came here - I'm here to have a good time!" She touched Andrea with two fingers on the shoulder in a friendly gesture and said, "Oh, Andrea, if you see me flirting with him tonight, don't get excited - at this point, I don't think there's anything I can do to get him back - just look at it as a last ditch effort." She jumped up from her chair and made a beeline for Steven.

Gina's activities were not lost on Bob Rosenberg, who was standing on a balcony above the crowd, nursing a drink and broodingly watching her every move. When he saw her head for Steven, the glint in his eyes expressed the heat of his emotion.

Steven may have been the object of Gina's attention, but Andrea was attracting admiring looks from a great many of the men present, and she soon had plenty of dancing partners. If there was a belle of the ball that night, it was Andrea, and she was radiant, enjoying every minute of it. When he had picked her up earlier in the evening, Steven had been well aware of how stunning she looked, but now, glimpsing her from time to time on the dancefloor, he realized, perhaps for the first time, how very special she really was.

As the evening wore on, Bob Rosenberg had taken just about all he could of Gina ignoring him. Gina had stayed pretty close to Steven as he performed his duties as a host of the affair. All evening, she had made it difficult for Steven to avoid her, since they had many mutual acquaintances, and now they were dancing together. Gina said, "Steven, I admit I've been wrong in the past, but now I don't give a damn who sees me with you - you've got to believe that."

"Gina, I don't think it's fair to do what you're doing."

"What do you mean, Steven?"

"You know that I'm here with Andrea, and you're here with that idiot who, by the way, is watching your every move."

"Well, you talk about fair! What do you mean? When it comes to you, I don't want to play fair. I love you, and I'm not going to let you go that easily."

"Aw, c'mon, Gina, give me a break. We've gone through this over and over, and I just can't take it anymore. I keep getting a mental picture of that scene at Lily Ryder's."

At that moment, Bob Rosenberg tapped Steven on the shoulder to cut in on their dance. Steven turned around, and their eyes met in mutual hostility. He turned her over to Bob.

As soon as Steven was out of earshot, Bob tore into Gina. "You're really asking for it, Bitch! I didn't come here to be humiliated by you. You haven't looked my way since we've been here. You've been hangin' around that black bastard all night. You're going to pay for this - I'm going to kill your fuckin' ass! I'm sick of this shit." He grabbed her by the arm and headed for the exit, pulling her behind him. Gina resisted.

Marybeth, being the busybody she was, had been watching the whole scene. By this time, Steven was back sitting with Andrea, and Marybeth ran over to them. "Steven, Steven, Bob's going to hurt her. He's dragging her out of here, and he threatened her. She needs help . . . please!"

By now, the commotion involving Bob and Gina was obvious. Steven looked in that direction and then rushed over to Bob. "Let her go right now, goddamn it! You remember what I told you. If I ever heard that you'd laid a hand on her again, you'd have to answer to me." In a fury, Bob took a wild swing at Steven and missed. Steven sidestepped the punch and delivered one of his own that landed right square on Bob's chin. Blood was spurting from Bob's mouth as he hit the ballroom floor. Steven stood over him, holding his fist in pain, and told the security guards who had just rushed up, "Get this guy the hell out of here." They dragged him out the exit.

Gina was very pleased by what Steven had just done, and there was a little grin of satisfaction on her face. Although Andrea believed that Steven was only doing what was right in coming to Gina's aid and that he had told her the truth about his relationship with Gina, nevertheless her eyes shifted back and forth from Steven to Gina with a look of uncertainty.

Seizing the drama of the moment, Gina threw herself into Steven's arms and cried, "Oh, Steven, I'm so glad you were here. Please, take me home. He might be out there waiting for me!"

This intensified Andrea's uncertainty until Steven took Gina by the shoulders and gently pushed her away from him, saying, "Okay, Gina, Andrea and I will take you home."

A look of disappointment fell over Gina's face, and she cunningly said, "Oh, don't spoil Andrea's fun - she seems to be enjoying all the attention she's getting - she doesn't have to come." Steven just motioned for Andrea to join them and

Chapter 21

went over to Talley and said, "We've got to take Gina home - would you mind taking care of things here for me? If it's not too late, we might come back."
Talley responded, "Go ahead, I understand. I've got it covered."
As they were leaving, Marybeth came up to Gina and asked, "Do you want me to come with you, Honey?"
"No, I'll be alright. You stay here and enjoy yourself. What's wrong with you, Girl? Can't you see I'm in good hands?"
Marybeth agreed and just shook her head in pity for her friend Gina as she walked away. She knew as well as Gina that the affair with Steven was over. As they were about to exit the building, Beth yelled out, "Steven, you take care of her - that's my best and only friend in this life, Chil'!"
"Yeah, okay, Beth."

Steven assumed that Gina would want to go to her mother's. On the route there, they passed by Steven's hotel, and Gina cried out in surprise, "I thought we were going to your place!"
"No, Gina, right now I think the best place for you to be is at your mother's."
Gina protested. "I don't want to go there - you know how badly we get along."
Andrea cut in. "Gina, she's your mother - someone who cares for you - that's what's important."
Gina ignored her. "Steven, I mean it - if I can't go to your place, stop this car and let me out right now."
Steven kept on driving, ignoring Gina's ranting.
"If you take me there, I won't go in - I mean it, Steven!"
When they pulled up in front of the house, Steven said, "Gina, stop this craziness - just go on in the house, Woman."

Gina didn't pay any attention to him. She jumped out of the car and walked up the street.

Steven jumped out after her, saying to Andrea, " Sit tight, I'll be back."

He caught up with Gina, took her gently by the arm, and pleaded with her, "Gina, please . . . go back to your mother's."

Gina screeched hysterically, "Let me go!" at the same time striking him across the face with her free hand. "You don't care about me, you son of a bitch!" Gina paused a moment and stared at him while Steven rubbed the spot on his face where she had just smacked him. Then she continued in a voice filled with rage. "You think you're really something, don't you, Steven?"

"What do you mean by that?"

"Just look at you! Hot shot lawyer! You'll never be the man I want - you're black as coal - kinky hair, big lips - no thanks!"

Her outburst left Steven speechless, but Gina could see the hurt in his eyes, and her anger quickly dissolved. She cried, "Oh, Steven, I'm sorry. I didn't mean any of the things I just said - please believe me! I just love you so much, Steven . . . " She hesitated and continued, her voice coming in sobs, ". . . that . . . that I don't want to live on this earth without you."

"Gina, don't talk like that!"

Gina went on, "You know that old saying, 'what goes around comes around.' Well, I really did it this time. What I dished out came back and hit me hard, didn't it? I never thought I would feel this way about a black man. And it's all my fault that it's over now." There was a pause, and then she said, in a voice of resignation, "Goodbye, Steven."

Chapter 21   247

Steven didn't want to walk away from Gina, but knew that trying to convince her to go to her mother's was an impossible task. He turned and headed for the car.

Andrea had been intently watching the scene up the street. As worried as she was about the possibility of Steven and Gina reconciling their differences, she was pretty sure that Steven had finally had it with Gina. When he returned to the car, she asked, "You're not going to just leave her out there, are you?"

"Well, there's really nothing I can do. I think she'll eventually come to her senses and end up back at her mother's." He put the car in gear, and they drove away.

Nobody knew it, but Bob Rosenberg had been following them from the hotel parking lot. After Steven's car had disappeared from sight, Rosenberg went after Gina. He caught up with her within a few blocks and pulled up beside her and slowed the car down to the pace that she was walking. "Gina, c'mon, Baby, get in the car. I'm very sorry - I really am!"

Gina yelled, "You stay away from me, you bastard, you! I don't want anything to do with you - ever again - do you understand? Just stay away from me!"

Bob continued to beg her to get in his car, but when he realized she wasn't going to comply, he slammed on his brakes. Gina knew what his next move would be and tried to get away, but before she could get very far, Bob had jumped out of the car, grabbed her, and put his hand over her mouth to keep her from screaming out. He put his other arm around her waist and started pulling her back to the car, saying in a chilling whisper, "You're coming with me, you nigger bitch!"

Gina kicked and squirmed to no avail, and before she knew it, Rosenberg had stuffed her into the car, got in himself and locked the doors. He pulled a gun out of the glove compartment and stuck it up to her face. "If you try to get out, I'll blow your fuckin' brains out - do you understand? You're mine, motherfucker!"

On their way back to the dance, Andrea said to Steven, "I'm really worried about her. I'm afraid something awful's going to happen to her if she runs into Bob again."

"I know. That bastard is crazy enough to try and kill her."

"Well, like you say, she'll probably end up going to her mother's."

"Yeah, I hope so. Andrea, I don't know about you, but I really don't feel like going back to that party - I just want to call it a night!"

"Whatever you want to do, Steven. You've had quite an evening!"

"If it's okay with you, I'll just take you home. I'm sorry things turned out the way they did. I really wanted you to enjoy yourself."

"It's not your fault - and until the trouble started, I had a ball!"

Steven turned the car around and headed for Andrea's.

Marybeth was very concerned the morning after the dance when Gina didn't show up to meet her as usual in the coffeeshop. She went to Steven's office and asked him, "Where's Gina?"

"Oh, she's probably still angry about our separation. I'll give her the time she needs, and she'll probably be in."

"Steven, I think it's more serious than that - I called her mother's, I called her apartment, and I called Bob's place. Her mother said she wasn't there, and there was no answer at Gina's or Bob's. Something is wrong. I know it is."

At that point, Steven explained what happened Saturday night after they left the dance. Hearing that, Marybeth was even more worried. "We can't just sit here - we have to find out where she is!"

"Well, maybe you're right - I'll call her mother."

When he called, he learned that she still hadn't been there. He was stricken with guilt.

Three days passed, and still nobody knew of Gina's whereabouts. By now, Marybeth was in a frenzy. Steven had told Gina's mother that she was missing, and she was worried sick. The police had been notified, and they had turned Bob's apartment inside out looking for any clue as to where he might be so that they could question him about Gina. Steven had enlisted the help of Sean Dickens to advise them and keep them abreast of any developments.

What they didn't know was that Bob Rosenberg was holding Gina captive in a house in Jenkintown, a suburb of Philadelphia, which belonged to a friend of his who was away. Gina was really in grave danger. Bob beat her savagely whenever he felt like it. He knew there was no chance of salvaging their relationship, and all he wanted now was revenge. Gina had tried everything to free herself. She had begged and pleaded with him, attempted to reason with him about the consequences of her kidnapping, and tried on several occasions to escape. Each failed attempt only resulted in another beating.

On the fourth day, Bob had to leave the house. He gagged Gina and tied her up to a radiator, telling her that he would be back in a couple of hours. He warned, "This is just a sample of what will happen to you if I come back and find that you've tried to get away." He then proceeded to punch her in the stomach as hard as he could and growled, "You know I'm going to have to kill you, don't you?"

Gina could hardly speak, but she did manage to say, "Bob, please let me go - I won't tell anyone you did this to me."

Bob responded, "Fuck you," and slammed the door and locked it.

He needed some cash and headed to Philadelphia, stopping at the first ATM he came to at the Cheltenham Mall. Upon returning to his car, he opened his car door with the remote on his keychain, unaware that he was being stalked by three black youths who had watched his visit to the ATM with great interest. He heard a voice say, "Okay, motherfucker, keep walkin' to your car. Don't turn around, or I'll blow your fuckin' face off."

Bob's legs turned to jelly.

Another voice said, "Man, that's a bad motherfuckin' car - we got it now!"

Another ordered, "Get the fuck in the car, Bitch!"

Bob was deathly afraid and did exactly as the young man ordered. He started for the driver's seat, but one of them shouted, "Go 'round the other side and get in the back seat, motherfucker, back seat! When you get in there, empty your fuckin' pockets - we know you got money!"

It was a two-door sedan, and Bob was thinking about his gun in the glove compartment. Maybe he had a chance to grab it. As he leaned over to get in, someone shouted, "C'mon, motherfucker, hurry up!" Bob made a desperate attempt to get his gun. He managed to pull it out of the compartment, but one of the boys saw him. "He's got a gun! He's got a gun! The motherfucker's got a gun!"

Before Bob could even turn to point the gun in their direction, two of the boys who were armed shot him in the back five times, fatally wounding him. They pulled him out of the car, threw him to the pavement, got in, and sped off. Bob could hear the boys cackling as they drove away, shouting obscenities. He died within minutes.

Chapter 22

That evening, Andrea was looking at the six o'clock news on television when she saw a story about a carjacking and heard that someone named Bob Rosenberg was the victim. She called Steven right away. "Are you watching the news, Steven? Channel Six!"

"Yeah, I just heard the same thing you must have heard - Bob Rosenberg, right?"

"Do you think it's the same guy?"

"Yeah, that's him - they showed a picture. I know one thing, whoever did it saved me the trouble - I was worried I might spend time in jail for killing that goddamn son of a bitch myself."

"But, where's Gina? They must not have been together."

"Let me hang up now, Andrea. I'll try to find out what's going on."

He called Lieutenant Dickens. "Sean, I need to find out if there were any other victims involved in that carjacking of Bob Rosenberg."

"No, not that we know of. I assume you're thinking of Gina Epps."

"I sure am. If you hear anything, please get back to me."

"You got it, Buddy."

Minutes after Steven hung up the phone, Marybeth called. "Steven, I'm worried. I take it you saw the news. I have a feeling that something's wrong."

"I understand. I just talked to Dickens - he's going to keep me informed."

Chapter 22

Later that evening Steven and Andrea were at his place anxiously watching the late news. The disappearance of Gina was now the lead story on all three of Philadelphia's major local TV stations. The anchorperson on the station they were tuned to announced: "Our top story today is the carjacking and murder of a Philadelphia man, Bob Rosenberg. As this story unfolds, we've learned that there's more to it than meets the eye. Now it's believed that there is possibly more than one victim involved: Gina Marlene Epps, a woman who has been missing since Saturday night. A police source states that it is believed that the carjacker has taken her with them and that hope of finding her alive is fading."

Hearing this, Steven flopped down into a chair, put his head down between his knees and cried out, "Oh, no, no! It's my fault . . . I should've never left her alone . . . it's my fault!"

Andrea came over to him and sat down beside him. She put her arm around his shoulders and pleaded, "Steven, please, don't do this - you did everything you could to make her go in the house that night. Don't torture yourself this way."

Andrea's attempt to comfort him did not do much good. He continued to feel despondent and very guilty. He also felt betrayed by Dickens and decided to call him. When he came on the line, Steven jumped down his throat. "Lieutenant, I thought you were going to keep me abreast of any developments - now I hear on the news that the carjackers took her and there's not much chance of her being alive. Why didn't you tell me?"

"Wait a minute now. Slow down, Richards, slow down. In the first place, don't tell me how to do my job. We're pretty busy around here. If I said I would keep you abreast, I meant it. I don't know where the press got that, but, as usual, they're just hyping the story."

In the meanwhile, Gina was of course unaware that Bob had been killed and, despite her injuries, was anxiously chewing at the thick rope he had used to tie her to the radiator. She had been drifting in and out of consciousness ever since Bob left, but she knew that the time he said he'd be back was long gone, and that he must be going to walk through the door at any moment! Although she was very weak, she persistently gnawed and gnawed at the rope until she finally broke the knot, thinking to herself, "Oh, thank God! . . . I gotta get out of here before he comes back!"

She struggled to her feet to look for an easy exit. Bob was so sure that she would not be able to escape from the radiator that he hadn't secured the house very well. When Gina staggered into the kitchen, she found that she was able to get the back door open. She fled the house and worked her way through a wooded area until she came to a well-lighted street. She was in terrible pain now and urgently needed medical attention. Being very late at night, there was no one around to ask for help so her first instinct was to locate a phone which she found at the edge of a car dealer's lot. There was no doubt in her mind that Steven would be the one she would call. She dialed him collect, but made a mistake in the number, and no connection was made. She decided to call Marybeth.

Marybeth and Arthur Gwaltney had grown pretty close and had been spending a lot of time together. This evening, Arthur had been trying to get Beth's mind off Gina so he could make love to her, but Beth wasn't having any of it. Arthur had finally given up and fallen asleep, but Beth was wide awake when the phone rang at two o'clock in the morning. Before the first ring had stopped, Beth anxiously snatched it up. "Hello, hello, who is it?"

She could hear a faint voice on the other end. "Beth, it's me . . . it's me . . . Gina!"

Beth screamed out, "Oh, my God, Gina . . . Gina, is that really you? Where are you, tell me - tell me where you are!"

Gina looked around and saw a street sign. "I'm at Old York Road, and . . . and, I don't . . . I don't know."

"Gina, Honey . . . Gina, listen. As much as we've been up and down that road, I'm sure you can tell me what township you're in."

There was a pause while Gina looked around some more, and then said, "I think . . . I think I'm in Jenkintown."

"You stay right where you're at. I'm on my way."

As Marybeth was coming up Old York Road in Jenkintown, she saw Gina on the other side of the street on a bus stop bench, slumped over, looking as if she were about to fall to the ground. She sped up, crossed the median strip and stopped, facing the oncoming traffic. She jumped out of her car and raced over to her. "Oh, Gina, Baby . . .what on earth happened to you? Gina . . . Honey . . . we have to get you to a hospital!"

At that moment, a police car pulled up. "What's going on here, Ladies?"

"This is Gina Epps - the woman they've been looking for. She's been beat up pretty bad and needs to go to the hospital."

"Who are you?"

"I'm her friend - she called me to come get her."

The policeman helped Gina into the squad car and told Marybeth to follow him, saying, "I'm going to need some information from you."

Gina was rushed to the Abington Hospital emergency room. She had been severely beaten about the head, and her body was covered with welts and bruises. One of the doctors commented, "Whoever did this was really trying to kill her -

it's a wonder she's still alive." Before long, it became evident that there must be internal bleeding; her vital signs were very poor, and it was decided she would have to be taken to the intensive care unit. Beth was pulling on the sleeve of one of the doctors. "Is she going to be alright . . . is she?"

"We're going to do the best we can, ma'am." After emergency care was completed, they wheeled her away. Beth followed, but when they got to the doors of ICU, they told her she couldn't come any further.

As Beth walked back down the hall, she was so upset she was almost incoherent, murmuring to herself, "Oh, God, please let her live . . . please let her live!" and in the same breath, "I've got to call Steven - he has to know." She found a waiting room and ran to the phone.

Steven picked it up on the first ring. "Steven, it's Beth. You've gotta get up here. I found Gina. Hurry!"

"What! Slow down, Beth, what are you saying?"

"I found her, Steven . . . I found her."

"Well, where are you?"

"I'm at the hospital!"

"What hospital, Beth . . . please!"

"Oh, oh . . . oh, Abington."

"I'll be right there!"

Steven and Andrea had been asleep in bed when Marybeth called. Andrea had been listening to his end of the conversation with Marybeth, and when he got up and started to dress, she asked, "What's wrong? Where are you going?"

"That was Marybeth. They found Gina - she's in the hospital."

"Well, you're not leaving me here. I'm going, too."

"C'mon, Baby. I want you with me."

Chapter 22

Lickety-split, Steven and Andrea were at the hospital. When they got off the elevator and went to the ICU area of the floor, the first person they saw was Marybeth, pacing back and forth in the hallway. As soon as she saw them, she broke out in a run and ran straight to Steven's arms. "Oh, Steven," she cried out. "I'm so glad you got here! It's really bad . . . they don't know if she's gonna make it or not. Maybe seeing you might lift her spirits a little - the doctor says she's been asking for you."

"Can I see her now?"

"I don't know. You'll have to go to the nurses' station and ask them."

After Steven rushed off, Marybeth turned and looked at Andrea as if to say, "If it wasn't for you, none of this would've happened!"

Andrea knew what Marybeth must be thinking and tried to avoid eye contact with her and simply said, looking in another direction, "What's the matter, Beth? Did I do or say something that didn't meet with your approval?"

Marybeth just rolled her eyes and went to sit on the opposite side of the waiting room.

In the meantime, Steven was trying to explain to the nurse in charge who he was. "Would you call her doctor out here? I understand she's been asking for me."

He managed to convince her, and when the doctor came out, he introduced himself as Dr. Pyle.

Steven asked anxiously, "Can you let me see her, Doc?"

"First of all, who are you?"

"My name is Steven Richards."

"Oh, I guess you're the Steven she's been asking for. Well, Mr. Richards, right now she's heavily sedated and needs the rest. So I don't think it would be a good idea to disturb her."

"Well, what's it look like, Doc? How bad is it?"

"To be honest with you, it doesn't look very good at this point. There have been severe internal injuries. Tell me, is there any immediate family who should be contacted?"

Steven mumbled to himself, "Oh, my God . . . her mother . . . I forgot all about her."

"What did you say, Sir?"

"Oh, I'm sorry, Doc. There's only her mother as far as I know."

"Well, I think you should get her in here."

Steven hurried back to the waiting room where Andrea and Marybeth were. Both women jumped up at the same time, asking, "How is she . . . how is she, Steven?"

Steven heard them but their words didn't penetrate, and he went straight to the phone. In a panic, Marybeth ran after him, "Steven - Steven - tell me, please tell me - how is she?" He just mumbled, partially to himself, "Not good . . . not good!"

Marybeth fell to her knees, and, almost like a child not able to have its way, put her face in her hands and cried out, "I told her to get away from that fuckin' bastard - Goddamn it, I told her . . . " and then, almost in a whisper, "I told her . . . I told her!"

Impulsively, Andrea came over to comfort her. She knelt down beside her, putting one hand on her shoulder and patting her on the back with the other. "I understand, Beth . . . I understand!"

Marybeth turned and buried her face between Andrea's breasts and cried like a baby until she suddenly realized who was holding her. She pushed away from her and jumped up. This time, she didn't just think it; she said exactly what she felt. "Yeah, I'll bet . . . you understand alright . . . if it wasn't for you she wouldn't be in there lying on death's bed right

Chapter 22

now. You knew how much she loved Steven, but you went after him anyway, didn't you? I wanted him as bad as you, but when I saw how much it meant to Gina, I stopped chasing him. You could have done the same! Why didn't you? ... why didn't you?"

Andrea wasn't surprised by how Marybeth felt, but didn't think she'd pick a time like this to express it. She backed off and said, "Beth, please, you're wrong - you're dead wrong! Besides, this isn't the time or place for this. Gina wouldn't like what you're doing now."

"Don't you dare tell me what Gina would like - she's my friend, not yours!"

By now, the women had drawn the attention of the staff on the floor, and one of them approached them, saying, "Please, Ladies, you've got to keep it down - after all, this is a hospital!"

While Steven was breaking the news about Gina to her mother, he could hear the argument between Andrea and Marybeth and was anxiously waiting for Mrs. Epps to hang up so that he could try to restore the peace between them. He finally cut her short, saying, "Just get over here as fast as you can, Mrs. Epps! I'll be looking out for you."

Then he went over to Marybeth, took her by the arm and they went out into the hall. "Beth, there's another waiting room. I think it would be best if you waited there, don't you?"

Marybeth, still not composed, sobbed, "I didn't mean to create a scene - I really didn't - I just . . ."

Steven cut her off. "I know you didn't, Beth - don't worry about it . . . but, for now I think it would be best if you waited down the hall. Okay?"

Soon after, Mrs. Epps arrived and was allowed in to see Gina who was still too sedated to be aware of her presence. Mrs. Epps knelt beside the bed and said prayerfully, "Please,

God, don't take her away from me now. Since you took Gilbert, she's all I have left. I know she's learned her lesson. Make her well for me. Please, God, make her well!"

By now, Steven had talked his way into Gina's room and saw Mrs. Epps kneeling at the bedside, with her head buried in her hands on the bed, weeping. He went to comfort her and gently raised her and led her to a chair in the room. She reached up to him and took his face in her hands and pulled him toward her, "Oh, Steven, why did this have to happen - just when her attitude about what she is seemed to be changing? Since you came into her life, she's been a different person - she seemed so happy. Do you know that you're the only black man that she's ever cared about, including her father?"

"Oh, no, Mrs. Epps, on the contrary. I do believe she did love her father. She may not have shown it, but I think she did. It was just her own poor self-image that didn't allow her to express it."

Mrs. Epps replied skeptically, "Well, I hope you're right about that, but I've known Gina a lot longer than you have." She changed the subject, saying, "I know you kids must have set a date by now for the big day - haven't you?"

Steven was taken aback and realized that Gina had obviously not told her mother they had broken up. He decided not to reveal it and stammered, "Uh . . . uh . . . I'm afraid we haven't, Mrs. Epps - not as of yet, anyway."

"Well, Son, I just talked to God, and I know my baby's going to be fine. He promised me you kids would have your day in the sun."

At that point, the nurse came into the room and asked that they leave because she had to give Gina some personal care. Steven and Mrs. Epps returned to the waiting room where Andrea was. He settled Mrs. Epps in a comfortable seat and then motioned for Andrea to follow him. He led her down the hall to where Marybeth was waiting.

As soon as Marybeth saw them, she jumped up and ran over. "Andrea, you were absolutely right. This isn't the time for that."

Looking relieved, Steven said, "I'm glad you see it that way, Beth. That's why I brought Andrea down here. Gina's mother is here now, and I don't want her to see any dissension between you guys that might upset her. Oh, and one other thing - Gina didn't tell her mother that we had broken up, and I think it would be best if we just left it that way. Are we all on the same page?"

Both of the women nodded in agreement. Marybeth started to cry, saying, "I have a bad feeling about this; I don't think Gina's going to pull through."

Steven tried to reassure her. "It's too soon to talk like that. As long as she's alive, there's always a chance."

They returned to the waiting room where Mrs. Epps was, and the next couple of hours were spent by the four of them, waiting and worrying. About six o'clock in the morning, a doctor came in and told them, "Gina has regained consciousness. Now would be a good time to go and see her."

All four of them immediately jumped to their feet. Mrs. Epps cried out, "Oh, thank you, God. I knew you would answer my prayer. Thank you, Jesus! Thank you, Jesus!"

They rushed down the hall to Gina's room. Mrs. Epps was the first at her bedside. "Gina, Gina, it's me, your mother. I just knew you were going to be alright. I knew it."

Gina clutched her mother's hand and whispered, "I'm sorry, Mom. I'm sorry for all the hurt I caused you."

"Now, Honey, you didn't do anything wrong - don't start that!"

"No, Mom, I gotta tell you - I know now that I loved Daddy."

Ms. Epps squeezed Gina's hand. "That means the world to me, Honey. It was his heart's desire."

Marybeth was standing behind Mrs. Epps, looking over her shoulder at Gina. As soon as she caught Gina's eye, she interrupted Mrs. Epps and put on a cheerful voice, "Howya' feelin', Girlfriend? Soon as you get outta here, we goin' celebrate!"

Gina smiled faintly and whispered, "What we goin' celebrate, Chil'?"

"You gettin' outta here - that's what!"

Steven couldn't help but notice the sad contrast of Beth's vibrant voice and Gina's feeble response, and he felt the tears well up in his eyes. He heard a little sigh from Gina and saw her eyes close.

Suddenly, the machine in the room which monitored Gina's vital signs sounded a loud, persistent alarm and the impulses on the screen started to flatten out. Mrs. Epps cried out in fright, and Steven ran out to the nurse's station. Before he could get there, he saw a team headed toward him, dragging equipment behind them. He watched as they ran into Gina's room and Mrs. Epps, Andrea and Marybeth were ushered out. As they stood in the hallway, they heard frantic voices inside the room and the harsh sounds of a resuscitator, working to bring Gina back to life.

Another nurse led them back to the waiting room where the next few minutes seemed like hours. When the doctor finally came in to the room, he looked grim, but said, "We've got her breathing again." He looked at Steven. "She's asking for you - just you this time."

As Andrea watched with anxiety all over her face, Steven eagerly left the waiting area and went down the hall to Gina's

Chapter 22

room. He went to her bedside, and, when he once again saw her ravaged face, he cried out, "Oh, Gina . . . who did this to you?"

Gina replied weakly, "Steven, I don't want you to seek revenge - but . . . it was Bob."

Steven didn't tell her that Bob was dead. He just reached for her hand and squeezed it gently, as if to say, "It's okay, he won't ever hurt you again."

Gina looked up at him with an exquisitely tender expression. As Steven was about to speak, she put her finger to her lips in a gesture for him to be silent. "You have all the time in the world - I don't have much time left, so let me go first."

Steven protested, "Gina, don't say that! Honey . . . you're gonna be okay!"

Gina sighed very softly and started speaking in a quiet voice. "I think Andrea always deserved you more than me; she's loved you from the very beginning, but I was too stupid to realize what I had in you." She was silent for a moment and then cried in a little voice of despair, "Oh, Steven . . . why couldn't I have met you earlier in my life? I probably wouldn't be lying here like this now!"

Steven searched desperately for something to say which would comfort her. Gina looked longingly into his eyes and then whispered, "I don't want you to say anything now, Steven . . . just kiss me for the last time."

He took her hand in his, caressed it softly and leaned over and kissed her lips. Gina squeezed his hand ever so faintly and murmured, "Goodbye, sweet black man." The breath left her body, and her hand went limp in his.

In the meanwhile, Andrea who had slipped away from the waiting room after Steven left, had been drawn to Gina's room. She had opened the door a crack and peeked in, listening to their conversation. She watched him kiss her and then saw him sink to his knees beside Gina's bed and heard him howl out in pain. She wanted desperately to go to him - to comfort him and to be with him - but she knew as sure as life itself that this moment of death belonged to Steven and Gina alone - this was truly the last time they would be together.

As she backed slowly out of the doorway in tears, Mrs. Epps and Marybeth appeared. They had been alerted by the nurses' response to Gina's monitor that something was drastically wrong. Now their fears were confirmed - Gina was gone. Steven slowly rose from Gina's bedside to make room for Mrs. Epps and Marybeth.

Outside, Andrea was waiting for him. She took him into her arms and said, "I know how much it must hurt, Steven. I'm so sorry."

Steven gave her a look of appreciation for her understanding, and they walked slowly down the corridor together.

Chapter 23

As the months passed after Gina's death, life went on. Marybeth and Arthur announced their engagement. Martin Pollock received a life sentence for the murder of his son. Dillenbeck and Grundage eventually came to trial, and, despite Steven's vigorous defense, were found guilty of violation of federal election laws and sentenced to three years in the federal penitentiary. Andrew Talley and Steven Richards ran the firm in their absence. Their employees were delighted when they ordered that the elevators run all through the day, instead of just at certain hours, and that the one-way mirrors in the executives' offices be removed. A new day had indeed come to Dillenbeck, Talley, Grundage and Richards!

As for Andrea and Steven, they had solidified their relationship; she moved into his suite at the Four Seasons, a place where she had once longed to spend even one night.

One particular night, about two o'clock in the morning, Andrea woke up to find that Steven was not in the bed beside her. Alarmed, she sat up and, by the moonlight streaming in the room, she saw him staring out the window, lost in thought. Andrea got up and walked across the room and put her arms around his waist. She whispered, "What's the matter, Sweetheart? . . . are you thinking about her?"

"Yes, I was," Steven admitted. "After all, I did love her . . . although not in the same way I love you. When I think about my relationship with Gina, it was like having forbidden fruit. Something I always felt guilty about - knowing how she felt about me and what I was . . . and I was always afraid of losing her. It was almost like she wasn't real - somebody I

Crisis of Identity

would never be able to spend my whole life with. . . . but you, Andrea . . . I feel that you love me for who I am and what I am . . ." Steven paused and then continued to let his thoughts flow. "I was never able to talk to Gina the way I'm able to express myself to you . . . and if you can't do that with the person you really care about, then the relationship isn't worth having . . . but, Andrea . . . I miss her" . . . his voice began to fade a little . . . "she was a part of me, and now she's gone." He stopped talking altogether.

She gave his hand an encouraging squeeze, and he started speaking again. "You know, Andrea . . . all of us have some of the sickness Gina had - that lack of esteem for ourselves and each other. We've been brainwashed by this society to the extent that none of us is completely free from it - no matter how much we accomplish. Gina was a black woman, but she had very white features, and I'm afraid subconsciously that's what really attracted me to her. I just didn't have the insight to realize that I too was a victim of the sickness."

Andrea didn't say anything; she just drew him closer to her. There was silence as they both looked out of the window into the night, enjoying the beauty of the darkness.

THE END

USE THIS FORM TO ORDER COPIES OF CRISIS OF IDENTITY OR TO ORDER ZURO!, ALSO WRITTEN BY WILLIAM A. SIMMS

FILL IN THIS FORM AND MAIL TO:
Waverly House Publishing, PO Box 1053, Glenside, Pa. 19038
For information call: 1-800-858-2253

Method of Payment: ☐ Check   ☐ VISA   ☐ Mastercard   ☐ American Express   ☐ Discover

Card Account No. Please list all numbers on card.   Exp. Mo.   Exp. Yr.

_____   _____
Customer Name   Customer Signature

_____   _____   _____   _____
Street Address   City   State   Zip Code

Day Time Phone (include area code)   Night Time Phone (include area)

Note: Your name and address must be filled in even if you are sending to another address.

Order #1 - Please send the following to the address below:

Qty	Description	Price	Subtotal
	Crisis of Identity, softbound	$12.50	$
	Zuro!, A Tale of Alien Avengers, softbound	$14.95	$
	Add shipping and handling (see below)		
	Add sales tax if required (see below)		
		Total	$

Ship to arrive week of _____ to: Name _____
Address _____ Apt. # _____
_____ Zip _____
Card to read: _____
You may enclose your own card or we will enclose a handwritten one with your personal message.

Order #1 - Please send the following to the address below:

Qty	Description	Price	Subtotal
	Crisis of Identity, softbound	$12.50	$
	Zuro! A Tale of Alien Avengers, softbound	$14.95	$
	Add shipping and handling (see below)		
	Add sales tax if required (see below)		
		Total	$

Ship to arrive week of _____ to: Name _____
Address _____ Apt. # _____
_____ Zip _____
Card to read: _____
You may enclose your own card or we will enclose a handwritten one with your personal message.

SHIPPING AND HANDLING: For single book, add $3.50; each additional book, $1.50 more
SALES TAX: Add 6% sales tax if being shipped to a Pennsylvania address.

USE THIS FORM TO ORDER COPIES OF CRISIS OF IDENTITY OR TO ORDER ZURO!, ALSO WRITTEN BY WILLIAM A. SIMMS

FILL IN THIS FORM AND MAIL TO:
Waverly House Publishing, PO Box 1053, Glenside, Pa. 19038
For information call: 1-800-858-2253

| Method of Payment | ☐ Check | ☐ VISA | ☐ Mastercard |
| | ☐ American Express | | ☐ Discover |

Card Account No. Please list all numbers on card.   Exp. Mo.   Exp. Yr.

_____   _____
Customer Name   Customer Signature

_____   _____   _____   _____
Street Address   City   State   Zip Code

_____   _____
Day Time Phone (include area code)   Night Time Phone (include area

Note: Your name and address must be filled in even if you are sending to another address.

Order #1 - Please send the following to the address below:

Qty	Description	Price	Subtotal
	Crisis of Identity, softbound	$12.50	$
	Zuro!, A Tale of Alien Avengers, softbound	$14.95	$
	Add shipping and handling (see below)		
	Add sales tax if required (see below)		
		Total	$

Ship to arrive week of _____ to: Name _____
Address _____ Apt. # _____
_____ Zip _____
Card to read: _____
You may enclose your own card or we will enclose a handwritten one with your personal message.

Order #1 - Please send the following to the address below:

Qty	Description	Price	Subtotal
	Crisis of Identity, softbound	$12.50	$
	Zuro! A Tale of Alien Avengers, softbound	$14.95	$
	Add shipping and handling (see below)		
	Add sales tax if required (see below)		
		Total	$

Ship to arrive week of _____ to: Name _____
Address _____ Apt. # _____
_____ Zip _____
Card to read: _____
You may enclose your own card or we will enclose a handwritten one with your personal message.

SHIPPING AND HANDLING: For single book, add $3.50; each additional book, $1.50 more
SALES TAX: Add 6% sales tax if being shipped to a Pennsylvania address.